Arrivals & Departures

A NOVEL

Also by Patti Hill

The Garden Gates Series
Like a Watered Garden
Always Green
In Every Flower

Stand-alone Novels
The Queen of Sleepy Eye
Seeing Things
Goodness & Mercy
The San Clemente Bait Shop & Telephony
Out of the Silence

Arrivals & Departures

A NOVEL

PATTI HILL

Garden Wall Press
Colorado

Arrivals
and
Departures

To the seen and unseen
who languish in places
not of their choosing

Each day holds a surprise. But only if we expect it can we see, hear, or feel it when it comes to us. Let's not be afraid to receive each day's surprise, whether it comes to us as sorrow or as joy. It will open a new place in our hearts, a place where we can welcome new friends and celebrate more fully our shared humanity.
~ Henri Nouwen

1

Floating in the open ocean—all that blue, above and below, the utter immensity of it all—served only to confirm my sense of insignificance. Thinking about what might eat me didn't help either.

So I didn't.

Instead, I conjured a list of things that are blue and reinvented Chicken Parmesan. I recited poems, like "Paul Revere's Ride" because it's long, and doing so required concentration. I often rehearsed what I should have said when my husband declared our marriage D.O.A. If especially desperate for distraction, I sang "One Hundred Bottles of Beer on the Wall," switching to a new beverage with each subtracted bottle.

Have I sung about guava juice today?

While I refrained from thinking of sharks too awfully much, I didn't leave safety entirely to chance. For one, sharks love seal meat, so I worked hard at *not* looking like a seal. Akimbo stripes of white tape on my wet suit disturbed the outline of my decidedly seal-shaped body.

For another, I didn't wear sparkly jewelry to avoid looking like a silvery fish—the Doritos of the sea. And splashing attracted the wrong kind of attention, so I kept all movement to a minimum. I'd considered buying a gun, but the probability of shooting myself outpaced running into a shark, even in his natural habitat.

Why was I floating off the coast of Baja California at Puertecito,

Mexico? I'd inherited the ability to travel anywhere in the world by simply touching a map from my father and his father before him. That may sound wonderful, but the landings were hard, sometimes resulting in injury. The trick was to plan travel so I landed in the water.

Magical travel held another disappointment: My stays were too short for any real exploration. The length of my visits was determined by the latitude, which gets too map-nerdy and cumbersome to explain. Suffice it to say, I had no control over how long I stayed, but it was never more than an hour. As magic goes, mine seemed pretty stingy.

I'd actually believed the traveler gene had skipped my generation or petered out, which I would have preferred. After all, I was rather ancient for starting something like this. I was a grandmother, for goodness' sake. I exploded with heat at the slightest hint of emotion, and my eyebrows grew in as stout as fire hoses. Staying home, in my cabin, with my moving boxes and the mice family in the kitchen wall seemed the wisest course for me.

Fighting magic proved futile, however, so I tried to be prepared. Since my departures were usually haphazard, I only wore shoes from the sale rack at Target. My feet killed me, but I didn't cry over lost shoes anymore.

On days that I opened the map shop, The Traveling Man, I wore latex gloves to prevent an accidental departure, as well as a life vest for the inevitability of an accidental departure. I couldn't risk ending up in the middle of the Indian Ocean with nothing but my heightened survival instincts to keep me afloat.

My water treading skills embarrassed me.

The only thing more unsettling than a departure was an arrival, as I always landed on the deck of the *Zella Francine*, Dad's fishing boat. The red cedar deck had been shaped, sanded, and varnished by Dad and me. Since the boat remained parked in my ex-husband's garage, I couldn't pad the planks for my arrivals. The wetsuit and the life vest cushioned the parts of me that are already padded but did little to protect my boney spots. I paid for my brief visits to Doug's garage with plenty of bruises. Yes, you heard correctly, I traveled to my ex-husband's garage via the Sea of Cortez on purpose, regularly.

Yep, pathetic.

I rode the swells like a plank of wood. Anyone else would let the pull and push of the waves massage the weariness clogging her muscles. I was not made that way, so I recited, yet again,

> *Listen my children and you shall hear*
> *Of the midnight ride of Paul Revere...*

My peripheral vision fogged, and my bones felt as if they were being pulled from my body.

2

My arrival on the *Zella Francine* punched the air out of my lungs and stirred the contents of my stomach.

I chewed a mouthful of oyster crackers, making a mash that absorbed the acid etching my stomach. When I poured the last of the crumbs and salt into my mouth, I sat up slowly. Doug's garage shifted and tilted, so I closed my eyes, waiting for all sense of motion to cease.

When the glassy planks of *Zella Francine's* generous deck felt firm below me, my thoughts slid back to the barn behind my parents' house, where I'd spent three summers sanding, gluing, and clamping her together with my father. And over the years, how we added three coats of new varnish to her hull and deck each spring before we put her in the water. Oh, how she rumbled as we raced to shore against a rising squall, and how the silence cocooned me when Dad and I fished. Emotion squeezed my throat.

This is not helpful.

I dried off with one of the towels I kept stored under the aft bench and swabbed the deck with another. I peeled off the wetsuit, rolled it into a ball, and packed it into a nylon tote I'd stashed up one sleeve.

I sat in the captain's seat and rested my forehead on the steering wheel. The heat of sunburned shoulders and endless days on the lake returned to me.

Those were the silken days of my childhood, impossible to

recover and just as impossible to relinquish. Why did I insist on trying? I climbed down the swim ladder.

Wanting to recover a childhood was fraught with problems, but traveling to Doug's garage was plain stupidity, even when I knew he wouldn't be there. I'd promised myself never to do so again, but there I was, squeezing the brake of his mountain bike, hanging his pruners back in place, and slipping on his golf jacket, the one I'd given him for our twenty-fifth wedding anniversary.

I buried my nose in the collar and breathed deeply. Where there should have been a mixture of sweet grass, sunscreen, and sweat doused in Old Spice, expensive perfume and hairspray lingered. I let the jacket slide off of my shoulders to the floor and riffled through Doug's golf bag. He kept a windbreaker in there for afternoon thunderstorms at the Grand Lake Golf Course.

My hand found something soft. My heart leapt. I tugged at the cloth, thinking and hoping it was the sweater he'd worn at St. Andrews on our first trip to Scotland. We'd discovered I was pregnant with Lauren, our oldest, on that trip.

Instead, I held a pink scarf embroidered with daisies.

Doug had never allowed me to store so much as lip balm in the pocket of his golf bag. A scarf? A *pink* scarf? There had to be an explanation.

Perhaps Doug had found the scarf laying near a tee box. He had two daughters. He knew how they treasured little things like scarves and how tears would flow once the loss had been realized. What else could he do? Of course he stuffed the thing into his bag, determined to find its owner and return the scarf. After all, the scarf looked homemade, treasured, very pink.

Doug would never.

At best he would have lifted the scarf off the turf with his three iron and hung it on the ball washer. Doug didn't fuss over someone else's carelessness, especially if the object of someone else's carelessness happened to be pink, and most especially in the middle of a golf game.

The scarf definitely belonged to *her*—the Tiffany, the second wife. I looked around the garage. Everything belonged to her. The woman was living my life, waking up with the man I should have been waking up with, and, more importantly, pleasing the man I could only disappoint.

I suddenly felt very conspicuous.

Zella and I didn't belong in that garage. She sat in sorry need of a good sanding and refinishing. The seat cushions had cracked at the seams, and her Bimini faded to lavender along the folds. Saddest of all, the paint of her name had blistered and flaked.

Zella's condition shouldn't have surprised me. Doug had never taken much interest in the boat until its value was assessed for the divorce. Everything is split down the middle in the state of Colorado, his and hers, with no grace for being a good egg and no penalty for infidelity. With the debt on our plumbing supply business paid, my column out-weighed Doug's, mostly because we'd never gotten around to deeding my family's cabin—where I now lived—and The Traveling Man, the map shop I'd also inherited from my father, in both of our names.

In truth, I would give up the roof over my head for the *Zella Francine*, but Doug saw the boat as a balancing of scales. I'd begged him not to sell until I could buy her back. He knew better than anyone what *Zella* meant to me. He'd watched the kids while I helped Dad get her ready for each season of fishing.

To be completely honest, I had no idea how Doug felt about anything anymore. I'd promised myself not to try to figure out the craziness of the last months of our marriage or how the world had slipped into a parallel and rather confusing reality in the two years since the divorce. I only got monkey-headed when I tried.

I dropped the pink scarf back into Doug's golf bag and used his driver to pack it onto the bottom. I scanned the garage to make sure I'd left nothing to let Doug and *her* know I'd visited. I locked the door and left.

At the road, barely wider than a footpath, I listened for approaching cars. I didn't want to explain to a passing neighbor why I was coming out of Doug's garage. Explaining anything about Doug or our marriage drained the life right out of me.

Not one over-sized SUV traveled the road, so I turned toward the cabin and walked double-quick. I would never forgive Doug for having an affair with someone from our lakeside neighborhood or for maintaining that affair for three years, or for deciding that he loved her most.

I swallowed down a sob and made a promise to myself: No more departures only to arrive in Doug's garage. Sniffing a perfume-doused golf jacket had ripped my heart open, again. That probably meant rethinking my time at The Traveling Man as well, because no matter where I traveled, I would always end up on the *Zella Francine*. Until I managed to buy the boat back, I would avoid maps at all costs.

How hard could that be? It wasn't like maps could sprout feet and walk up to my door.

3

I could count on one hand the number of times someone had knocked on the cabin's door. Plenty of signs warned looky-loos from daring to drive on the lane that edged the southernly side of Grand Lake. And if this guy would have knocked, I would not have answered. Instead, he found me bending over the mess the raccoons had made around the trashcans.

"Is Dr. Deering home?" he said.

As first impressions go, the man seemed a contradiction. Athletically built and tall, he stood with the confidence of a warrior. But his beseeching eyes reminded me of a child asking for a second cookie before dinner. Although, from the gray peppering his scruffy beard, he was long past begging for cookies.

"He's not here," I said, dropping a yogurt carton into the trashcan.

"He does live here, then?"

My throat tightened. "Dad passed away three years ago."

A shift of weight, a puckered brow. "I'm very sorry. I took a bunch of classes from him at CU. He sure knew his geography, and he made sure his students knew the world. I never worked harder. I'd always hoped to look him up, to tell him what his classes meant to me."

Other students had come looking for Dad. He'd been a popular professor of geography and advised grad students working toward becoming cartographers. Years had passed since the last student had come, which was a shame. Dad would have enjoyed their company.

"I guess you waited too long."

The man registered hurt, but the look faded quickly. He took a step toward me. "Are you a map person, too?"

I could not have grown up in my father's household and not been a map person. Maps hung from every wall, stood rolled up behind the sofa, and collected dust under the beds. We talked maps over every meal. To get our driver's licenses, my brother and I had to master drawing the world from memory, including every country, its capitol, and label any body of water larger than a horse trough. Dad gave me a map on every birthday, one a map of the Gettysburg battlefield that Colonel Joshua Lawrence Chamberlain of the Union Army had carried.

"What do you want to know?" I said.

The man squinted into the afternoon sun. I should have invited him into the shelter of the cabin, but I hadn't made the futon, my bed, in the living room. Dad would have offered the man a tuna fish sandwich with a thick slice of tomato. Maybe the mice had missed a box of macaroni and cheese.

The man patted his pockets until he found what he was looking for, a folded piece of paper. "This is going to sound a little weird."

It struck me then that I had no idea who this man was. He could have been ... "Are you a mass murderer, by chance?"

"What? No. Oh man, I'm sorry. I get single-minded sometimes, forget the niceties. I'm Callum Branigan." He reached out to shake my hand. "Cal. No one calls me Callum. And you are ... ?" His hand swallowed mine. It was surprisingly soft.

"Robin."

With the threat of murder out of the way, I invited Cal to the deck on the lakeside of the cabin. He stopped short, like most people did, when they rounded the corner and came face-to-face with Grand Lake and the Never Summer Range beyond. "Wow, this is quite the view."

Some of Cal's surprise probably came from the mismatch between the cabin and the view. The cabin was basic, possessing all the architectural surprise of a doublewide. On a lake populated with the Halls of Kansas City (yep, the ones of Hallmark cards and sappy movie fame), Texan oil barons, and rich doctors from Denver, we added an element of humility.

The Deering brothers of Nebraska built sturdy and functional cabins with no attention to frills. They'd managed to satisfy the aesthetic values of the neighbors by using the same planked siding that covered most of the cabins around the lake and adding a red roof, but they'd fallen far short of accomplishing anything close to Colorado chic.

On the other hand, the lake spilled before us, intensely blue and glittery. The mountains rose precipitously, shaggy with lodge pole pine from the lakeshore to the bare rocky slopes above. The pines served as a backdrop to all of my summers. They'd heard all of my secrets and provided a sheltering place for my dreams.

It must have been Tuesday because Mrs. Terry waved from her canoe as she paddled by. The octogenarian traveled two miles across the lake and back each week to buy groceries. I admired her vigor but could not imagine imitating her.

"That's where I'm headed," Cal said.

I followed the length of his arm to Mt. Baldy, as the mountain was known to locals, and Mt. Craig to the rest of the world. "That's an ambitious hike."

"You've been to the summit?"

"Not recently." Small talk wasn't going to get Cal off the deck and on the road. "You have something to show me?"

"Sorry, your view distracted me." He opened the paper to reveal a hand-drawn map, colored with crayons. He made to hand the map to me.

I stepped back, held up my hands, still sticky with goo from the trash. "Why don't you lay the map on the table?"

The map turned out to be a color copy of the original. "I found this on a beach in Sumatra. In a bottle," he said.

I stepped closer, clasped my hands behind my back. A child had drawn an island as a blob of green in a sea of scribbled blue. Across the top of the page—in the expanse of water—were the words "please to help!"

"Where is this?" I said.

"I've been pouring over maps, but I can't make a match. I was hoping your father would recognize the island. His students never stumped him, although we sure tried. Does it look familiar to you?"

"Nothing comes to mind. The knobs on the east and west shores might be a hint, but there's no scale. This could be a child's rendition of Iceland or Australia or one—egad, there are tens of thousands of islands in Indonesia. What about the islands off the coast of Sumatra?"

"The Mentawi Islands. I've looked and looked. None match this."

Dad would have loved a mystery involving a sketched island tossed to sea in a bottle. Looking at the map made me tired. "Couldn't this be a child playing at being a castaway?"

"I'd hoped to look through your father's maps, start with Indonesia, move west with the currents."

Cal's ambitious hopes were starting to irritate me. "Dad's collection is a mess. He wasn't capable of cataloging his acquisitions in his last years. Finding anything specific would be plain impossible. Mr. Branigan, Cal, I'm afraid I'm not going to be much help to you."

He held out the map. "Can I leave this with you? Perhaps you'll see something in your father's maps as you're sorting. I'll be on the mountain a week. I could stop by when I get back to civilization."

I waved off the map. He looked confused.

"I don't go to the shop any more than I have to," I said.

Cal folded the map along the creases. "It's the plea for help. My wife says I have a strongly engrained hero complex."

I couldn't explain to a stranger how much I risked each time I entered the map shop. I stepped off the deck and made for the front of the cabin, where Cal had parked his vehicle.

He followed me. "Can I stop by, Robin, when I come off the mountain?"

I turned to him. "You're asking more than you know. I wouldn't count—"

"Do what you can. That's all I ask."

I stepped behind the front door, using it like a shield. "I rarely go to the shop. I'm so sorry. Thank you for stopping by. Dad would have been pleased." I closed the door with enough pepper to discourage Cal from knocking again. His footsteps crunched in the gravel, stopped, and returned.

He shouted through the door, "I put the map under the mat. My number is on the back. I'll see you in a week."

To touch the childish map meant an unplanned departure, ending up God knows where, so I tugged on two pairs of latex gloves to retrieve the map from under the doormat. I dropped it into a plastic bag and zipped the bag closed, only to throw it away under the sink.

No traveling to scribbled islands for me.

4

I loathed the dinner hour.

The gray hours, from right after sunset until night dropped like a boom, filled me with dread. There was nothing to anticipate in the coming darkness. Dinner was whatever I scrounged from the last reception I'd worked—plus an apple, probably pithy, or an orange, probably woody. I finished eating in five minutes. Going to bed had once been an irresistible invitation. Now, I slid under the covers when my eyes got too blurry-eyed to read.

There were days when I fought against the aching darkness. As the light grayed, I carried a mug of orange-spiced tea to a deck chair and wrapped myself up in a sleeping bag against the coming chill. I lit a candle and watched the flame gyrate in the evening breeze. Spotting the first star over the Never Summer Range triggered a minor celebration. I counted meteors as they swiped the sky. Something close to contentment settled on me on those days.

To be honest, those evenings were rare.

Five candles flickered on the table beside me to no effect. An ache opened in my chest and drilled toward my spine. I fingered through my layers of clothing, expecting to find my eternity ring hanging from a chain, warmed by my flesh, resting in the canyon between my breasts. Sliding the ring over my index finger and rubbing it with my thumb usually helped me reset to something resembling calm. I felt for the chain, ran my hand into the cups of my bra. Nothing. Perhaps it had slid to my back.

But no.

I rushed inside and stripped to my underwear, shaking out my blouse, shoes, and socks, and turning out pockets. Nothing.

My dinner curdled in my stomach. I sat on the edge of the tub with my head in my hands.

When Doug had presented the ring, he made sure I'd noticed the Cherry Creek box and insisted that I keep it in the safe when I wasn't wearing it. But I wore the ring every single day. It broadcasted that after twenty-five years of marriage, Doug still believed me worthy, desirable, a treasure to behold.

Sure, the ring was audacious. Thirteen diamonds circled the band, totaling five carets. I had been slightly uncomfortable showing it to friends when Doug insisted. A recession mired most of the country that year, and Nicci, our youngest daughter, reminded me the thing dripped the blood of the oppressed.

I wouldn't find the ring sitting on the tub.

I checked the fish-shaped bowl by my toothbrush, where I parked the ring and its chain whenever I took them off. In the living room, I shifted boxes to search ravines of cardboard. I shook out bedding and ran my hands over the linoleum in the kitchen. I ripped the shower curtain down, spread it across the kitchen floor, and dumped the contents of the trashcans. Finally, I leaned against the kitchen cabinets, my hands mucked with butter and coffee grounds, and walked back through my day.

When had I last seen the ring and chain?

It very well could have hung around my neck that morning. When I dried off after a shower, I had to lift the chain, but I hadn't showered yet that day. The pesky raccoons had distracted me.

I redressed quickly and pedaled my bike to the food market on Main, sucking breaths to compensate for the thin mountain air. I asked the cashier, a young woman with no discernable pores and the urgency of a tortoise, if anyone had turned the ring into lost and found. Her nametag labeled her as Chenoa. She cast a casual glance at a battered box under the cash register.

"Do you mind if I take a look?" I said, nodding toward the box.

"It's not in there," she said. "I've been here since two. Someone would have said something." Chenoa looked longingly at the screen of her smartphone and woefully back to me, totally unmoved.

Perhaps if I added some heartbreaking details. "My husband gave the ring to me, Chenoa. He died a horrible death last month. Right before his last breath, he slipped the ring on my finger. Could I look through the box myself, just this once?"

Chenoa raised one eyebrow. "Your husband died? He came in here last week, Mrs. Connelly. With his new wife. The redhead."

I studied her more closely. "Do I know you?"

"Vacation Bible school. Maybe sixth grade. Lauren was in my class. You were our teacher."

Oh. "It's good to see you again."

I wandered up and down the market's aisles, scanning the floor for the ring. I dug through the Fuji apple display and stirred the bulk items until the manager asked me to leave. As I crossed the Rainbow Bridge back toward the cabin, I remembered tucking the ring into my wetsuit. I'd had the ring when I left for Doug's garage via Mexican waters. I stood to pedal faster.

Either the ring rested on the floor of the Sea of Cortez or in Doug's garage, maybe under the pink scarf at the bottom of Doug's golf bag. If it lay on the bottom of the sea, the ring was lost to me forever. But if I'd dropped it in Doug's garage ...

The only way back inside the garage was via the Sea of Cortez. I didn't especially like the idea of floating in the ocean in the dead of night, but I hated even more the idea of losing that ring.

I splashed into the night-cooled waters and floated for the longest five-ish minutes of my life. Only a few lights winked on the shore of Puertecito, and the moon was nothing more than a shy smile. Not one line from "Paul Revere's Ride" formed in my head. I willed myself to float as high as possible on the rolling waves, until I was pulled back to *Zella* and Doug's garage.

I rubbed the back of my head and swept the deck with my hands, feeling for the ring. I pointed the flashlight into Doug's golf bag and shook out the pink scarf. Nothing. I switched the beam to high and worked the area like a crime scene. I was about to surrender to defeat when a glint caught my eye.

My eyes burned from sea water, but sure enough the flashlight's beam had found the ring. It rested in the track of the Land Rover's rear tire, which, of course, was *her* vehicle. If I hadn't found the ring, *she* would have crushed the thing when she'd gone to the market for gin. Again.

I slipped the ring onto my quivering finger and hugged my hand to my chest. As tempting as it was to crawl back onto *Zella* to sleep on the aft bench, I hefted myself off the floor and walked in the flashlight's tremulous beam back to the cabin.

I sunk into a fitful sleep and dreamed of petting hairy dolphins with puppylike tails. Even in my dreams, the world refused to be what I expected it to be.

5

Carolyn was uncharacteristically quiet as she drove us toward Spirit Lake Lodge.

"Is something wrong?" I asked.

She groaned. "Don't ask, okay? If we're friends, don't ask."

We were friends, all right. In fact, Carolyn was my only friend.

Any assumptions made about how utterly miserable I was for company would be correct. After the divorce, I avoided going out in public for fear of being asked the wrong sorts of questions about Doug's new redhead. And if I successfully chided myself into meeting friends for lunch, I always canceled at the last minute. I maddened absolutely everyone.

I would have stopped calling me, too.

And then came Carolyn Truelove. Yes, Truelove, and never has anyone lived up to her name more than she. She was, after all, a retired kindergarten teacher. Being kind to snot-filled and headstrong children came naturally to Carolyn, which prepared her perfectly for being my friend. Kindergarten teachers must be encouraging and patient, but they must also say the hard things without leaving a scar.

The Mini Cooper rode low to the ground, so she slowed to ease past a puddle. The underside of the car scraped, and her cargo slid and scuffed. Curious. I was about to tell her the tale of the lost but recovered eternity ring.

"This road is terrible," she said. "It's barely a road at all. It's more like a bike trail." She shot me a look. "Okay, you're right. Our fearless leaders keep bike paths better maintained than the roads."

My heart caught. Carolyn only turned contrary when she was afraid. "Carolyn, sweetie, you aren't sick, are you?"

Carolyn sniffed and swiped at escaping tears. "If only! I'm completely mortified. I've gone and done it again."

"But you got rid of the ax, didn't you?"

Her shoulders shook and the tears redoubled. "This is much, much worse."

The car swerved into the opposing lane, not a huge deal on the quiet residential streets of Grand Lake, but the shoulder sloped sharply down to Shadow Mountain Lake. "Stop, for heaven's sake!"

Carolyn braked hard. Before us the lake winked in the morning light, and a westerly breeze pushed lazy swells toward us. In the distance, Table Mountain heaved toward the sky.

There would be no retelling of the ring scare. I touched her shoulder. "Tell me," I said. "You'll feel better once you do."

She dabbed at her tears and shifted the Cooper into gear. "You remember, don't you, that Wayne and that *woman* have a listing at the end of my street, that hideous modern thing with pink trim? The for-sale sign is as big as a billboard, for crying out loud.

"If *she* could truly see herself in those pictures, she would forbid their use. Her head is like a melon, I swear. Have you noticed? And her hands, they're more like talons, don't you think? And that diamond! Good grief, it's huge! He never gave me a diamond, not ever. He blamed the DeBoers for manipulating women's expectations. And I believed him!

"Anyway, I might have had more than one glass of wine before dinner last night. And I might have slammed a few drawers and cursed the day that *woman* was born."

We came to a stop sign. Carolyn dug through her purse until she found a package of tissues and blew her nose. "The thought of driving by that stupid sign every day for the rest of my life—okay, so I wasn't completely rational at this point—drove me to madness. That gap between her teeth. Her smooth skin, which you know has to be Photoshopped, unless she spent her whole life in a cave. Do you think she's a vampire? Don't answer that! I'm being stupid again."

"What did you do, Carolyn?"

"I had another glass of wine and went to bed, but once I laid down, I could barely breathe. All I could see was that sign polluting my view. You understand, don't you?"

I understood perfectly. Carolyn needed out of Grand Lake. Everywhere she went Wayne's face graced real estate signs and brochures, even bus stops. And now, that woman's face smirked back at her, too. I could have suggested a move to Carolyn, but if she took my advice, I would lose her. "Have you considered using the sign for target practice?"

"I did toy with the idea, actually, but rifle shots attract needless attention. Instead, I put on my Sorels, marched down to the corner, and yanked that sign out of the ground. It came out a lot easier than I'd expected."

"That's all? You pulled a sign out? Boy, that's not as bad as I'd feared. We can put the sign back before anyone misses it."

Carolyn drummed her fingers on the steering wheel. "I might have pulled out a few more."

"A few? Like three?"

"More like thirteen."

I gestured toward the cargo area. "Is that what's sliding around?"

"Maybe we should stop by the landfill."

"What landfill? The closest dump is in Granby."

"Oh Lord, what am I going to do?"

Carolyn should not have been driving. I switched places with her and steered the car back to my place. Once there, finding niches to hide fifteen—not thirteen—real estate signs proved harder than I'd anticipated. We ended up sliding the signs between stacks of boxes in the garage. With a few carefully draped towels, no one would be the wiser.

Carolyn considered the contents of my garage. "I can't let you harbor my stolen goods forever."

"Not forever. We'll think of something."

Carolyn had never faced anything like the acrimony of a shattered marriage. Kindness was her core belief, the compass that guided her professional and personal lives. She admitted, once we'd known each other for nearly a year, that Wayne hadn't been the easiest of husbands. From the stories she told, he was moody and cruel, always at the ready with the perfect zinger to deflate her. But she truly believed she would win him over, sort of like Belle and the Beast.

Unfortunately, Carolyn's marriage wasn't a Disney movie.

Wayne remained a beast, and Carolyn hadn't a clue how to manage her feelings of hurt and anger. Ironically, we worked together every Saturday making sure brides got the wedding receptions of their dreams.

Carolyn threw up her hands. "This is not the person I want to be. I am not the kind of person who exacts revenge. I bake muffins for new neighbors. I pick up trash as I walk. People trusted me with their children for thirty-five years. I've never said a harsh word to anyone. Well, that last part isn't exactly true. I gave my brother heck on a regular basis, but do brothers really count as people?"

We'd had this conversation many times. Our unspoken agreement forbade judgment in our friendship. "You are most definitely not that kind of person," I said. "You're wonderful. In fact, you're almost too good. That's your only real problem. What could have prepared you for the kind of heartache you're living? Nothing, I tell you, absolutely nothing. You're doing the best you can under the circumstances."

"Do you really think so?"

"Of course I do."

We both went silent. I mentally flipped back through the days since my marriage had turned to powder. I wasn't proud of how I'd handled myself. I repeatedly said ugly and plain stupid things that could never be taken back. I'd stomped like a child and grown petulant when Doug went superior on me.

Most disturbing was that I didn't remember my marriage correctly. Perhaps I'd ignored Doug's slights and his lapses in judgment for thirty-three years. But I honestly didn't think so. Does believing that make me stupid? He slept with another woman for three long years—three Valentines, three Fourth of Julys, three Thanksgivings, and three Christmases and New Years—while coming home to me every single night. There had to have been clues, right? Was I that trusting, or was he that devious? I hated this second-guessing.

Carolyn parked the car in the back of the lodge. She put her hand to my arm to stop me from getting out. "Before we go in," she said, "I've been very selfish, carrying on about what I couldn't stand another minute. How are *you* doing? Have you been traveling?" She used air quotes around the word "traveling."

The last time we'd talked, I'd pledged to never travel to Doug's garage ever again. "I, uh, well ..."

"You think I don't understand? You want to be near him, right? Well, honey, I know you'll do better."

Would I?

She touched my arm. "Tell me this: Did you feel better after visiting his garage?"

"*She's* been wearing Doug's jacket, the one I bought for him. It smelled like her. And she'd stuffed a pink scarf into his golf bag." I lifted up on the car handle and turned back to Carolyn. "Well, actually, I'm the one who stuffed the scarf. But I really shouldn't jump to conclusions. The scarf could have belonged to someone else, right?"

Our eyes met and widened with understanding. "Now, that would be some sweet kind of justice," Carolyn said.

Carolyn only asked about my traveling to be polite. She didn't believe I touched a map and magically arrived somewhere. But fortunately, her students' imaginary friends had prepared her to be my friend. To believe that I touched a map and traveled to that exact spot wasn't so much more of a stretch. Not really.

6

"Mother, what the hell is going on here?" Nicci threw up her hands. "Have you lost your mind? Normal people, and by that I mean women with spines, do not live barricaded behind moving boxes. You're starting to freak me out."

As my tornado child, Nicci tempted me to run for shelter. Unfortunately, the cabin didn't have a basement.

Nicci continued. "Mom, it's been two years. *Two* years. This is pathetic. Yes, you had a beautiful home, which Dad totally screwed you out of, but this is not helping. Either get rid of this crap or—" She looked around. "Mom, you do realize that half of this stuff won't even fit in here?"

A fiery rash filled the crooks of Nicci's elbows and spread from her collar bone to her chin. I kept one eye on Nicci and one on Alex, my granddaughter, who slumped on the futon between my folded bedding and a box labeled "MISC."

"I've been pretty—" I started.

Nicci sniffed the air. "Do I smell mouse piss? Crap, Mother, this place is a pit."

Nicci pushed boxes aside to make a path to one of the two bedrooms—the front room with the window to the lake we'd always called the Lakeview Room. We named the other, the one with a window to Jerico Road, the Pollywog Room, as my brother and I were just out of diapers when Dad built the cabin.

Alex chewed at her cuticles, and her bangs covered her eyes.

She looked pale for a fourteen-year-old. And taller than when I'd seen her last. That had been Christmas. Six whole months earlier. Where had the time gone?

"Alex needs a place to sleep. You'll have to clear off the bed." She studied the doorknob on the Lakeview door. "Does this door have a lock? You can't take your eyes off Alex for a minute, unless you can lock this place up. She's turned into a monster."

Alex rolled her eyes. "Mother, I'm right here."

"See what I mean? She's absolutely hateful. She has no idea what she's doing. She appreciates nothing. I'm working two jobs and going to school. I only ask her to come home from school, do a few things around the house, and, oh yeah, not run away."

Alex met my gaze, pleaded with her eyes. But I couldn't capitulate yet. Nicci had to believe she'd won a hard-fought battle. "Nicci, honey, wouldn't Alex do better at home? That's where her friends are."

"I can't drop everything when she gets squirrely and blows."

"I went to Kaelyn's," Alex said, spicing her voice with contempt. "There was no mystery, no subterfuge. I spent the night with Kaelyn, my best friend since first grade."

"Don't you dare patronize me. And don't play little miss perfect in front of Grandma." Nicci turned to me. "I called Kaelyn. She had no idea where she was. And, Mom, Alex doesn't get what guys want. They'll say anything."

I loved hearing my words parroted out of Nicci's mouth, but I dared not say so, especially with Alex's eyes glistening with tears. She pleaded with Nicci, "Mom, ask Sean to leave, and I'll never run away again, I promise."

"Are you crazy? Sean is the best, and you know it." She turned back to me. "He's got a good job, a nice car, and he doesn't spend half of his life wasted."

Nicci's boyfriends usually populated America's Top Losers list, but Sean seemed truly different. He was settled, dependable, not a drunk, not on parole. He was a sigh of relief that I took as a sign for better things to come. Alex's face told me something different. If possible, more color drained from her face. "Alex, honey, what's wrong with Sean?"

Nicci stepped between us. "Do not listen to her. She can't get away with anything with Sean around. He pays attention, makes sure she gets her homework done." Nicci stepped closer, lowered her voice. "Listen, Mom, I need your help here. I'm real, real close to getting my degree. I have to do well in these last two classes. Worrying about Alex, trying to keep the peace at home, it's too much. I'm going a little crazy.

"You have to let Alex stay," she said. "She can help you. She's great at organizing stuff. Hell, she'll get these boxes emptied in no time."

Over Nicci's shoulder, Alex clasped her hands in prayer and mouthed "please."

Nicci continued. "I don't know what I was thinking. There's plenty of room for your crap. Mom, your life is in these boxes. You'll feel better with your things out where you can see them. Maybe if you painted the paneling. This old place would look like a little French cottage, especially with all of your pillows."

I'd given my pillows to my sister-in-law, every last fringed, bejeweled, shimmering, and ruffled pillow that I'd bought on our travels. After she'd helped me box up my life and listened to all of my theories as to why Doug had turned into a person I no longer recognized, she deserved my fabulous pillow collection.

Alex would definitely stay with me. When Nicci fixed an idea in her head, I went along with her, or she disappeared for a week or a month or a year. No mother can stand against that kind of estrangement. But I wanted Alex to know I cared about what she wanted.

"Alex, are you okay staying with me for the summer? I'm pretty strapped for cash. There won't be much to do. I don't have

Internet and no cell service here at the cabin, but we can walk to the library. Life on the lake could get boring. I'm working weddings every weekend."

Nicci scowled at her daughter. Alex rolled her eyes as if on cue. "What choice do I have?"

"Do not cop an attitude with your grandmother. Is that understood?" Nicci hefted her sizeable purse to her shoulder, slid her sunglasses into place, and dug for her keys. She opened the door and turned back. "You've saved my life, Mom. I don't know how to thank you."

Alex rushed into my arms before the door clicked closed. "Grandma, this is so great. Thank you. I'll do anything you say."

Her exuberance squeezed my heart and something warm poured into my chest. And yet, a niggling doubt tapped on my shoulder. I held her at arm's length. "This is a fast turnaround, even for you."

"You know Mom. She likes to think she's sticking it to me. I love the idea of a summer on the lake with you. Thanks so much for letting me stay." She flipped her hair over her shoulder. "Can we go down to the lake?"

"Sure. I guess. We should make some sandwiches. My friend, Carolyn, says there are bluebirds in the meadow. We'll hike up there, too."

Alex helped me shift boxes to find Dad's binoculars. The bread bag had been nibbled by mice, so we packed saltines and a jar of peanut butter. We took an apple to share.

There would be time to discover Alex's real problem with Sean, and whether or not he had anything to do with Alex's wanderings. But not that day. The local Audubon group had installed new nest boxes, and the bluebirds were gathering materials to set up housekeeping. The sun gently warmed the earth, and a breeze slid across the lake to bathe us with the scent of percolating life.

I wished Doug were there. He had been the one constant male influence in Alex's life from the day she was born. He'd played dolls with her, made her lunches, attended all father-daughter events. Best of all, he got all dreamy-eyed whenever she came into a room. Every little girl needed a prince like that.

When Lauren and Nicci had started to blossom, as Alex was now, Doug became awkward with our daughters. We'd talked and he'd promised to do better before they found all-too-willing boys to satisfy their need to be adored. I saw Doug try, but his efforts fell flat. Had he felt the same ineptitude with Alex? Or had he been too distracted by *her* to keep in touch with Alex?

Whatever the reason, Doug had gone AWOL, again.

THE CABIN PERCHED ABOVE the lake on a narrow shelf, so we descended sun-bleached stairs to reach the dock and the boat garage, where we had once parked *Zella*. The bay stood empty, except for a tiny rowboat filled with mildewed life jackets and fishing tackle.

When Dad built the boat garage to protect Zella from the harsh winters, Mom saw an opportunity. She insisted Dad add a screened room on the flat roof for a bug-free view of the lake. It became our sleeping porch, Rocky-Mountain style. I kept the room shuttered.

That afternoon, Alex and I sat on the end of the dock, warming like lizards in the sun. Speedboats whined in the distance. A drowsiness came over me that I welcomed, but Alex groaned and jogged up the stairs to the sleeping porch. The door opened with a screech, and she disappeared inside.

What is she up to?

I was suddenly homesick for my loneliness. She poked her head out the door. "Grandma, this is perfect. There's a daybed, a chair, and a table. I can sleep in here."

An alarm sounded in my chest. "The lock's broken."

"What could get me? No one comes down the road."

I gathered the book she'd abandoned and stood. Nicci had, in her own irresponsible way, given me a sacred trust. Keeping Alex safe in the wilds of Colorado fell to me. "There's wildlife, Alex. Bears. Coyotes. Skunks. Moose. Mountain lions. And snakes."

"I won't keep food up here. That's all they really want."

I stood at the landing, peering into the small space where I'd spent so many summers, reading on rainy days and playing monopoly with my brother by candlelight. Doug and I made out for the first time on that very daybed. "This place freezes at night. There's not a lick of insulation in these walls."

"We slept in here during the reunion. I used Grandpa's sleeping bag. I never got cold or scared."

"That was August. This is June. The wind blows over the ice fields and drops the temperature into the thirties every night."

"I won't open the shutters."

"There's a health concern here, as well. The city doesn't issue permits for enclosed structures like the porch over boat garages anymore. They worry about carbon monoxide, Alex, from boat exhaust. People die from CO_2 poisoning." *Please, be reasonable.*

"But *Zella's* not even here, Grandma."

"I saw a fox the other day, walking down the road like he owned the place."

Her face darkened. "You believe her! You think I'll run away! I thought you would be different, but you're not. I should have gone home with Mom." Alex pushed open the door and clomped up the stairs to the cabin, her long hair swinging across her back.

I followed her, slowly, rehearsing words I didn't want to say. I found her sitting on the futon with her nose in another book. I sat on a box across from her. "Wildlife is a real concern, Alex. I keep my doors locked. I hear things in the night. The raccoons outsmart me on a regular basis."

"And?"

"And I would feel better if you weren't down there by yourself."

"And?"

"And you think you know all the threats in the mountains."

"I know how convincing Mom can be. I get that. I just want to be judged for who I am, not who she is."

She had a point. "That's fair."

"But?" she challenged.

"But you're a little bit infuriating in your own way."

A small smile. A glint in her eye. "That's what my teachers tell me."

"You've had to grow up too fast, Alex. I'm sure that being on your own feels good and natural to you, but I'm not quite ready to put you in a screened porch all night."

"I won't run away, Grandma. I love being here with you."

"I know." *Did I?* "Listen, Alex, can we revisit this question in the near future?"

She surveyed the room clogged with moving boxes. "So where am I supposed to sleep?"

"Good question." If I emptied a bedroom of boxes, those boxes would fill the kitchen and, possibly, the bathroom. If I gave her the futon, that meant hunting for the blow-up mattress. This fifty-four-year-old body had no business sleeping on the floor. "For tonight, we punt. I'm pretty sure I know where more blankets are. I'll make you a nice bed on the floor."

Alex was content with popcorn for dinner, but I couldn't expect the girl to survive on a diet of beans and rice with a smattering of buffet-line leftovers, as I did. I would buy groceries, do some cooking.

Who am I kidding?

The thought of cooking three meals a day flattened me. Was I too tired to take care of my granddaughter? No, not that tired. Never that tired. Only too tired to take care of myself. For Alex I would pump my bike along the road—a mule track, really—to where the pavement began, cross Rainbow Bridge, and press on to the market, where I would navigate narrow aisles and questioning glances. Buying the kind of groceries a growing girl needed would undercut my savings, which meant buying back *Zella Francine* from Doug would take longer.

Having Alex's company more than made up for any delay.

7

Teenagers are sleep anarchists.

They resist the urges of their growing bodies to rest, only to lie comatose well past the soft hours of morning. Alex was no exception. She'd read a hardback that crinkled as she turned the pages well past two. With the lamp on.

I didn't sleep until she did.

The next morning, I dressed quietly and poked through the trash to find Cal's map. All those hours of wakefulness had given me plenty of time to revisit the question of the map, which I'd almost decided had to be a child's dream. Neverland? Narnia? Oz?

Or perhaps not.

What if the plea for help proved bona fide? The child could be in all manner of duress. Perhaps his mother languished with fever, or a horrible storm had left him orphaned, or he needed a pen pal for his English class.

The Girl Scout in me demanded action.

I rode my bike along the road that paralleled the lakeshore, passing what some called cabins on Colorado's largest natural lake, only they cost millions. The dirt road hadn't been graded after the winter snows, so I dodged puddles and dirty slush until I hit pavement, right in front of the snootiest house on the lake.

I pressed hard into the pedals, hoping to beat the stream of tourists in and out of Rocky Mountain National Park. Trail Ridge Road had only been open two weeks, but the increase in traffic through Grand Lake made me irritable. Gawking drivers tended to drift toward parked cars and pedestrians as they read signs along the boardwalk, looking for a restaurant or a motel with a vacancy. Riding a bike in the business district could be classified as reckless at certain times of the day. Only a few mud-crusted trucks grumbled through town at this early hour. I cut across Grand Avenue, turned onto Garfield, and parked my bike outside The Traveling Man.

Inside the door, I breathed deeply of ink, paper, and dust. Before taking one step, I pulled on rubber gloves and slipped on the life vest I kept beside the door. A heap of glossy mail covered the floor. Nothing looked all that important, so I stepped over the pile.

This was no quaint lakeshore shop. A warren of aisles and chests of shallow drawers, all under hooded lights that intensified shadows, made The Traveling Man chaotic for the uninitiated. Cardboard tubes of maps leaned against the wall. Stacks of maps with worn folds lay on every surface. I smoothed Cal's map on the viewing table.

I walked my fingers through a pile of Indonesian maps until I found a topographical map of Sumatra. I pulled my sleeves to my wrists to avoid touching the map with my bare arms and bent closer, comparing Cal's island with each of the Mentawi Islands. A satellite map would have been more accurate, but still, none of the islands even came close to matching.

A sharp rap of knuckles against the glass door startled an expletive out of me. A woman with a stocking cap pulled low looked back at me. Panic creased her features.

"Hello?" she called through the glass. She jiggled the doorknob. "Are you open?"

The main street attracted all sorts of tourist business with sports outfitters, antique stores, and restaurants. The Traveling Man wasn't any of those things. Housed in a deep, narrow log cabin, off the main drag, few people mistook us for an actual place of business. We hadn't posted operating hours, nor bothered with an open sign, in a very long time.

She knocked again. "I know it's early, but I'm desperate."

I unzipped the life vest and let it slide off my shoulders to the floor and tugged the rubber gloves off before opening the door, but only wide enough to show my face. "We're not a real store."

"You have to understand. I went to close my suitcase, and the zipper broke. My ride is picking me up in a half hour. I have to repack everything for three weeks in Europe. This is a nightmare. Will you sell me a large suitcase or not?"

She held a common misconception. With a name like The Traveling Man, she expected us to carry overpriced luggage and plastic bottles approved by TSA.

"I would be happy to if I stocked luggage. And I can't think of any place in town that does. There's a Walmart in Granby."

The woman groaned. "Too far."

I dug deeper for suggestions. "There's that nice mall in Golden, right off the interstate. They have a Target—"

"You're worse than no help at all." She turned sharply for her car, so I closed the door.

I pictured the woman in airport security with a suitcase held together with duct tape. That made me smile. And then, without thinking, I picked up Cal's map with bare hands. My vision blackened and the sucking pull lifted me from the floor. I pinched my nose.

And then I plunged under the water in a rush of gurgling and the fizz of bubbles. I kicked off my shoes and clawed for the surface. Once breathing sea air, I did what I always did on an unplanned departure, I looked for land. An island within easy swimming distance rose from the sea, which had to be Cal's island, didn't it? Not the product of a child's imagination but small as islands go.

I would never reach the shore with saturated jeans, so I sank under the surface to unsnap the pants and work the zipper down. Up I came for another breath and another and another until I worked out of the sodden jeans—the only jeans I owned that fit my waist *and* my hips—and let them sink to the bottom of the sea. Refracted light played off the sandy bottom. The jeans had come to rest too far below for me to retrieve.

Oh, how I regretted sliding out of the life vest, and how I wished I'd mastered treading water. I sank like a stone no matter how many swimming classes or personal trainers I went through. I wasn't that good of a swimmer either. The thought of going ashore, however, didn't appeal. Whoever had drawn the map had called for help. Who knew what awaited a traveler?

The island looked peaceful enough with densely packed palm trees and large fleshy bushes that could have hidden anything. A sandy beach extended a welcome, and a dock jutted out into the water from its generous shore. Two huts, one with a curl of smoke coming out of the chimney, squatted on the beach. I noted, also, an open-sided shade structure.

Going ashore was out of the question, not with people present.

Still, without a life vest, solid ground held great appeal. Just not this particular beach in front of those very lived-in huts.

With a gliding sidestroke, I swam parallel to the shore and away from the dock. Hopefully, I would find another sandy beach where I could wait to depart for *Zella*. I kept an eye on the dock for any sign of people. My heart pounded and my chest burned, so I switched to a lazy breaststroke.

Movement drew my eye to the dock. A slight woman in a long dress walked with fretful steps to the end. I feared she would see me, but she seemed intent on looking toward the last bit of brightness on the horizon. Wherever this place was, the day was waning, while the day in Colorado had only begun. I was far, far from home.

The woman looked over her shoulder toward the huts on the beach. She pulled something out of her dress and dropped the small object into the water, then walked quickly back to the shore, where she ducked into the hut with the curl of smoke.

My arms and legs felt like lead. I had no idea how much longer I would be in that place, and this would be my only chance to learn something about the island for Cal. I rolled onto my back to frog stroke, resting between pulls, inching my way toward the dock and whatever floated in the water among the pilings.

Only a small bottle, corked and stuffed with a folded paper bobbed in the shadows of the dock. Gratefully, the piling hid me from possible lookers on shore, but if someone walked down the dock, I wouldn't have a moment's warning or a place to hide. I couldn't stay there.

By my watch I'd been in the water for just under thirty minutes. I could have another half hour to go, depending on the island's longitude. I reached for the bottle. Before I could capture it, my vision turned fuzzy, and I was wrenched back to *Zella*.

I landed hard, the deck grinding against my spine, my head bouncing against the boards with a crack. I stifled a moan and settled in to wait for the nausea to pass. When I finally opened my eyes, Doug glared over me. My confused heart lurched with joy and drummed with alarm.

"What the hell? Robin, this has got to stop. You can't keep breaking into the garage." His face disappeared below the gunwale. He jiggled the doorknob of the side door. "It's locked," he said with befuddlement. "This is happening too much."

If he'd noticed I was sopping wet, that was a much smaller mystery to him than how I'd gotten into his garage. Even though the world spun crazily, I reached for a towel and rubbed my face and body. I then realized I wasn't wearing pants. I wrapped the towel around my waist and started down the swim ladder.

"Why are you wet?" His face registered disgust before it went unreadable and distant. "This is weird behavior, Robin, even for you."

Doug didn't know I was a traveler, and he didn't know about my father either. I held this truth about my father and me to my chest like a great poker hand. I hadn't started traveling until after the divorce. As a super power goes, traveling confounded the heck out of me. What good was it, really? Until I had all of that figured out, I planned on keeping my cards breasted.

Besides, Doug would never believe me.

Might as well revisit our timeworn discussion. It was what Doug expected. "Sell the boat to me, Doug. I have about five-hundred dollars to give you today. Maybe a little less, I haven't checked my account in a while."

Doug heaved a weary sigh. "You'd be floating in cash if you sold the cabin."

Only the cabin remained solid under my feet. I couldn't let it go. I put my hands to my hips. "And you feel perfectly comfortable asking me to sell off all that remains of my life?"

"The cabin is wood and plaster, Robin, wood and plaster that could rake in a cool million or more. There isn't a better view on the lake." He leveled his gaze at me, looking me up and down. "How are you living, anyway? You're clearly not working. You can't survive off sentimentality, you know."

Sentimentality? Me? Doug was the one who cried through truck commercials. Clearly, he wasn't the same man I married thirty-three years earlier. I blamed *her*, of course. She'd sashayed over to the cabin one time too many, looking for a sympathetic ear for her troubled marriage and found Doug a willing listener. I suspected voodoo on her part. After all, she was only a year younger than me and about twenty pounds heavier—in one rather advantageous area. Doug had been complaining of feeling his age. I must say she perked him up better than those horrid protein shakes and testosterone patches he'd tried.

I squared my shoulders. "I'm working, and you know it." I served at wedding receptions all summer long at the Spirit Lake Lodge and worked on the banquet line in Winter Park during the ski season. The pay barely kept the lights on and covered the taxes, but I took home all the food I wanted. I ate a lot of Chicken Parmesan. I tried to find a full-time job, but I'd worked for twenty years at our supply shop for no pay whatsoever. Potential employers took one look at my résumé and assumed I'd never worked at all. And there was my age.

"Listen, Robin, I know this is hard for you." He gestured at *Zella*. "You loved your dad, and the boat means a lot to you. I get that. But you can't come back here, not to this garage, ever, and I certainly can't wait for you to squirrel away enough to buy the boat."

He feigned understanding my feelings, but he extended not a whit of compassion. The woman had hijacked his soul. Plus, I suspected a brain disorder had made him vulnerable to her wiles. "Have you gotten that MRI yet?"

He looked at his feet and shook his head. "I don't have a brain tumor, Robin."

"A bladder infection, if left unchecked, can alter your personality. Dad went a little loose right before he died. Antibiotics fixed him right up."

"This is who I am, Robin. This is who I've always been. I simply saw my chance at happiness and took it. That's all that happened. If you could move on, that would help me very much."

He couldn't, or wouldn't, see how much his happiness had cost me, and I was foolish to ask him to. What he wanted blinded him. How had she done this to such a good man? "Can we talk about those payments? Don't make me beg, Doug."

"You're not in much of a position to uphold a commitment like that."

I ran my hands over the starboard rail. "You're letting her rot in place. Let me take her. I can get her pulled out of here by this afternoon."

"Using what? You don't own a vehicle."

"I have friends, good friends." I had one friend who drove a Mini Cooper.

"You have to believe me. I would really like to see you get the boat back, but time isn't on your side. Tiffany wants *Zella* out of the garage yesterday. I've put her off as long as I can."

"You've got your truck, don't you? She won't have to look at *Zella* one more day. I'll put her in the boat garage. You get a happy wife, and I get the boat I built with Dad. We both win, Doug. Well?"

Doug hemmed and hawed like he did when he had to say something he did not want to say. "I don't have the option of being a nice guy here. It's like this—I need the cash. I have to sell the boat, end of story."

I had saved the business with brilliant repositioning of assets and clever marketing during the great recession. "Cash? What's going on?"

"We've hit another slump, that's all."

"A slump? That's impossible." Denver boasted one of the most vibrant economies in the country. For a plumbing supply company to hit a slump in the middle of a building boom smacked of mismanagement. "And your only source of cash is *Zella Francine*? Really?"

What about your wife who ended up with half of Colorado in her divorce settlement?

"I'm doing the best I can. The boat has to go." He opened the garage's side door and with a sweep of his arm gestured me through.

I stood my ground. "We've always been able to talk about anything. Remember Nicci in rehab? Mom's diagnosis? Our own rough patches? That part of who we were doesn't have to change. How much cash do you need?"

Doug sucked in his lips, studied his shoes. "A lot. I can't wheel and deal my way out of this one. I'm truly sorry. I put an ad for the boat online, and I've had a couple calls. A guy is coming by to look at her after lunch. That's why I'm up here in the middle of the week. I can't help you. I'm sorry."

My throat tightened. "Doug, you're a reasonable guy. A good guy. I'm not sure how we ended up like this, but I know you're still that good guy. You know—"

"You need to go, Robin. Don't press me about the boat again. I can't change anything that's happened."

I walked the three doors to the cabin and planned on a really good cry when I got there. But I wouldn't be alone, would I? Alex would still be sleeping at 10 o'clock.

I tiptoed into the cabin, but Alex's bed on the floor was empty. No Alex. She wasn't there. Not in the bathroom or either of the bedrooms, as if she could move in there. Not on the deck or in the dappled light of the forest or skipping stones across the still lake from the dock.

I lost my granddaughter in less than twenty-four hours. Nicci would kill me, or worse, she wouldn't acknowledge my presence on the planet for a very, very long time.

I stood at the back door. "Alex!"

"Grandma?"

Alex's voice came from below. I leaned over the deck's railing. There she stood on the landing to the sleeping porch, waving like a homecoming queen. "Come see what I've done!"

She'd arranged her bedding on the daybed, and honestly, I'd never seen a bed made with more precision. A mason jar of dried pods and pine boughs sat on the table with a pitcher of water and a glass. Where had she found a tablecloth? And she'd commandeered the bathmat to lay inside the door.

"It looks cozy, right?" she asked, her eyes pleading for approval.

I hadn't noticed until that moment how much she looked like her mother, plus Alex used Nicci's playbook: *Whatever you do, do not take Mom seriously. She never means no when she says no. She means go ahead and do whatever you want.*

An ember of anger caught and flared. "You didn't hear a word I said. We discussed this, and I haven't changed my mind. You are not sleeping in the porch."

Alex had even mastered the mock hurt that had melted me into Nicci's hands a million times. My anger sputtered and died, not for lack of wanting but for lack of determination. "Alex, I have nothing left in me to fight you. It's been a bone-crushing morning. There's nothing left in me to argue. You're going to gather up the bedding, the rug—definitely the rug—whatever knick-knacks you've brought down and haul all of it back up to the cabin."

"But—"

I raised my hand like a stop sign. And she sucked in her bottom lip. *Good girl.*

"I'm going to save you the trouble of making childish arguments that will only embarrass you later. I'm in desperate need of a shower."

"Grandma—"

"I'm quite out of words, Alex. Quite out." I put my finger to my lips and backed out. The girl's eyes glimmered with tears. I was being horrible, and her only offense was being too much like her mother. "Give me a few hours," I said and hauled myself up the twenty-three steps to the cabin and headed for the shower.

The tears didn't come. They rarely did anymore. By the first anniversary of the divorce, I'd run out of tears. The truth was worse than that. All of the broken places where tears used to leak out had hardened to a crust. What used to hurt me only left me empty and tired. A hurricane could blow right through me and not disturb a thing.

My body ached to lay down, but closing my eyes would only

start the questions, like how did you end up in this place? You're not that far from retirement and you haven't a penny set aside. What sort of cat food do you prefer? And really, hadn't there been clues?

Gah!

Besides, where would I lay down? Alex had folded my bedding and claimed the futon where she now read self-consciously and avoided eye contact.

"Alex," I said as cheerfully as possible, "Let's go to town." To my utter amazement, she closed her book on a bookmark and slipped her feet into her flip flops. We retrieved my bicycle from The Traveling Man and headed to the grocery store for some real food.

On the way home, I explained to Alex why I didn't own a car, how I got angry when I was actually hurt, and that we would both sleep in the sleeping porch when the nights got warmer, and by warmer I meant forty degrees or better, which might happen by mid-July.

Alex held herself protectively around the waist as we walked. She wasn't Nicci. How could I ever have thought so? The child had managed to stay tender and vulnerable until, of course, I'd squashed her flat, and then I yammered on and on. Regaining her trust would take weeks, and I sensed she had something important to tell me.

I let Alex ride the bike home from the grocery store. She carried the perishables, and I followed with the rest. All the while, I watched the road for a truck towing *Zella*. Doug selling the boat to a stranger created a huge problem. If I happened to touch a map again—and speculating that I wouldn't was ridiculous—I would return to *Zella*, wherever her new owner had parked or docked her.

I had to get *Zella* back.

Besides, there was more to learn about Cal's island, and I

would need a landing place if I planned to visit it again.

8

Lying isn't always bad.

Lying can be a role played to accomplish good, something important. And it was very important to find Cal's island. Someone on that island needed to rescue the whip of a girl who tossed pleas for help into the ocean. That meant another trip to The Traveling Man to study maps of Indonesia and nearby locales. But I couldn't exactly leave Alex alone again, especially now that I'd given her actual cause to run away. She would have to accompany me to the shop, where caution required me to wear rubber gloves and a flotation device. You can see why I had to lie to my granddaughter.

Outside the door to the shop, I donned rubber gloves and scrubbed the doorknob down with spray bleach.

"How long have you been like this?" she asked.

"What do you mean?"

"Grandma, you're sterilizing the doorknob."

"Oh, that. Well, not so long. Maybe a couple of years." I misted the doorknob again.

"I saw you flick a mouse turd off the kitchen counter with your bare finger."

Oops. "There's something about the shop. So many hands have touched the maps. And wait until you see the dust."

"You know, don't you, that this has nothing to do with germs? Maybe you should talk to someone."

I hadn't counted on my fourteen-year-old granddaughter

being well schooled about odd behaviors. Nicci let her watch too much television.

I pushed the door open with my gloved hand. "You're right, I'm not making sense. My fear embarrasses me, but I can't seem to stop myself. I can only enter the shop with gloves and a gallon of bleach."

"Maybe I could clean while you're looking at the maps. Would that help?" she asked, all bright-eyed and earnest.

How many ways could this child best me? "Actually, I could use your help with the maps. I hate touching them." I showed her Cal's map and told the story of its discovery. "It's nothing but a hunch, really. I don't know what degree latitude we're dealing with, but I believe the island is between twenty-five- and thirty-five-minutes longitude."

"How have you figured that?"

I couldn't exactly explain to Alex that I stay at my destinations for the number of minutes longitude of the location, and I'd stayed at Cal's island for about thirty minutes. That had given me the range of degrees longitude where the island was located, which is almost a worthless piece of information.

"Like I said, just a hunch."

Alex scanned the store. "Okay, so where do we start looking?"

I took a globe down from the shelf and dusted it with my sleeve. "We're talking a ten-mile swath to search for each longitude, and there are 360 degrees of longitude. The island could be off Tierra del Fuego—that's at the tip of South America—here."

"I know where Tierra del Fuego is, Grandma."

"Of course you do, so you know there are a gazillion islands off the coast of Chile, too."

"I'm not getting why the longitude is so important. Couldn't we just try to match the shape of the island?"

Looking for a tiny island in the world's oceans would certainly keep Alex busy. She would have to proceed without anymore information from me, as I couldn't tell her why I knew what I knew—that the island was twelve hours ahead of us and probably near the equator. All those palm trees.

"You're probably right." I slipped on the life vest, trying my hardest to act as if I'd done nothing stranger than putting on an apron.

I felt Alex's eyes on me as I bent over the map, my hands clasped behind my back. An unspoken question hung in the air between us. I probably wouldn't be able to answer why I wore a life vest in the Never Summer Range of the Rockies and retain any standing of sanity in her eyes.

I asked her to unroll a map of the world. The map covered the display table and hung down on both ends in graceful curls. "We can narrow down the search by sticking close to the longitudinal lines. Draw a circle around any island you find."

"Won't that ruin the map?"

"This isn't a rare map, only a big one."

"Are rare maps valuable?"

"They can be. A map's value depends on who wants it and how much someone is willing to pay."

Alex took in the shop. "If you're not selling maps on eBay, you should think about it. That's where people who are looking for rare stuff go to look. Some of what you find is plain weird, but maps are cool. I remember listening to great-grandpa's stories. Maps are history, right? Maybe you could sell enough maps to buy a car."

"Or another bicycle."

She smiled wryly. "A car would be better."

A car would require me to sell thousands of maps, not only to save for the purchase price but also for insurance, tax, license, registration, and gas. But if I could earn enough to do all that, I could earn enough to buy *Zella Francine*. She was my priority.

"Tell me how this eBay works."

As Alex ran her finger along the 75th meridian from Baffin Bay to South America, she explained how online selling sites worked. I would need a good camera, a way to display the maps for photographing, and an online account for payment. She spoke of possibilities and not one obstacle, which made me suspicious of the whole scheme.

"I could do all of that for you, Grandma. Maybe not the good camera part, but I do lots of stuff online. Setting you up would be easy."

I could still see my father bending over the shop's drawers of maps, his dimples betraying the pleasure of finding a just-right map. Selling maps to buy back *Zella* seemed foolish but somehow right. How many would I have to sell? My heart wouldn't let me consider not trying.

"Geesh, Grandma, Chile has a lot of islands."

I WILL SAY THIS much about having Alex with me: The week flew by. She dug through boxes until she found the camera, and now she wanted to spend all of her time at the shop, scouring maps or photographing maps. A light sparked in her.

The camera didn't have a great flash, so we carried lamps from the cabin to create a light booth. That sounds technical, but we simply hung lamps over the viewing table to eliminate shadows. Extension cords wound around pipes and draped over map cabinets. All that bare-bulbed light improved the quality of the pictures. I prayed the building-code inspector wouldn't make a surprise visit.

Alex shot the pictures by standing over the maps, zooming in and out to frame each map. She knew to take close-ups of tears and worn folds and any stains on the maps to provide the best as-is photos. We didn't want any dissatisfied map collectors leaving cranky reviews. At least, that's what she insisted.

We established a rhythm. I selected the maps to post, and Alex unfurled them on the viewing table. While she photographed each one, I compiled information, making sure to include everything a potential collector would want to know. Research revealed how to grade the maps for condition, too. Working together erased the weirdness between us far sooner than I'd ever thought possible.

I bent over an engraved map of Cape Breton Island in Nova Scotia. I never tired of how the cartographers blended science, math, and art to create a beautiful and useful masterpiece. For that map, someone back in 1752 had trudged through the northern wilderness, encountered wild animals, gotten eaten by mosquitos, and, perhaps, negotiated safe passage with the native peoples. All for an accurate map of a port. That took grit and commitment.

The mapmaker had labeled the waterways and landforms with spidery letters and washed watery colors over the land and sea. An inset provided details of Fort Dauphin, so the maker exceled in architectural drawing as well. I could sell the map for less than a hundred dollars, which hardly seemed enough for its artistry or enough of an award for surviving intact for 265 years.

I knew exactly what had attracted my father to the map. He would have reveled in the accuracy of the surveying and compared the map to a modern rendition made with satellite images and the benefit of GPS coordinates. Mostly, he would have enjoyed the finesse of the maker.

A rap on the door interrupted my thoughts, and I prepared to turn the knocker away. Cal looked even scruffier than he had when he left on his hike up the mountain, and now he was also sunburned. I welcomed him inside.

"I hoped you might be here," he said with a warmth that disarmed me.

I gestured him in, introduced him to Alex. Suddenly shy, she looked unsure of what to do with her hands, her eyes, her feet. She wanted to be polite, that much I could tell, but she kept looking over her shoulder to the map.

"You can keep working, if you want," I said, releasing her.

"I need to catch up to you." She slipped on cotton gloves and rolled up the map of the Cape Breton Islands to slide it into the cardboard tube I'd already labeled.

When I turned back to Cal, his bemused smile reminded me that I still wore rubber gloves and a life vest. More than I wanted to appear collected and capable, I didn't want to end up back in the ocean without a life vest. I brushed dust off the front of the vest and gave him a look that dared him to say something. "I suppose you're here about the map?"

"Have you discovered anything?"

"Not really."

Alex's head snapped up from the map she was unrolling. "What about your hunch, Grandma?"

"It's less than a hunch, really. More like a wild guess."

Now that Alex knew Cal was the man who had delivered the mysterious map, she set the camera down and stepped easily away from the viewing table. She peppered Cal with questions. "Exactly where were you in Sumatra when you found the map? Do you live there? Could the map be a hoax? If not, what kind of trouble could the girl be in?"

"Why do you assume the map was drawn by a girl?" he asked.

"The printing is childish but neat, and the letters have shape. They're round and full. Guys wad their letters up."

Cal smiled. "That's a great observation."

"So what do you think happened to her?"

"I travel a lot, mostly Asia." His eyes flitted to mine. He seemed to be asking for permission to keep talking, but before I could respond, he continued. "There are places in this world, and to be honest, in this country, where being a girl is a handicap. When things go bad, it always goes worse for girls. Sadly, that's the way it is.

"I fear this map is a cry from a girl like that. And there aren't many people who can help her. She might be hidden away by her captor, or one or both of her parents are dead or too sick to do anything. Sometimes girls are sold into slavery to provide food for younger siblings."

The blood drained out of Alex's face. "By her parents? Why would they do a thing like that? Where are the police?"

Cal answered with the steady tone of someone who'd repeated his speech many times. "There's not one place in the world where slavery is legal, but enforcing laws takes extraordinary will. Powerful people manage to get their way in most places, even here. They use their money, their muscle, or they go very deep where good people won't go. Laws are written to protect all citizens, but in much of the world being poor means you're less than human."

Alex's eyes welled with tears. I put an arm around her shoulders and gave Cal a pleading look, hoping he would stop talking. "And the map comes from a girl like that, someone considered less than human?" she said.

"There's no way to be absolutely sure. Like your grandmother, it's a hunch. I've spent a lot of time in those places, so that's where my mind goes. I've seen very young girls in horrendous circumstances. Once you know their names, there's no going back." Cal pulled off his cap, ran his hands over his face. "Truthfully, I needed a break. Hiking usually gives me that. With no cell phones, there's no news. The beauty lulls me, you know? But I dreamed every night—they were nightmares, really—about the places I've seen. All those faces."

"Grandma, you have to tell him about your hunches."

Cal turned to me, his eyebrows arched in a question.

To tell him anything useful, I would have to tell him about traveling to the island. My father had warned me not to tell anyone outside of the family about traveling. No one else needed to know, although I had told my friend Carolyn. "I'm embarrassed I ever said anything. Sometimes I get these—I don't know— impressions? They never mean anything, but that doesn't stop me from following a thought trail. I'm big on futility, if you know what I mean."

"I know what you mean, Grandma. I spent hours circling islands along the longitudinal lines."

"Why longitudinal lines?" Cal asked Alex.

"It's hard to explain," I said.

He shrugged. "So what are you finding?"

"About a million islands," Alex said.

Alex retrieved the world map she'd worked on, and Cal leaned over to run his finger over its surface, stopping to note the names of the islands. He raised his head. "Do any of these match the drawing I brought?"

I nodded toward the world map. "This map isn't scaled right for that much detail, and I haven't had a chance to look online."

"I'll look for you," Alex told Cal. "I'll make a list and compare your island to satellite images on the Internet."

"Could you email me the list? And anything else you find?"

Cal handed Alex his business card.

Was that wise? The man didn't sleep for all he'd seen in the world, and he was a grown man, not a tenderhearted girl like Alex. If Alex lost sleep, let it be over something she could actually change, like poor cafeteria food or daylight savings, which I would love to see abolished. Not trafficking, not the basest of human behavior. No girl should have to look through such a window.

Cal put out his hand to shake. I ripped off the rubber gloves.

"Thanks for trying," he said. "I'll be back through in a week or so. I'm doing some training in Fraser. I'll stop by." And off he went.

Alex frowned and stared at my hands. I'd made a big mistake by taking off the gloves. I slathered sanitizer all over my hands and forearms and quickly donned new gloves. False cases of OCD are tough to maintain.

When Alex finished the list of islands, she begged me for her own library card and access to the Internet. "Grandma, that girl is waiting for us."

The only thing I'd been dedicated to saving at her age was my dignity. My hair was thin and straight, and I wore my love of ice cream on my thighs. I also wore hand-me-downs from my much older sister. My twin brother played the role of golden boy, athletic and incredibly bright. The word *average* defined me perfectly. I tripped over cumbersome thoughts and my feet. Only constant vigilance had kept me upright and somewhat invisible.

What would have happened if someone like Cal had stumbled into my life with news that little girls were sold into slavery? Could I have been distracted from my own misery? Would I have grown into a stronger, more capable woman? A crusader? I had no way to know, except by watching Alex. She started rising early enough to eat a good breakfast and get to the library by opening time at nine.

She scrolled through satellite images until she met me at The Traveling Man for lunch, stopping only when another library patron claimed their time on the computer. We photographed and cataloged maps all afternoon. She finally receded into her novels—always two or more going at once—after dinner. Her stories seemed a place for her to hide. I hated to think from what.

I started waking each morning, not asking myself how I'd ended up in such a bad place but wondering about the girl on the island, wondering what forces pressed on her. Did her mother pray for her daughter to be returned, if she had indeed been trafficked, or had she given up on ever seeing her again?

Instead of my worst fears, I hoped the girl lived on the island with her family, that she strung shells on string to wear around her neck, that she fished with her father and played with her younger siblings in tide pools. Perhaps the bottle she'd dropped into the sea held what amounted to a lonely girl's shout into the expansive universe.

But I didn't think so. I'd seen her constricted gait, her furtive glances, her hurried retreat.

She needed help. I also wanted Alex's diligence to be rewarded, but she wouldn't find that island without more clues, so I would definitely visit the island again. This time, I would take my diver's watch to time how long I stayed there and swim ashore to ask the girl many questions. Surely, she knew the name of the island. Who doesn't know where they live?

I truly hated to consider the answer to that question.

9

I planned my trip back to the island with scrupulous care.

Since I always returned to *Zella*, I paid an early morning visit to Doug's garage to see if he had indeed sold her. On a previous trip to the garage, I'd bent a couple of slats in the side door's blinds for such a time as this. I scrubbed at the dirty window with the sleeve of my hoodie.

My heart sank.

A rowing machine filled the space where *Zella* had always been parked. *She* had pushed Doug to sell *Zella* for a place to put a stupid rowing machine. Had *she* not noticed a perfectly wonderful lake not twenty yards away? She could row and row and row out on the water until her heart burst. And actually get somewhere, leaving *Zella* here for me.

I slumped against the door. *Zella's gone.*

But where? Moored in Florida? Lake Michigan? On the leeward side of the San Juan Islands? Finding my way back from someplace like Washington state would take time, a long time, and I didn't dare leave Alex on her own for that long.

Job one: Find Zella.

I texted Doug no less than a dozen times. Silence met my requests for a buyer's name, or an address, a phone number, or a city. He finally answered a terse, "Yes" when I asked if *Zella* had ended up in Colorado. *She could be in Grand County, right?* The possibility that *Zella* might reside in my home county filled me with enough confidence to plan another visit to the island. Never mind that I only knew for sure that *Zella* was in Colorado—a state bigger than all of the UK.

I packed a change of clothes in a watertight bag, along with a credit card and what cash I had on hand, thirteen dollars and change. In another bag that I tethered to my ankle, I packed a hairbrush, identification, and—very importantly—a hat. No one, not the most generous cowboy on earth, would offer a ride across Grand County after I'd taken a dunk in the ocean. I looked exactly like Gollum with my hair pasted to my head.

I planned to depart during Alex's deepest sleep, about three in the morning. That would get me to the island midafternoon, if I'd figured the time difference correctly. And if *Zella* wasn't too far away, I could get home long before Alex woke up.

Moments after three, I slipped off the futon and dressed for the bike ride to the map shop. I taped a note for Alex to the refrigerator, saying I would be gone all day working a wedding reception in Kremmling, in case getting back to the cabin proved tougher than I'd expected.

I carried a duffel with the strap across my chest. Inside, I'd added a pair of fins. My time on the island would be short. Fins would get me ashore much faster. I prayed no sharks fed in the vicinity.

Not one soul stirred on Grand Avenue. The bars had been closed for over an hour, but someone had left their truck parked in front of The Tipsy Moose, a demonstration of sound judgment. I pedaled through amber pools of light to The Traveling Man and let myself in.

All of my planning would be wasted if I touched the map prematurely. I donned rubber gloves and plucked Cal's map off the bulletin board behind the cash register. With the map on the viewing table, I used a tack to prick a hole in the tip of the glove's index finger. I'd learned this trick from my travels to the Sea of

Cortez. The hole limited how much of my finger actually touched the map, and thus gave me more control over where I landed.

I held my hand over the map, careful to align my index finger with what I believed to be the north side of the island, the side opposite the dock and the two huts. Since I didn't want to spend all of my time swimming to shore, I aimed for what I estimated to be fifty yards offshore.

My heart pounded in my chest as I lowered my finger to the map. The pull crushed my ribs. Several vertebrae popped. My nostrils cramped against the biting cold.

Aquamarine water. Azure sky. Emerald green. A fiery sun. I splashed into the water and almost immediately hit my shoulder hard on the bottom. My lungs emptied with a glug of bubbles and burned for air. I pushed off the bottom and soon broke the the water's surface, but I could not draw a breath. I flailed, begging myself not to panic or to splash too awfully much—to wait, to wait for my lungs to expand with a blessed breath.

I sucked in violently, only to bark out seawater. My head called for deep, even breaths; my lungs could only spasm. I rolled onto my back, letting the life vest do the work of keeping me afloat. Only then did a softness come. I filled my lungs greedily.

I turned my focus to the island. A girl crouched at the plant line. She stood after a time, lifting her skirt to wade into the water. I should have been afraid, swam—where? The ocean was a monotonous plane of blue in every direction. I watched her through each shuddering breath, until, finally, the burning ceased. If this was the young woman I'd seen on my first visit, she was much younger than I'd thought and as insubstantial as a vapor.

Yet somehow formidable.

Without the distraction of suffocation, my shoulder throbbed for attention. I gingerly rolled it. The joint was hot with insult but didn't grind in its socket. I hoped that meant my shoulder wasn't broken.

The girl shielded her eyes from the sun to watch me bob in the water. Did she see me as a threat? Would she respond to such a threat with violence? My pulse quickened. Perhaps the map had actually been a lure to entice good-hearted people to the island, only to be exploited, or worse.

I should have thought all of that through before I touched the map.

The girl held her hands over her heart, watching me, chewing on her lower lip. She turned quickly, bent to run into the brush, and disappeared. Had I scared her? Was she going for help? I wouldn't find the answers to my questions in the water.

I left the fins in the duffel and kicked toward shore, holding my left arm to keep my shoulder motionless. When I paused to scan the brush for the girl, my feet settled on a firm shelf, so I waded to shore, careful to keep an eye on the tree line.

Once on the beach—a startlingly white crescent of sand—I backed into the shelter of the palms to be less conspicuous and to find some relief from the sun that hung brashly in the sky. Even in the shade the heat squeezed me. Of course, my estrogen-starved body chose that moment to stoke a hot flash that ignited a flame between my shoulders. The wetsuit had to go.

I kept an eye on the path the girl had taken, anticipating her return and, more honestly, hoping she never returned. I eased the wetsuit off my shoulder. Blood oozed from striations and a bruise had spread a ghastly purple. The joint was stiffening, which made peeling the wetsuit off even slower and more agonizing than usual. I slumped to the sand with the wetsuit only half off and gathered at my waist.

The breeze stirred a stew of shadow and light. Belatedly, I wondered if tigers lived on the island. I longed to return to the relative safety of the sea. Instead, I pushed into the low foliage, nesting into the broad leaves.

"Hello?" I whispered into the rustling fronds. "Don't be afraid.

I'm here to help you."

Movement caught my attention, not at all close to where I'd been looking. The girl stood only yards away, studying me with obsidian eyes, breathing heavily with her hand to her heart. She was the color of oiled walnut with full brows that arched pleasingly over inquisitive eyes. I looked past her to the dense foliage. "Are you alone here?"

"How did you come here?" she said, looking to the sea and back to me.

I hadn't anticipated explaining my sudden appearance. I couldn't very well tell the girl that I'd traveled to the island by touching her map a half world away. Such information could only muddy our interactions. Besides, I didn't have time to do much clarifying.

"You are much smaller than I expected," she said, "and I am most surprised you are a woman of sorts. I am not complaining. I am very pleased to see you at long last. I hope not to offend you, honored one. Please, wait here."

The girl darted back into the trees, weaving around corpulent plants and kicking up sprays of white sand. There was a snapping of twigs, and then all went quiet except for the rattle of palm fronds in the breeze.

She remained out of sight for what seemed like an eternity. I sat as still as stone—listening, watching, looking longingly over my shoulder to the welcoming blue.

The girl returned alone. She carried an elaborately carved wooden tray with a teapot and two cups. She knelt in the sand and set the tray before me. Her sari stretched over her stomach to reveal a baby bump.

"Is there anything else you require?" she asked.

She couldn't be much older than Alex, but she carried the experiences of a much longer journey on her narrow shoulders. "How old are you?"

She followed my gaze to the rise of her belly. "I am not so young as I look, I do not think."

"You don't know how old you are?"

She held me with pleading eyes. "I have been away from my family long enough to forget my mother's face."

Letting the girl distract me wouldn't help her. "Please, before we continue: Are you alone on the island?"

She looked to where she had just emerged from the trees. "You have picked a good day to come. Shaitaan is far from here, to a place he calls Main Land. He would not be happy to see you. Not many come here and only those he chooses. Men with money, mostly. And girls. Very young girls." She studied me. "Please to drink your tea. We should be on our way. How will we go? Will we fly from this place? Or is *Bapa* God to send a boat like the ark? A boat might be better." She nodded toward my shoulder. "Because your flying is not so good."

I didn't appreciate the girl's riddled answers to my questions. Shaitaan wasn't here, but what about the other men or girls she mentioned? She expected to travel with me? That wasn't going to happen. And an agent of God? Me?

I shook my head. "I'm not who you think I am. I'm certainly not from God. I'm from Colorado, in the United States, a small tourist town in the mountains."

"Who but one from God would come for me? I pray only to my Father. He alone knows where I am. His eye is on me. He has told me this. How else would you come to be here?"

The girl surely lived a very simple life, and she couldn't have been very educated, although she spoke surprisingly good English. Such quaint ideas about God and heaven, especially that I could be a supernatural being. Misleading her felt wrong. "A map of this island was found in a bottle. By a man. On a beach. Very far from here."

The girl prostrated herself at my feet. "You *are* from *Bapa* God, for I prayed and prayed someone would find one of my messages. Thank you, most gracious Father."

Arguing with her wasted what little time I had on the island. I pulled her to standing. "What is your name?"

The girl frowned. "I am called Bimala, but I am in need of a new name. Bimala is no longer who I am."

The girl darted along one rabbit trail after another. "No one likes their name," I said.

She sucked in a breath as if to argue with me. A touch to her hand silenced her.

"Bimala, my time here is short. I wish I could answer your questions, explain all that is unexplainable, but I need some information, or I can't help you. You must not answer my questions with more questions or riddles."

"We are leaving today, are we not? I should pack." She made to turn but stopped. "Packing won't take me long. We are going now? Before Shaitaan returns?"

"Bimala, please listen to me. I cannot take you with me, not today. I came for information only. If you can tell me what I need to know, a good man will come for you."

Bimala fell to her knees and grasped my hands. "Dear, dear Angel Lady, one who is from *Bapa* God, we cannot—we *dare* not—wait another day." She looked across the water. Her eyes welled with tears and spilled down her cheeks. "This is a bad place, Angel Lady. I did not choose to come here, as some suppose. Hear my story. You will see.

"My *pita* was very sick. He could not work at the brick factory, although he tried for a time, but then he died. My sisters cried for rice. *Mata* stopped making milk for Charvi. She had no other choice but to take me to the brick factory. The foreman said I could work there, to take the place of *Pita*. He gave me a hammer to break the coal for the oven. I was to live in a house for young girls. He promised to send my wages to *Mata*." She lowered her head.

"None of that happened—"

"Bimala," I pleaded. Her story ate a hole in my chest.

But the girl was relentless. "The foreman took my hammer and dragged me to a house with many, many girls. Some were younger and others older. All of them missed their *maaji*. They cried until they had no more tears. Shaitaan took me from that place to here.

"I worry my sisters have no one to watch over them. Who will take them to school when they are old enough? It is most hard in this—I fear my sisters may be in a place like this or like that house for girls where the shame was thick."

This was the sort of story that could conjure nightmares, like they had for Cal. "I will work hard to get you off this island, Bimala. I'm not sure how, but I will get you away from Shaitaan."

"Won't you take us with you today?"

"Us? Who else is here?"

She pulled me by the hands. "I will show you. You will meet Pooja."

I dug in my heels. I hadn't learned anything useful, not one thing. Not yet anyway.

Bimala released my hands and ran again into the palm forest. "I will bring her to you," she called over her shoulder.

I considered following Bimala through the brush to where she gathered Pooja, but I checked my watch. Time had run out. And I was thirsty. I dipped a finger into the tea. It was cool enough to drink but very bitter. Still, the wetness washed the salt out of my mouth.

I feared the tea had been poisoned when my vision dissolved around the edges, but the wrenching pull awakened the pain in my shoulder, so I knew that I was headed for *Zella*, wherever she might be.

And the name of the island remained a mystery.

I should have kept the wetsuit on. Without the cushioning neoprene, my shoulder slammed against *Zella's* deck. I covered my mouth to keep from screaming out. In the discombobulation of my arrival, I wasn't sure I'd succeeded.

I lay stock still in the swallowing blackness, waiting for someone to discover me. The air was stagnant and cold, not one degree above freezing. I breathed in oil and dirt, which proved strangely reassuring. I thought instantly of Dad's workshop in the barn. I ran a hand over *Zella's* familiar deck. "Thanks for catching me, old gal."

Outside, a passing car's engine silenced chirruping crickets. I clicked on the flashlight that hung from my neck. Above me, the beam revealed rafters laden with ladders, an old bed frame, and many tattered and stained boxes. My nose had placed me correctly in a garage or a shed.

My shoulder burned, but I had to get my bearings. I rose with some difficulty, careful to keep my left arm immobile against my chest. The only exit lay through large, double garage doors.

I climbed down *Zella's* swim ladder to put my face to the gap between the doors. Even cooler air seeped in. Where was I? Wherever in Colorado I'd landed, my watch told me I had just over a hour until sunrise. I pressed against the doors with my good shoulder, only to hear a jangle of chain and to meet resistance. Hopefully, there was another way out.

My flashlight shone on walls built of splintering wood, then on an oil-soaked dirt floor. The slat walls would not stop a driving rain from seeping in. Not one light disturbed the darkness, nor did I sense the nearness of another building. I pressed into the locked doors again. The hinges creaked but didn't budge.

I took stock of what tools hung on the shed's walls. The hammers could easily break through the slats, but that would be a noisy affair. I scraped at the dirt floor with my heel. They called these the Rocky Mountains for a reason. The floor could have been concrete, and it wouldn't have been harder. The gardening tools— trowels and a cultivator and a shovel—could be used to dig my way out, which would be a protracted affair with my injured shoulder.

But not impossible. And, really, digging out was my only good option.

The back of the shed would be positioned away from the road and would shelter me from curious eyes. I roughed up the dirt with the tines of the cultivator and dug one pitiful shovelful after another, leveraging the shovel under my good armpit.

I'd barely dented the hard-packed floor when gray light bled through the slats. I squinted through the narrow gaps. A stand of lodge pole pines filled my view with a lake beyond. A big lake. Only a handful of lakes in Colorado fit that description. My lake, Grand Lake, was one of them. Could I have landed that close to my cabin? Was I in a neighbor's shed?

I moved to the adjacent wall to look for a landmark. Some yards away, closer to the lake, a log cabin stood with dark windows. Ten yards out the double doors, a narrow road led into even more trees. There was nothing to prove this was Grand Lake, but nothing to prove it wasn't.

Where the heck am I?

I continued my work, stopping frequently to check for light or activity in the cabin or to spot anyone walking their dog down the road. A car rolled to a stop in front of the cabin, and my heart nearly exploded. The passenger pitched a newspaper out the window and continued on. I scratched more vigorously at the earthen floor and heaved dirt out of the hole.

The moment I decided I'd dug the hole big enough—and you can bet I made plenty of promises to diet my generous hips away—a light clicked on in the cabin. I held my breath. An older man with a purposeful gait and square shoulders walked out to collect the newspaper, paused to take in the morning, and headed back inside. I fought an impulse to hide myself under *Zella's* aft seat, which would have helped absolutely nothing.

With some difficulty, especially with my shoulder complaining with every movement, I pushed my way through the hole, dragging all that I'd taken to the island with me. I walked away quickly, brushing dirt from my clothes, my face, and out of my hair. The air smelled of wood smoke, and the moon hung pale against the morning sky.

I kept the lake on my left, hoping for a break in the trees. Surely, I would recognize a ridgeline and determine my location. Instead, a split-rail fence seemed familiar. And then a group of newspaper boxes, one hand-painted with the name "Laubscher" lined the road. I knew some Laubschers! They lived on Shadow Mountain Lake, the reservoir connected to Grand Lake. As I continued walking, Shadow Mountain rose sun-kissed through the trees. Glory be, I wasn't that far from home. I reversed and walked in the right direction toward Grand Lake.

Finally heading toward home, I let myself think of Bimala and the promise I'd made her. I knew more but nothing that would help Cal find her. And yet, I felt a new urgency. I would return to Bimala soon but only once my shoulder healed. I would also have to find another way to return back from the island. Landing in a stranger's garage was painful and too much work, maybe dangerous.

On the other hand, I'd dug an impressive hole that might go unnoticed. The sooner I traveled to Bimala's island, certainly before someone had a chance to fill in the hole, the better. Only this time, I would be better prepared to get answers from the girl.

BY THE TIME I got back to the cabin, Alex was pouring batter onto the griddle.

She took one look and started grilling me with questions. Never one to maintain clear thoughts with bacon frying, I asked if I could eat before I answered. Besides, I couldn't exactly tell her the truth. I needed a full helping of animal fat to keep my wits sharp.

She narrowed her eyes. "You should probably shower first."

A mixture of salt, sweat, and a thick layer of oily dirt coated my arms and legs, probably my face. Everything I'd concocted to tell Alex during the long walk home had already dissolved under her steely gaze. The shower gave me time to finesse an alibi for the last five hours.

The shower felt heavenly, and the breakfast of eggs, bacon, and pancakes slid down sweetly. Alex stilled her fork and watched me eat. "Feeling better?"

I kept my eyes on the last strip of bacon. "I'm very tired."

"You said in your note that you had a wedding reception in Kremmling today. Shouldn't you be there already?"

Lie number one. "I'm not feeling all that well. I think I'll stay home."

"You're holding your arm funny."

Lie number two. "I fell. I was speeding up the Tonahutu Creek trail. I didn't see where the trail had washed away. I took quite a tumble and hit my shoulder on a rock." The part about the rock was true, although technically coral isn't a rock, it's a skeleton. But that was splitting hairs.

"You didn't mention a hike in your note. Besides, hiking alone seems like a bad idea. You said something about bears, right? And mountain lions?"

Lie number three. "My friend Carolyn was with me."

"Shouldn't you see a doctor?"

Young girls shouldn't be troubled by their grandmother's lapsed health insurance. "I'll be fine. All I need is some ice, maybe some ibuprofen."

Alex studied me, blinking sparely. She was too kind to point out the very large holes in my story, but that didn't stop her curiosity. To interrupt her questioning gaze, I pushed the chair back. "Let's get this day going."

Alex spent the rest of the day at the library and The Traveling Man, as she'd done for the last week. She'd compiled quite a list of islands to shoot off to Cal in installments each day. I stayed at the cabin, where I applied ice to my shoulder. Every time I closed my eyes, I saw Bimala pleading with me to take her from the island. And no matter how hard I tried not to think about the home for girls where Shaitaan had taken Bimala, I could think of little else.

I gave up on sleeping by two and followed Alex into town. We photographed a collection of maps Dad had kept in a locked cabinet. Alex speculated on their worth, wondering out loud if we needed to offer insurance with shipping. The girl's business sense amazed me, but as I watched her, I couldn't help noticing that she wore the miles of her journey much like Bimala had.

I brushed her hair off her forehead. "You know you can tell me anything, right?"

"What do you mean?"

"I mean, sometimes sharing secrets helps."

Alex adjusted the focus of the camera. "What secrets? I'm fine, Grandma. Really." Her jade eyes held a hint of a smile meant to reassure me, but my time with Bimala had left its mark. Little girls, the innocents of this world, were especially vulnerable to the appetites of evil.

How was I to protect my granddaughter?

God help me, I didn't know.

10

Carolyn winced at my shoulder. "It could be broken."

"I can move it." I demonstrated with a shoulder roll, careful not to give away how much the movement hurt. "Besides, it doesn't feel broken, just bruised. Give me a few days and I'll be as good as new."

She frowned at my reflection in the mirror. "An x-ray wouldn't hurt."

Alex looked up from her book. "That's what I said."

I pulled my T-shirt back in place. "You promised Alex some ice cream."

"And I have an ice pack left over from my knee surgery." Carolyn sent Alex to retrieve the ice pack from the freezer. She bent to whisper in my ear. "Robin, honestly, how did this happen?"

I explained how I had misjudged the depth of the sea and smacked into a coral shelf. "I understand if you don't believe me. In fact, I wouldn't believe me either. It's okay, Carolyn."

"I do believe you're in some kind of trouble, Robin. I only wish I could help. I'm not big, but I am wily. I'll go anywhere with you, stand up to anyone, or press the pedal to the metal and speed you out of danger. You only have to ask."

I didn't doubt she would do all of that and more. "We are a danger to evil everywhere, you and me. I'm glad we're friends."

Alex returned with the ice. "I'm going outside, Grandma, to sit by the fire ring."

"Keep an eye out for that fox that comes visiting," Carolyn said.
Alex brightened. "A fox? Really?"

"You'll have to sit very still."

Carolyn had grilled hamburgers and roasted potatoes like
she'd seen done on a cooking show. An arugula salad with grapes
and almonds made me wonder if she hadn't written a recipe down
incorrectly, but the flavors melded beautifully. Alex ate every last
bite. I made a silent promise to hunt for my packed cookbooks.

The residents of Grand Lake called their homes cabins, but
Carolyn's home only pretended to be rustic with a paneled ceiling
and the requisite wood-burning stove. Before Wayne had walked
out, their plan had been to update their 1980s house to appeal to
Denver families looking for a mountain cabin, with the hope of
selling at a handsome profit and purchasing a smaller house more
suitable for retirement.

That plan died with the divorce.

The renovation changed every surface, but the cabin was still
a vault for Carolyn's memories. The same view of Shadow
Mountain Lake—joined with Grand Lake by an umbilical of
water—and the mountains beyond had back-dropped all of the
important events of her life and the lives of her children. Their
voices bounced off the walls; their steps resounded in the
floorboards.

As unreasonable as a four-bedroom home seemed for one
woman, Wayne's pestering to abandon the seat of her memories
was cruel. When I'd locked the front door of my marriage home
for the last time, I'd felt as if I'd been ripped in two.

Carolyn joined me at the kitchen sink, where I watched Alex
through the window.

She sat as still as stone on a small deck off the kitchen. A fire
crackled in the fire ring, the orange light illuminating her face.
Dark hadn't yet settled, but the house and yard sat fully in the
shadow of the mountain. Encased in a Bronco blanket, Alex waited

for the fox."

"She looks a lot like your daughter," Carolyn said, offering a glass of red wine.

I searched Alex's face for echoes of Nicci. Yes, their noses were similarly straight. Yes, they shared green eyes, but Nicci's were sun-scorched leaves and Alex's a springtime forest. I could hardly remember Nicci's natural hair color. She'd been a towhead until she started school, growing darker through the primary grades until it was a silvery mink. I loved the color, but she had said, "Mother, this is the color they dye an actress's hair if they're trying to make her plain and dull." I ran my fingers through my hair. She'd gotten the color from me.

"You'll go back to this island?" Carolyn said.

"I have to. The girl is expecting me. We spent too much time trying to figure one another out, and I need to know the name of the island to help her. Even better, I hope she can tell me something about the island's location."

"You'll wait, won't you, until your shoulder heals?"

I could not think of wiggling in or out of the wetsuit without wincing in pain, and I'd been noodling over how to achieve a softer arrival at the island. That meant studying how the island sat in the sea, especially how far out the coral shelf extended. Without such knowledge, I could only aim for another fifty yards from the shore and hope for the best.

Arriving that far from shore would definitely require fins. I liked anticipating a soft landing, but swimming to shore without fins—my kick was deplorable—would be a colossal waste of time when time on the island was already limited.

The biggest problem, truthfully, was arriving back on *Zella*. The deck was rocklike. And what would meeting *Zella's* new owner be like? Yes, I would absolutely wait until my shoulder healed.

"Robin?" Carolyn conveyed worry and warning in the way she

said my name.

"You have nothing to worry about. Bimala is a young girl, and by that I mean a teenager. She's absolutely no threat to me whatsoever. Now that I know what I'm up against, there will be no more injuries." Or so I hoped.

The cool evening air followed a breathless Alex into the kitchen. "He came. The fox came. I didn't move, just like you said, not a muscle. Oh my goodness, he was gorgeous and so very red. He didn't seem scared at all, like he owned the place. But then he saw me. He totally froze. I thought, *Please don't go.* He watched me, and I thought maybe he would sit. I didn't even blink. But he turned and ran back around the corner of your house."

"Come with me," Carolyn said, beckoning Alex. We followed her into her bedroom. She opened a journal she kept on her nightstand. "I write every sighting of wildlife in here. I started when I was a student at CSU, so I've had this journal for, well, a very long time. We don't have enough magic in our lives." She looked at me. "Well, some people do, I suppose. But we mere mortals, we have to gather what we can along the way. That fox came to you, Alex. You waited, expected him, and he came. That's magic, isn't it?"

Alex leaned into a mob of teddy bears—all gifts from Carolyn's students—at the head of the bed to write about the red fox in the journal. Her smile deepened a dimple as she wrote.

A magical fox indeed. I would have stood there all night watching my granddaughter, but Carolyn tugged on my sleeve and jerked her head toward the door. I stopped at the doorway to watch Alex for one moment more.

She tapped the pencil against her chin in thought. I understood her dilemma. What to compare his red coat to? How did he move? Did firelight reflect in his eyes? If I possessed the power, I would herd a thousand red foxes to trot before her because when something as unexpected as a red fox shows up, we are reminded that encountering the wondrous is possible. And young girls should always have that hope beating in their hearts.

In the kitchen, Carolyn spilled Bananagram tiles in the center of the table. I thought we'd escaped playing an educational game that night. I always lost. I started to protest, knowing my argument would be futile, but Carolyn spoke first.

"I need to warn you. Wayne came to the house this morning, looking for his precious signs. He pushed his way in—he fancies himself a bulldog—and ranted as he went room by room, opening closets and looking under beds. Like I would leave evidence around the house. Does he think I'm stupid?" Carolyn screwed up her face. "Actually, he probably does, now that I think about it."

"And I need a warning because ...?"

She grimaced.

"Carolyn?"

"I might have mentioned your name."

I leaned closer, lowered my voice. "In what context?"

"You can be sure I didn't pin the blame on you."

"But ...?"

Carolyn filled the kettle at the sink. "He had advice for me. Can you imagine? He knows exactly how I should live my life. He sees me as some kind of recluse. He actually suggested that I go to the senior center—the *senior* center, mind you—to make some friends, play a little canasta, join a knitting circle. Is that not ridiculous?"

"And you told him you had a friend?"

The flame lit under the kettle with a whump. "Of course I did, a very good friend who would do anything for me."

"Like hide a fortune in real estate signs in her garage?"

"Don't be silly. I said nothing of the sort, only that you were a very, *very* good friend."

Alex stepped into the kitchen. "Are we playing a game?"

I considered bowing out of Carolyn's game to watch

something inane on the television, but a change had taken place in Alex that proved much more intriguing. She no longer looked dystopian. The crease she'd plowed between her eyes from entering maps into a data base had softened. And her shoulders no longer orbited her ears. A smile tugged at her lips. She stood straighter. She nearly sparkled.

A fox did all that?

Watching the transformation in Alex recalled how Bimala had stood before me—eyes wide in fear, her hand resting on her swollen abdomen, her pleas for help. The child she carried belonged to the man whom she feared. That much was clear. What would make Bimala smile? More than a visit by a fox. My heart thumped wildly when I considered how she would spend the days until my shoulder healed, and I could return to the island.

I stood abruptly, tipping my wine glass and sent a rivulet of wine toward the game tiles. "We have to go. We have to go, now."

ONCE SETTLED IN OUR beds, I could feel Alex's eyes as I stared at the same page in a book for over an hour. I did my best to look relaxed and focused, but my brain buzzed. To pass the time until Alex fell asleep, I made a mental list of all I needed for my trip to the island in the early morning, including my best fins, which I hadn't seen in ages. Were they behind a map display? In the bathroom, otherwise known as my changing room? The cupboard by the back door? I gave up figuring out where I'd stowed the fins and forced myself to actually read. The story wasn't half bad.

I woke suddenly to a dark room. The clock read 4:00 AM, two hours later than I'd planned on starting for the shop. I briefly considered staying in the warmth and safety of the cabin.

How long would it take me to get to the shop, and once there, to prepare? Traveling took no time, and I expected to be on the island no longer than thirty minutes. That reminded me to strap on the watch with the stopwatch feature.

I rolled my shoulder gingerly. Nothing a generous dose of Tylenol couldn't quiet to a roar. I couldn't know, however, how much time I would spend in the garage with *Zella*, digging out.

One problem at a time.

I could not stop thinking of Bimala's hand on her belly and her face both hopeful and wary. I unfolded myself from the bedding and made for the door. Alex's face reflected the blue light of the nightlight. When I saw her eyes closed, I left the house silently.

At the shop, I found the fins behind the mop bucket. I dressed quickly in my bathing suit and fought my way into the wetsuit, stopping only to cradle my insulted shoulder until the worst of the pain passed. I tied a change of clothing to my ankle, and before putting on the life vest, I stuffed bubble wrap inside my wetsuit to add a layer of protection for my shoulder. Finally, I draped the duffel with the fins over my chest.

When I touched the map and felt the first tug, I turned to see Alex staring through the shop's window, her mouth agape and her eyes wide with surprise.

11

I clenched the duffel as I dropped into the water, immobilizing my arm to my chest. Down and down I sank, expecting at any moment to collide with coral. When the buoyancy of the vest paused my descent, I swam for the surface with one arm and started the stopwatch. The first milliseconds blurred by.

I used my second lungful of air to groan at the memory of Alex's shocked face. I'd observed my father depart many times. His body dissolved until I could look right through him. I never got used to him fading like that. Panic bubbled in my stomach each time and simmered there until he'd returned.

What must Alex be thinking?

I couldn't help her. I couldn't answer her questions or reassure her. Not until I got back.

I turned toward the island, only a nosegay of palms against a sky as blue as larkspur. The distance to the island distressed me, but for the first time I saw how truly small it was, no bigger than a football field. Bimala lived in a very small world.

There was no time to spare. I wiggled into the first fin, but the second resisted and popped out of my hand. I dove after it. Below me, the coral ended abruptly, a cliff of light that dropped into blackness. The sight of all that emptiness, which most certainly was not empty, froze me in place. I watched the fin twist down into the abyss and disappear. One fin would have to do.

I swam for shore, pulling with my right arm and kicking with my left leg. My kittywampus stroke made for slow progress. Five minutes ticked off by the time I reached shore. Once out of the water, the heat pressed me with a menacing hand. So much for protective padding. The sun threatened to parboil me, so I pulled down the zipper and struggled out of the gripping neoprene.

Another four minutes. Gone.

I stuffed the wetsuit, the one fin, and the change of clothes into the duffel—and stared into the palm forest. The trees nodded in the breeze, and light skittered across the sandy ground, but nothing—more importantly, no one—moved in the trees. The ocean was a blue void behind me, the keeper of secrets.

Stop wasting time!

I ran into the forest. A startled bird returned the favor with an insistent, rasping call that sent me back to the beach, where I contemplated the absurdity of my mission.

"This is stupid. So, so stupid."

I'd been on the island 13 minutes 45.995 seconds. Heading into the trees and to the huts beyond was the only way to make the trip worthwhile, if doing so was even possible. I swept aside a palm frond and charged in. Before long, a clearing opened, and there stood the huts I'd spotted on my first visit. I squatted behind a dense bush to watch the yard. Bed sheets on a clothesline snapped in the breeze, and a goat slept in the shade.

An open structure with a thatched roof and a sand floor, stood closer to the shore. A scattering of folding chairs, large white coolers, a trash can, and several tables filled the space. An eighties-styled boom box with a mangled antenna sat on one of the tables. Heaped in a plastic laundry basket were multi-colored bottles, much like the one I'd seen Bimala toss into the sea on my first visit.

Liquor bottles. Lots and lots of liquor bottles.

Large containers of water filled another table. The sight of them made my tongue stick to my teeth. Two other structures—enclosed huts with corrugated roofs—stood at awkward angles facing the dock, which seemed to be the center of attention. A sigh of relief escaped when I saw no boat moored to the dock.

Besides the bird that continued to scold me and the lapping of genial waves, Bimala's world was silent.

Sixteen minutes, 53.632 seconds.

"Bimala," I called in a stage whisper and waited, listening and scanning the beach, the trees, the doors of the huts. My heart raced. I sifted through the sand until I found a pebble. I tested its heft in my hand, stood, hesitated, and tossed it onto the closest roof. Before the pebble plunked on the tin, I collapsed behind the bush again. I made ready to run, although I knew not where—if someone other than Bimala came out.

Bimala stepped into the sunshine, scanning the trees for the source of the sound.

"Bimala, it's me, Robin," I whispered.

She spotted me and her hand flew to her mouth. She fell to the ground before me, crying into her hands. "I thought you had forgotten us. I came back to the beach with Pooja, but you had gone. I saw the marks your feet made in the sand. I was happy to realize I had not dreamed of you. Oh, most favored Angel Lady, thank you for returning."

Twenty minutes, 6.203 seconds.

I pulled her up by her arms, determined to draw out all she knew about the island. "Do not speak. We don't have time for small talk. The only thing I must hear from you is the name of the island."

"I am sor—"

"Don't speak!"

She lowered her head in submission and covered her heart with her hands. I didn't like being another person who demanded Bimala's obedience. But I had to.

"What is the name of this island?" I asked.

Her eyes searched mine.

"For heaven's sake, say it."

"Kuna."

"Koo-nah?"

"Yes, Kuna."

I dug for the Ziploc bag with the paper and pen and wrote the name out to show to her.

She corrected my spelling. "The name of the island is K-u-n-a, Kuna," she said, and dipped her head again.

"You've done well, Bimala." I touched her shoulder. "This is exactly what I needed. I will give this to a man who likes to help."

"I will not leave without Pooja."

The other girl. Another potential complication. "Where is she now?"

"Sleeping. We rest in the heat of the day before the evening meal. I will wake her. You will see how beautiful she is. You will see that she is attracting Shaitaan's attention."

I wasn't anxious to meet another girl. Already, Bimala's face haunted me. I prayed this would be my last trip to the island, and Bimala and Pooja would be Cal's problem. I wiped the sweat from my forehead and checked my watch. Twenty-one minutes, 10.118 seconds. "I haven't much time. Maybe ten minutes."

The heat cocooned me in a woolen blanket. My breaths came labored. The world tilted.

"You need a drink. I will return." Bimala ran to the shelter and filled a container with water. I poured some over my face and drank long and deep. The water tasted of hot plastic.

She looked over her shoulder to the dock "Will the man come soon, the one who likes to help? Shaitaan is never gone this long."

I had no idea when Cal would make his way to the island. I supposed there would be funding to acquire and paperwork to submit—to whom I did not know—transportation to arrange. I had to admit, and this surprised me greatly, that I never doubted for a moment Cal would find his way to Bimala and Pooja.

My response was embarrassing in its ambiguity. "He will come as quickly as he is able."

"Supplies are running low. I stretch as much as I am able. Shaitaan will, when he returns, bring rice and water. Water is needed most of all. I do what I can to make each drop last. I do not ask for the man to come—"

"His name is Cal."

"You understand, do you not, that water is not what I need most of all? That is what I say. Asking for water is easy, also for rice and help to come. What is most difficult is that Shaitaan will return very, very soon.

"When he comes, he is hard. Nothing is right. He drinks. He cries sometimes. I wait outside his hut. I wait for him to call my name. I tell Pooja to stay in our hut, to not make a noise. She must not cool herself in the shallows. She must not milk the goat. She must relieve herself in the bucket and bear her thirst. Light no fire, I tell her. Shaitaan must forget you are here.

"There will be a day when Shaitaan calls Pooja's name, and she will have to go to him." Bimala stilled her quivering lips with delicate fingertips. "Cal will come this day?"

To tell her the truth, that I had no idea when Cal would come for her and Pooja would crush her. To lie with optimistic dates and times would crush her slowly. "He won't come today. A long time may pass. Many days. Perhaps a week or more."

"Months?"

I nodded.

"Oh, I see." She turned to the expansive ocean. The waves fluttered at the shore, barely stirring the sand. "All that is left to me is to wait, just as I have always done. I will wait for the man who is Cal, and I will remind Pooja of what she must do to be safe. What else can I do? *Bapa* God is always faithful, is he not?" She studied me, but I had no affirmation or rebuttal for her. "Will you return to heaven now?" The rebuke in her voice stung.

"I'll return to Colorado."

"Is that near heaven?"

I pictured the headwaters of the Colorado River, nothing but a stream that spilled out of a saturated meadow west of the Continental Divide. I have straddled that stream. Other streams converged to sing over boulders and carve canyons. There was the meadow where the mountain bluebirds returned each spring to have their young and, of course, there was the red fox that visited Carolyn's yard. The snow that frosted Mt. Baldy into summer. The trout that leapt for mayflies as the sun dimmed. And no Shaitaan that preyed on young girls there, that I knew.

"Yes, it is."

Twenty-eight minutes, 38.601 seconds.

My departure would frighten Bimala as it had Alex, and I wanted to make a pad of the duffel to ease the landing on *Zella*. "I'm going back to the beach to wait for my departure."

I realized tardily that I should have brought a gift of supplies, something to let her know that I understood, or at least appreciated, her suffering. I rummaged through the duffel for the oyster crackers—they were powder—and handed them to Bimala.

She frowned and handed them back. "Shaitaan must not find anything here from you. He is very suspicious. I am sorry for this discourtesy. I hope you will understand." Lacking anything I could give her, I pulled her into my arms and held her against my chest. Her heart fluttered against my heart, now beating like a war drum.

Just as I released her, my vision dimmed at the edges.

12

The old man aimed a rifle at my chest.

"You can lower that thing," I said over my pounding heart. "I can't hurt you and I want nothing."

"It was you who dug a hole in my garage?"

I nodded tightly.

"Well then, that gets us back to my original question, doesn't it? How did you get in here? I've checked all the slats. Nothing's loose. The doors were locked tight."

Alex waited for me at The Traveling Man. "Sir, please, the gun? I will tell you my whole history at a time of your choosing, if you would point that thing someplace else."

He looked at the gun with a question, like he'd forgotten what he held. "I didn't know who or what I would find." He lowered the barrel. "You look harmless enough."

He clicked on an overhead bulb and insisted I climb down the swim ladder to join him on the floor of the shack. He gestured toward the door, and I noticed it had been secured with a lock and chain, now from the inside. "I've been puzzling for two days over how you got in here. You didn't dig yourself in because you used my tools. You tried to clean them up, but it's clear you used the hand cultivator and the shovel. Am I right?"

"If I've damaged them in any way—"

"Those tools have been around a lot longer than you. They were my father's." The man moved into the circle of light. He wore a Patagonia fleece over khaki pants with a smart crease down each leg. He studied me with deeply set eyes whose color I couldn't determine in the low light.

"My father left his tools to me, too." I ran my hand over *Zella's* hull, loosening flakes of blue paint. "In fact, we built this boat together. We started after my senior year in high school. That, of course, was some time ago."

"Why should I believe you?"

"I know everything there is to know about this boat. I know where we switched from cedar to ash, and which planks had to be patched after a storm blew her onto the rocks. That storm convinced my father we needed the boat garage. My name is Robin, by the way. I live on Grand Lake, on Jericho Road. Do you know it?"

"You could be making that up. I don't know why you would, but nothing you've said proves you built this boat with your father or explains how you got in here."

I gestured to the swim ladder. "You'll have to climb aboard. When we finished the boat, my father burned an inscription on the underside of the engine hatch. There's the date we christened the boat, July 19, 1984. Dad signed it and so did I. Sam Deering and Robin Deering."

The man eyed me with suspicion. "Move on over there to the corner, where you can't do anything funny."

He climbed to *Zella's* deck with remarkable dexterity, keeping a wary eye on me. The hinges screeched, and then there was silence while he read the inscription. "Well now, this is curious. I don't suppose you have any identification on you?"

He leaned over the side, and I flashed my driver's license. "You've come to visit the boat, have you, in the middle of the night?"

"You bought *Zella* from my ex-husband. After the accountants and the lawyers had had their ways, Doug got the boat. And as I'm sure you will understand, *Zella* is very dear to me. I would like very much to buy her from you."

"I've searched all over for a boat as nice." He looked wistfully in the direction of the log cabin and back to me. "I'm not at liberty to travel like I used to. When I saw the ad online, well, I couldn't believe my luck. A boat, a wooden boat, right here in Grand Lake. In the end, I agreed to a much higher price than I should have paid."

My heart dove for my belly button. "You know my name. What's yours?"

"Richard."

"Well, Richard, I'm sure you now know that Doug is quite the negotiator, but whatever you paid, I'll happily match."

"Boats like this don't come around very often."

"Sir—"

"I'm not a heartless bastard. Some have said I'm a good man, although I'm not sure what I've done to deserve such a distinction. I live with plenty of regrets." He stopped talking, narrowed his gaze. "Now, tell me, how did you get in here?"

How could I tell him? "I'm really very sorry for the trouble."

Richard pulled a key ring out of his pocket and opened the lock. The chain fell away with a jangle. He pushed open the doors. The morning chill bit my nose.

"Clearly, there are things in this ol' world I do not understand. I'm getting more comfortable with ambiguity as the years add up. That's quite an admission coming from an engineer, I hope you know."

I gathered all of my supplies from *Zella*. With my arms full, I thanked Richard for his hospitality.

"If you must see the boat again, knock on the door of the cabin there. Not too early and not too late. And if a woman answers, tell her you got the wrong address and try again later."

"Should I call first?"

That seemed to make sense to Richard, so he waited as I laid my stuff in the dirt and dug for something to write with. I wrote my phone number below the name of the island and tore it off.

We stood in his driveway, both of us breathing in smoky air and getting our bearings from the lightening sky. Mt. Baldy, Shadow Mountain, the Never Summer Range rose above us. Our talk turned to what westerners always talked about.

"Look at that sky. Not a cloud in it."

"We could sure use some rain."

As I turned toward downtown and the shop, where I hoped to find Alex, it occurred to me that I'd come to an understanding with Richard. We both loved *Zella* for our own reasons. We both felt our claims more legitimate than the other's. And, in his own way, he was willing to share her with me. That would have to do for now.

AT THE SHOP, I found Alex sleeping in Dad's leather chair by the front window. She woke with a start. "Grandma, you faded like a ghost to nothing!"

After reassurances that I wouldn't disappear again in the next few minutes and with a promise to tell her everything, we made cups of hot chocolate and squeezed into Dad's chair. The leather still held Alex's warmth and released the sweetness of Dad's pipe. I explained about the maps, how I'd watched my father come and go, and how I always landed on *Zella Francine.*

"Grandma, I could have helped you," she complained. There's no one quite as indignant as a wronged fourteen-year-old.

She'd heard me bumping around the cabin early that morning, and because she'd considered my behavior at Carolyn's house strange, she'd followed me to the shop. "You seemed far away." The girl read adults and their hidden worries all too well for my taste. I vowed to be more sphinxlike.

She asked one hundred questions. "Who's a traveler in Mom's generation? Aunt Lauren? Is that how she got to Italy? It can't be

Mom. There's no way. She would tell the world. I would never see her again. She isn't a traveler, is she?"

I had no idea if Nicci was a traveler or not. If she was, she couldn't have traveled yet because, and Alex knew the truth, she would be long gone. And no, I hadn't told Lauren or Nicci about this inheritable trait. Being a traveler wasn't cancer, but it wasn't fairy dust either. Rough landings had broken bones of ancestors and worse. Perhaps I needed to come clean with my daughters.

Alex pushed herself out of the chair and walked to the viewing table where the map of Kuna still lay. "You went to the island? Is that where you went? Was a girl there? How old is she? Shouldn't we let Cal know? Have you been there before? Did she tell you her name? Is she going to be all right?"

Now what?

I told her everything, except about Bimala's desperate pleas for Pooja. Neither did I tell her about Shaitaan or the way my skin crawled upon hearing his name, or how he'd invaded my dreams.

In my retelling he was a run-of-the-mill bad guy, who needed Bimala to cook and clean for him but didn't pay so well. And most especially, I couldn't tell her how the light drained out of Bimala's face when I'd told her Cal would not be back in time to save Pooja from Shaitaan.

Alex gathered her hair into a knot held by a pencil and shed her hoodie. "We'll be at the library when it opens. Until then we'll study the maps—Grandma, where do they wear saris? We could look for Kuna there."

I only knew for sure that women of India wore saris, but perhaps women of other South Asian countries also wore them. I put on rubber gloves and pulled out maps of India, Sri Lanka, and Bangladesh—all countries of South Asia with a coastline and, possibly, islands. The scale of the maps meant many of the smallest islands—and Kuna definitely fit in that category— probably wouldn't show up. The impossibility of our task frustrated us within minutes.

"This is crazy impossible without the Internet," Alex said.

"We can't get into the library for another hour," I said. "Let's put this aside for now. We'll go to the Timberline Café for some breakfast. By the time we finish, the library will be open."

She looked me up and down. "Your hair, Grandma. Do you have a hat?"

My fingers tangled in my salt-crusted hair. "I have a bandana around here somewhere."

IN LESS THAN FIVE minutes at the library we discovered Kuna wouldn't be easy to find, even with an Internet search. Lots of things were called by the name Kuna. The Kuna Company made security lights. We read reviews about their porch lights on CNET. Kuna is the currency of Croatia. There's a brand of alpaca clothing called Kuna. Not Peruvian women in bowlers, either. The scarves and sweaters would appeal to hipsters with bulging wallets. Also, a weasel-like animal by the name of *kuna domova* popped up. We got excited when we found the Kuna people on the San Blas archipelagoes until we saw pictures of how they dressed. Nothing like Bimala.

"Maybe Cal will know where Kuna is."

There were people—like my father—who knew every place name on the planet. Unfortunately, I didn't know them, nor did I think Cal knew them. "I'll call him when we get home."

"Shouldn't you call him now? I mean, this is urgent. Who knows what could happen if we wait?"

TO CALL CAL REQUIRED wrestling with what to tell him about Kuna and Bimala. How could I explain what I knew? I regretted ever telling him that I sometimes got impressions. I needed—Bimala and Pooja *needed*—for him to take me seriously. Would he?

I saw Bimala's trembling fingers every time I blinked.

Oh God, I'm so tired. And my shoulder...

I scrolled through my contact list until I found Cal. I closed my eyes for a moment before tapping his name.

"Is this a hunch?" he asked.

"No."

"But you don't know where this Kuna is, right?"

"I'm mostly sure the island is in South Asia. And that the need is great."

"I'm preparing for an operation now. In fact, I leave in the morning. If you can get more information before then, I'll pass it on to the right people."

"Listen, Cal, I know I must sound crazy, and I don't especially like sounding crazy. I've spent most of life securing my position among the rational and trusted. You can't run a business otherwise. Knowing the girls' situation is making me a little reckless. I'm sure you understand."

The phone went quiet. I pictured Cal with his head in his hands, wondering how he might end this conversation gracefully. I appreciated that he didn't hang up immediately.

"Robin, the people who rescue girls ... this is very dangerous stuff. We're talking lots of money exchanging hands, very high stakes. The men in charge of the brothels are trying to protect their livelihoods. As reprehensible as that is, they are highly motivated and armed. We depend on the local authorities for protection.

"As guests in their countries we can't carry firearms, so we have to be extremely careful. The best we can do for ourselves and our families is to have good intelligence. We never jump into a situation. That's the quickest way to end up dead, and we all want to come home to our own little girls."

"The girl's name is Bimala," I blurted, desperate to convince Cal to take me seriously. "She's young, probably still in her teens. She was sent to work at a brick factory by her family, but she was taken to a house and then to the island. There's another girl. I haven't seen her—"

"You've actually been to this place?" Disbelief saturated his words.

"Uh ..."

"This girl sounds like a thousand girls. They're all over Asia. Hell, they're all over the world."

"What are you saying? Do you think I made her up?"

"You have a good heart, Robin. You want to help. I get that. But this is not helping. Thank you for all your work with the map. I truly appreciate your efforts. And thank your granddaughter. That girl has a head on her shoulders. I'll try to stop by when I come through again."

Translation: *You're a little nuts but your granddaughter has potential. You'll never hear from me again.*

I hung up first.

Alex was incredulous. "He's not going to help?"

"We can't be too hard on him. He's in a difficult place. I couldn't tell him everything without explaining how I knew Bimala, and he's responsible for the safety of his team."

"You have to go back. You have to find something to help Cal get to that island. You are the girls' only hope."

"Not today. We both need rest, and I have to work a wedding tomorrow. We'll aim for Sunday. My shoulder will be better by then, too."

To be completely honest, I had no hope of finding out anything I could pass on to Cal. Explaining my life as a traveler would not convince Cal to help. He would never believe me. How could he? I would definitely go back to Kuna, though. Alex saw me as a minor superhero, which frankly felt good. I didn't want to disappoint her, although surely I would.

Thinking about traveling back to Kuna made my heart pound. The fear that dogged Bimala proved Shaitaan was dangerous. I had no desire to meet the man face to face. Also, the ocean and its inhabitants posed a real threat, in a variety of ways. I made the mistake of checking out what sorts of creatures lived in the South Asian seas. The thought of swimming with a beaked sea snake gave me sweaty palms. And I could hit that coral shelf again, only with my head this time.

But like I said before, I would go. I wasn't a superhero, but Alex didn't need to know that quite yet.

13

Wayne Truelove was the last person I expected to knock at the cabin's door.

And I didn't invite him in. I couldn't betray Carolyn with any sort of courtesy to the man. Instead, I gestured him to the back deck. He shrugged and led the way. Tall and generously stout, Wayne struck a pose of nonchalance, leaning against the deck's railing. Behind him the lake roiled in anticipation of an afternoon squall. Even on my deck, with the mountains standing proud on every side and the sky building thunderheads, the man commanded space.

Who was he trying to kid?

According to Carolyn, Wayne was a philanderer with a red-hot temper. All of the stories she'd told supported these assertions. I resisted a squirm under his gaze and charted two potential exits.

"I want to thank you for befriending my ex-wife," he said. "These have been difficult days for her. Most of her teacher friends have retired and left for warmer climes. I'm glad she has someone to talk to."

I blinked so I wouldn't roll my eyes. "Carolyn is a good friend. We support one another."

"I realize it's a little odd for me to show up like this. But never forget, even though pancakes are thin, they always have two sides. If you only hear Carolyn's side, I'm sure I come off as a complete jerk."

"You underestimate her. You coming here isn't nearly as odd as Carolyn still loving you—she's the eighth wonder of the world, all right. Even if you've done only half of what she's told me, you have to agree that woman loves like a champ."

He nodded. "That sounds like Carolyn."

I loathed the man. He claimed to know Carolyn, actually understanding her devotion to him, and yet he had stomped, stabbed, and slashed her heart. To both appreciate her capacity for love and to dismiss it—what a creep! I crossed my arms and lifted my chest. "What can I do for you, Wayne?"

"I need your help."

"You'll have to be awfully convincing. Carolyn's friendship means the world to me. I won't violate her trust."

"Then you're the exact person for the job."

I shifted my weight, suppressing the urge to kick his little wanker out of service for a while. "Go on."

Wayne came away from the railing, leaned in, lowered his voice. "Carolyn hasn't been herself. She's doing things I never dreamed her capable of."

"Like?"

A sardonic smile played on his lips. "I think you know. She's not exactly subtle. And she is a talker." He smoothed his goatee with a swipe of his hands. "I loved her very much, you know. She was a wonderful mother. Our kids think she walks on water. Her students adored her. I suspect some of the parents worshipped her. They weren't above bribing the principal to get their kids into her class."

"Ya know, Wayne, you aren't helping your cause." The quicker this guy got off my deck the better.

"There was a time—" he started.

"You can't justify what you've done or who you are. Are we clear on that? There is nothing you can tell me that could make hurting Carolyn okay in any universe. You have about a minute to ask your favor."

He sucked in his lips and studied me for an uncomfortable moment. "All right then, here it is: Those signs she took will be expensive to replace. I'm getting pressure to contact the authorities and press charges. In the interest of our mutual history, I would rather not do that to Carolyn."

"Your benevolence is astounding."

He shook his head and made to leave. He stopped short of the steps and the path to the front of the cabin. "She can leave the signs someplace—anywhere, really—and let me know where they are. She doesn't have to bring them to me. That might be awkward. And if you could, please, ask her to stop. I can't protect her forever. Thank you."

His tires skidded on the loose dirt before they gripped the road. Thunder rumbled overhead and the first raindrop hit my cheek. The wind stirred the branches overhead into a frenetic whisper. I stepped into the protection of the eaves just in time. Lightning cracked over the water, and the sky released a torrent. I said a prayer that the storm wouldn't wake Alex.

Wayne had sounded reasonable and generous. He said lovely things about Carolyn. In his mind, he'd acted nobly in his efforts to protect Carolyn from the consequences of her actions. Did he really think he could shatter a woman's life and redeem himself with condescension? Poor little Carolyn? Things are rough for her? Had he forgotten how they got that way?

I leaned against the cabin, slid to the deck, and wept. I wish I could say that I cried for Carolyn, but my tears were for me. I could hear Doug as if he stood before me. *I haven't been happy in a very long time. You don't expect me to live as if I'm dead, do you? This was my one chance at happiness.*

Robin, I don't love you anymore.

If WAYNE BELIEVED HIMSELF a bulldog, Carolyn was one of those yappy terriers, digging incessantly for a bone. The woman did not back down, ever. We'd been preparing the lodge for a late-morning wedding and lunch reception to follow.

The bride arrived with boxes and boxes of centerpieces, favors, and place cards. Purple wine glasses. Purple candles. Purple bows. Table numbers printed on personalized wine bottles. Sprigs of lavender. Doily placemats. Lanterns etched with the couple's initials. In lieu of a guest book, the guests signed oversized Jenga pieces. A seating chart and a photo booth put the guests in their places and memorialized them. I stood over the heart-shaped advice cards on the entry table. I almost wrote, "Stay off Pinterest" on one of them. Carolyn stopped me.

The bride had everything under control, even the weather. The earth sparkled from the play of sunlight on the vapor rising from the warming ground. Pine pitch and humus scented the air. All was perfection.

Carolyn pulled me into the men's room, the only place not teaming with bridesmaids. "Something *is* bothering you. You're awfully quiet. Did you see Doug?"

I hadn't yet decided if relaying Wayne's message served Carolyn's best interest. More truthfully, a night and a day had passed since he'd visited, and I hadn't told her yet. She would likely see the delay as me keeping vital information from her. I mean, I'd had a visit from Wayne, *the* Wayne, *her* Wayne. That was big news. I would have questioned her loyalty had she forgotten to mention Doug visiting her. Such moral conundrums left me itchy. Better to redirect her anxiety for the moment.

"Alex saw me depart," I said. "Seeing me vaporize has traumatized her."

"Oh."

"It was an accident. I thought she was asleep, but she heard me leave the cabin, so she followed me to the shop."

"I thought you were—you know—not going places while she

was staying with you."

"On the other hand, being able to travel makes me the coolest grandma in Colorado."

"Excuse me?"

Urinals made me nervous. I pushed my way out of the bathroom and headed back to the main dining room. "Alex has been drilling me with questions. She's very intrigued, thinks I'm a rock star. I wish I'd been a traveler when the girls were young. I could have used the boost to my reputation."

"Do you think it's wise to feed Alex's curiosity?"

Mission accomplished. For the rest of the day, Carolyn took every opportunity to champion Alex's mental health. While we folded napkins, she questioned the wisdom of shoring an adolescent's misconceptions of reality without actually saying that I'd manufactured my ability to travel. She waxed on about Alex's newfound ability to understand abstract concepts and how too much fairyland thinking might dissuade her from testing hypotheses logically.

By the time we carried the last of the empty platters into the kitchen and the bride's mother thanked us for the most magical day ever, even my hair was tired. We lost interest in exploring anyone's emotional or cognitive development.

We rode back to the cabin in silence. Carolyn pulled me into an embrace that I returned with my good arm. "You're an amazing friend, and any girl would be lucky to call you grandmother, especially Alex. Sleep really well."

It wasn't every day that someone could believe you delusional, practically an accessory to the destruction of a young person's grip on reality and love you enough to also believe you're better than all that. Before I reached the cabin door, I'd decided. The next day I would invite Wayne over to collect his signs.

WAYNE ARRIVED AT THE cabin less than ten minutes after I called.

He wore jeans and a pair of work gloves. We didn't talk much. I uncovered signs, pointed out boxes that needed to be moved. We found eleven signs easily. Wayne seemed pleased, so I didn't suggest we keep digging for the remaining four. He leaned the last sign against his Escalade and slapped his gloves against his leg.

I pointed to the smarmy smile on *her* face. "Carolyn gets gut punched every time she sees one of your signs. You might consider that when you order new ones."

He loaded the last sign into the SUV. "Our daughter wants Carolyn to move to the Springs. She could use help with the grandsons, and Becca would feel better if Carolyn wasn't alone all the time."

"But she would have to sell her house," I complained. The thought of Carolyn moving turned my stomach to stone. "She loves that house. She feels connected there."

"I've seen lots of women hang onto homes much too long. Sentimentality can destroy a person." Wayne hefted himself into his SUV with a grunt.

I stood on his running board. "Are you kidding me? Men are the sentimental ones."

"You're talking through your hat."

"I have one word for you—*sports*. Men can watch the same play over and over. They read stories about games and gather in groups to watch. And then they talk and talk and talk—*ad nauseum*—about sports constantly. They get poetic about the strength of an offensive line or some baseball has-been's home run record."

Wayne cocked his head and shrugged. "I hadn't thought of it like that."

He revved the engine, so I stepped down. "Sentimentality doesn't destroy people, Wayne. Betrayal does."

"Maybe you can encourage Carolyn to move on."

Because I loved Carolyn, I would definitely encourage her to move on. But I knew my limitations. I couldn't heal her broken heart, and that pissed me off. I certainly wouldn't suggest she move to the Springs.

DREAMS ARE WHERE OUR minds rehearse the fears of our wakeful hours, the very things we do not name or acknowledge. So I wasn't surprised when I had the very, *very* bad dream after Wayne's visit.

Doug and I are still married in the very, *very* bad dream.

In this dream, Doug, a man who had always been kind and attentive, always eager to please, turns cold. I usually found the details of my dreams hard to remember, but not how they made me feel. Unfortunately, this time, because the dream was still fresh, I remembered everything with bruising detail.

I found Doug in our bedroom, which wasn't our bedroom— dreams! He folded his golf shirts into a suitcase for a vacation in Ireland, but I wasn't invited. At first, I was incredulous. How had he managed to forget to buy a ticket for me, his wife? Doug did not care that he'd hurt me with this sleight. He discounted my pain, scoffed at my surprise. His heart was a block of ice that no amount of pleading could thaw. His indifference was a javelin through my heart.

At first, his apathy angered me, but that soon turned to terror. I shouted and cried until my throat burned. When that didn't evoke a response, I hit him. He remained dismissive and utterly distant.

I woke up—this time and always—feeling horribly alone.

During the years of our marriage, the dreams had darkened my mood, made me fretful, and I'd eventually told Doug. He reassured me of his love with rib-crushing embraces, calls all through the day, dinner at our favorite restaurant.

Now, waking up put me right back in the moments after Doug had announced his intention to leave. We had not quarreled more than anyone else. We made plans for the future and bolstered the other's sagging dreams. Parenthood made us partners, a united front, especially with Nicci. The sex, because that's what everyone assumed had gone cold, was quite lovely.

We'd both sagged and pillowed in recent years, and Doug wore baseball caps constantly to cover his bald spot, but we managed one another's frailties with grace. I'd trusted Doug not to expose me, and his receding hairline remained our little secret.

All of my daytimes had been filled with the confidence of his love, so why had I dreamed Doug as a man of stone? Had I misinterpreted hints only my subconscious could decipher? Or hints my conscious mind ignored? Otherwise, how could my husband have slipped away for three years to sleep with another woman, and I never noticed anything amiss?

I worried for a time that I'd contracted a brain disease, my go-to diagnosis for strange behavior. If not a lesion on the brain, then perhaps a temporary psychosis. External realities can be so very raw and easy to dismiss. I feared most being stupid.

I'm probably not as dense as I'd once feared. And I'm definitely not as optimistic. Doug wasn't coming back.

14

The longer I stayed away from Kuna, the easier it was to stay away.

Instead of traveling, I posted maps from The Traveling Man on eBay, which meant doing research for pricing at the library and sourcing the materials for shipping the purchased maps to buyers. I focused on little else. I began to believe I might sell a few. In fact, we'd had inquiries on the Fort Dauphin map that convinced me to raise the price.

Am I kidding anyone?

Marketing maps did nothing to quell my anxiety over Bimala. It was quite simply the possibility of running into Shaitaan that kept me from returning to Kuna. When a log popped in the stove, or a door hinge creaked, or Alex snorted in her sleep—I startled, expecting Shaitaan to be the source of all that tormented me.

Fear, however, did not complicate Alex's compassion for Bimala and Pooja. She unpacked the produce we bought at the farmer's market—some too-early tomatoes, a quart of strawberries, and apricots. "Bimala's expecting you," she said, when I suggested I'd done all I could do to help Bimala.

"Actually, she's expecting Cal," I said weakly.

"But only you can find where she is, Grandma. You have to go to Kuna."

"It's possible that Bimala's kidnapper is on the island," I said, arranging the tomatoes in a bowl.

Alex had learned to argue from the best, her mother. "You're only there for thirty-one minutes. Can't you hide?"

"The island is very small, Alex. Very, very small."

Alex sighed heavily. "I've wondered what life must be like for Bimala, stuck on that island with a creep like him."

Wondering that very thing was why I floated in the turquoise waters off Kuna again. Bimala huddled on shore, crouched in a tight ball with her hands on her head. She rocked with the rhythm of the lapping waves. She looked as if she waited for the sky to fall on her.

I let the water roll me through mild swells. In my hurry to reach Kuna, I'd left my wetsuit behind, but no divide of temperature marked the place where my skin touched the amniotic water. Bimala's distress acted on me like an opposing magnet. I lingered in the warm waters.

Cumulonimbus clouds rose mountainlike with brilliant white peaks and shadowed valleys over the waters. But nothing moved on the island. No breeze stirred the trees. Shore birds had abandoned their dance with the waves. Even the grating calls of the birds had ceased. The stillness was a presence.

I'm stalling.

I swam toward the shore and Bimala. The injured shoulder tired quickly, but there was no pain. I scanned the trees for movement, the horizon for a boat, the clear, clear water for a shadow. Nothing threatening there.

I glanced toward the dock, which I couldn't see due to the island's dense foliage. Shaitaan's boat could be moored there. Should I wait until Bimala looked up? Perhaps she had a warning for me.

I'd traveled to Kuna to learn something that would help me locate the island, but I doubted Bimala knew anything more to tell me. She'd been a child when Shaitaan brought her to Kuna. I knew all I would ever know. The time for heroic measures had passed. I paused to watch Bimala, congratulating myself for such thoughtfulness and caution.

That was a joke. Terror gripped me. I could hardly breathe for the pounding of my heart. Whatever tormented the girl could easily torment me.

I turned and swam for the dark water beyond the reef, glancing over my shoulder every few strokes. Bimala stayed face down in the sand. When I rolled to my back to rest, Bimala raised her head and startled. She ran into the water, stumbling on her wet skirts, finally falling into the water in her reach for me. When her head popped up, her eyes pleaded.

I had to ask myself: If Alex was the one waiting for me on the shore, wouldn't I swim through a phalanx of sharks to reach her? I put my face in the water and clawed through the water to Bimala.

"Please, Angel Lady, exalted one, *Bapa* God has heard my prayers," she sputtered, guiding me to shore. "Can you help?"

On shore, she put a finger to her lips before squeezing water out of her skirts. I left the duffel and the life vest in the sand. She clasped my hand. "Please to come with me." She lowered her head. "Something very bad has happened."

As we wove through the palm forest, Bimala looked often over her shoulder, so I did too. Only what was typical of Kuna filled the scene—palms, sand, sky. We walked briskly away from the beach toward the north end of the island.

She stopped suddenly, and I stepped to her side. We stood as far from the dock and the huts as possible, but not distant. Nothing on Kuna was distant.

In the sand before us lay a young girl, her hands stretched above her head, her eyes staring without seeing into the palm fronds above.

I struggled against Bimala's grip. "No, no, no."

"Shh, Angel Lady, speak only with quiet words."

I pulled out of her hands and turned toward the beach. Bimala stepped instantly before me. "We must bury her. The Father sent you to help. I am most grateful."

I could not put my fear to words. I breathed, "Pooja?"

Bimala looked to the girl. "No. Another girl brought by Shaitaan. I do not know her name. She did not please him. Pooja is locked in a cabinet, the only way I have to protect her." She gestured toward the girl. "I did not want her to see this. And I did not want Pooja to face Shaitaan alone. I knew of nothing else to do."

A furrow in the sand marked the path where Bimala had dragged the dead girl to this spot. The girl's lips grimaced back from her gums, where the scalloped edges of adult teeth pushed through. "My God, she's a child."

"She is older than Pooja, I think."

I squeezed my eyes shut against the sight. I remembered Nicci's toothless second-grade picture. I vomited into the sand and backhanded my mouth. "Where is Shaitaan now?"

"He is sleeping. They all are. They drank too much beer in the night."

My stomach convulsed and spilled its contents again. Not only was Shaitaan on the island, but he'd brought other men. I backed from the grisly scene. "How many are here?"

Bimala tugged at my arm. "We must bury her, or they will drop her off the dock. She will float there. Sharks will come. Pooja played with the girl. You will help me?"

I looked at my watch. Only sixteen minutes left. "We must hurry."

I picked up a shovel Bimala had discarded and thrust the blade into the ground. Within moments, slick sweat and sand covered my arms and legs. Over and over, I plunged the shovel into the sand. My hands grew raw. I searched the trees as I threw aside each shovelful, keeping my back to the dead girl.

No birds sang. The palm fronds hung limp above me. Bimala scooped sand with a pie plate. I wiped away tears. I would do anything for a drink of water or to dip under the surface of the cool sea. When the hole was deep enough, Bimala stood and stopped my digging with a touch.

"What about her family?" I said. "Shouldn't they be told?"

She shrugged and moved to the girl's head. She gestured toward her feet. I hesitated, but Bimala did not, so I took the girl's cool ankles in my hands.

The girl's body didn't bend as we lifted and lowered her into the hole. Bimala folded the girl's hands over her heart and lay a sprig of greenery from a nearby bush on her chest. I put my fingers in my armpits to warm them.

We abandoned the shovel to bulldoze sand over the girl with our palms. The damp sand mounded over the girl's body. Bimala smoothed it like icing on a cake. "You should pray."

"What?"

"You are the only voice of heaven here. Please."

Not one word came to me.

"The time is now short," she said.

"Dear God ... dear, dear God ... God in heaven ... help us."

"Amen?"

"Amen."

Bimala turned toward the huts. "I must go to Pooja. You will leave soon?"

The stopwatch read 29 minutes, 23.0573 seconds. "Very soon."

"Tell *Bapa* God that we are waiting. We are ready for his deliverance. Pray for us, Angel Lady. The days are very long."

She gathered my sand-crusted hands and kissed them before she ran through the forest toward the huts. My eyes returned to the disturbed mound, where the child now rested in her unnatural sleep.

Such a weight—whether helplessness, fear, despair—I could not tell. Moving proved too herculean an effort until I remembered that I'd left the duffel and the life vest on the beach. I couldn't help Bimala, but I wouldn't hurt her by leaving evidence of my visit behind. I ran as fast as my chubby legs would take me toward the beach. My vision darkened as I dove onto my things.

I vowed I would never return to Kuna

BY THE TIME I arrived on *Zella*, Alex and Carolyn had found their way to Richard's house and convinced his wife, Sally, to let them into the garage. The two of them managed to pad the deck only moments before I landed, which rated as the one good thing that had happened that day.

Such an odd collection of characters sat around Richard and Sally's massive dining room table. My little house was a cabin because of where it sat beside a mountain lake. This cabin earned the description with log and chink construction.

Newly arrived from his errands and startled by the collection of women at his table, Richard glared at me and patted his wife's hand. She seemed to be adjusting quite well to a surprise visit by three strange women, one who had materialized from nothing. She kept calling me Becky and asking me to tell her about the grandchildren, Jamie and Tara. She wore an elegant bob of silver hair, and her eyes shone like sapphires.

Carolyn sat like a gargoyle at the end seat. "You weren't there, and then you were."

"Can we talk about this later?" I whispered through my teeth and not for the first time.

She made crescent moons of her eyes when she forced a grin. "You *will* answer my questions."

I scored a seat facing out the glass doors to Shadow Mountain Lake. On any other day, I would have reveled in the view. The sparkling lake. Shadow Mountain. Granby Mesa a hazy purple against the sky. My legs bounced. I felt underdressed in my damp bathing suit and shorts. And I could smell myself.

I saw the dead girl every time I blinked.

Of the three interlopers, only Alex seemed in her element. She passed the plate of macaroons that Sally had assembled and asked us what we wanted to drink. The girl was a cucumber on a hot summer day. I hated to think how she'd developed such skills.

Sally took my hand in hers. "My dear, you look ... well, you don't look like yourself." She brushed my bangs from my forehead. "Let me set up an appointment with Gloria. I'm sure she can get you right in. You'll feel so much better with your hair out of your eyes."

"Sally ..." Richard started. He played with the fringe of the placemat.

"It's a girl thing, Richie," Sally said and fixed her gaze on me. "You wouldn't understand. If we look our best, we feel better on the inside. Perhaps a color, too, Becky?"

Richard bit his lip, waiting for my reply. I remembered his warnings when we'd first met. He hadn't wanted me to bother his wife. Clear to me now, he'd been protecting her. How I managed that realization, I did not know. My head throbbed.

Sally waited for my answer, expectant as a daisy. Playing along—being her Becky—might be the fastest way out of there. "That's exactly what I need." I pushed the chair back as I stood. "I better get going."

"What's your rush?" Richard asked.

"Well, uh, I thought I should get going, leave you and Sally to yourselves? We've taken too much of your time."

"We have nothing but time, don't we, dear?" he asked his wife. He looked to me, imploring. "Your *mother*," he said and winked, "hasn't been this calm in a very long time. She's happy to see you. Maybe you could stay for a few minutes more?" His eyebrows rose in anticipation of my answer.

I looked from Richard to Sally. She wore hope like a new Easter dress. My hands stung from the blisters that had formed and then ripped with the shovel on Kuna. I sat down slowly. "I'm sorry, we can't stay long. We have a ..." I stared blankly into each face. An urgent reason to leave would not come to me.

I looked at my hands. Sand caked my fingernails, and deflated blisters oozed blood. Sand also flowed in my veins, thickened, and clogged. I could barely keep my head up. I had, I reminded myself, buried a little girl not more than an hour earlier.

With great effort, I put my palms to the table and pushed myself to standing. The pressback chair tipped and fell behind me. I closed my eyes. Chairs scraped the floor. "I'm so sorry," I managed to say.

Sally stood beside me, her warm hand on my back. "You must take care of yourself. You have so much on your plate. I worry about you, darling. Please let me help you."

She meant the words for her daughter, not me, but her kindness opened a spillway of tears. "I really, really have to go."

Carolyn wrapped an arm around my waist. She assured Sally that she would get me home safely and stay with me until I got to sleep. Alex's brow creased with worry. Still, she pushed in our chairs and returned the cookies to the kitchen.

"And make sure she calls Gloria, won't you?" Sally said to our backs. We left with a bag of macaroons and a business card for Gloria's Glory Station.

Richard leaned into the passenger side window. "I don't know what happened here today. My mind can't quite get around it all, but thank you for coming. You're welcome to return anytime. Be sure to bring your granddaughter. And that other lady can come too. She seems real nice." He patted my shoulder. "Get the rest you need. Everything will look better after a good night's sleep, whatever has happened."

15

A kind of sickness entombed me through indistinct hours. My stomach sloshed with a sour brew and purged anything I tried to eat. I avoided sleep. More truthfully, I avoided the dreams that terrorized me the moment I slipped the veil of wakefulness.

I drank coffee late and took cool showers, but I couldn't stay awake forever. The dreams that came were more real than anything that had happened since I'd returned from Kuna. Someone very strong—I assumed it to be Shaitaan—gripped my ankles and dragged me toward the end of the bed. I grabbed at the sheets and opened my mouth, but a scream would not sound. Inches from an abyss that had opened in the bedroom floor, I woke with a start.

In my rush to turn on a light, my arm swiped the lamp onto the floor, where the base shattered. I sat there in the distressing darkness, trying to convince myself that only a dream—my own imagination—had tortured me, not Shaitaan.

Carolyn refused to leave. She made tea and washed the dishes. She cleaned the bathroom, swept the deck, the stairs, and the dock. My windows had never looked cleaner. She purged the refrigerator and wiped out kitchen cabinets. Alphabetized spices. She laundered our clothes and made sure Alex ate well.

She did not ask questions, which tortured her.

Alex watched me, too. Her silence accused me more than any words she could have said. She wanted me to return to Kuna. She could not know what she asked of me.

Finally, after my stomach permitted toast with a light smear of raspberry jam, I sat in an Adirondack chair on the dock. The pitying sun warmed my skin but didn't reach my bones, and the lake sighed a half-hearted welcome. Carolyn left for the grocery store with a list she and Alex had compiled. Alex sat cross-legged at my feet, reading a library book.

Imagination—had tortured me, not Shaitaan.

She closed the book gently. "Is Bimala okay?"

"Alex, please."

"I talked to Mom yesterday. She misses me."

My heart fluttered. "Does she want you to go home?"

"She has mixed feelings, I think. She likes that I'm here with you. She told me a story about you and her, when you went fishing on *Zella* and caught a bunch of fish. She said it was the most perfect day of her life. She wants those kinds of days with me, too."

"Do you want to go home?"

"I miss her, but ..."

A flame of anger ignited in me. Nicci knew how to get her way. She didn't bludgeon me with a sledgehammer but with a memory, for a good memory was a rarefied thing in our relationship.

I remembered the day Nicci had referenced. She was in the eighth grade. The year that will live in infamy. We fought over everything. She could not walk out the door to school without exploding into histrionics.

I needed a good day with my daughter, so I took her out of school—who really needed eighth grade algebra?—and we drove the 100 miles from Lakewood to Grand Lake. She sulked the whole way.

We took *Zella* out. Rain had fallen the day before, so crystalline drops of water clung to the pines. The day sparkled. And the fish could not help themselves. They bit everything we threw at them.

At the end of the day, Nicci hefted a full string of trout. "This was the most perfect day of my life," she said. I took a picture of a beaming Nicci on the dock. I had a dozen copies of that photograph made. I tucked them into drawers, used them as bookmarks, and framed one for my desk at work. I'd often stroked the photo like a talisman.

The power of a good day with a difficult person must not be underestimated.

Nicci knew I coveted good memories and the connectedness they created more than breath. She wielded them like a club to get what she wanted. All these years later. Still. She wanted Alex home, for whatever reason served her purpose. I could only warn Alex.

"Alex ..."

"Things won't be any different if I do go home. I know that, Grandma."

This would have been the perfect time to ask about Sean and why Alex wanted him out of the house. A good grandmother would dig until she found out the truth. I promised myself I would do just that when I felt better.

"This can't be very fun for you, Alex. Tomorrow, I promise, will be better." Where this optimism came from, I did not know. "We'll get Carolyn to take us somewhere."

Alex rested her hand on my knee. "Something really bad happened on Kuna, didn't it? Carolyn won't tell me anything, either."

Before Alex had woken that morning, I told Carolyn everything that had happened on Kuna. I hated burdening her with such gruesome visions. Crying with her had finally blurred the memory somewhat and set my resolve.

"I'm never going back there." I sounded petulant rather than determined.

"Is Bimala okay?"

"Bimala looked fine when I left her. Please don't ask me

anymore. Tell me about the book you're reading."

"Did you see Pooja?"

The urge to stomp up the stairs to the cabin and lock myself in the bathroom burned deep, but my arms and legs were positively leaden. People say that, I know, like they're weary, but my limbs were sandbags. "Alex, do not ask me about Kuna."

"You want me to forget that two girls are slaves? Or how you looked when you landed on *Zella*? Do you want me to pretend I've never heard of Shaitaan, to forget how badly he has hurt them? They will never see their families again, not ever. There will be no birthday parties. Fear is all they'll know."

Children can be cruel, my granddaughter included.

"Grandma, I did some searching on the Internet."

"That's a mistake, Alex. There are things we're not meant to know."

"Bimala and Pooja aren't only washing this guy's laundry. You know that, right?"

I hefted myself out of the chair, and to my surprise, I stood. "We're done, Alex. I cannot go back to Kuna. We don't have the skills or resources to help those girls. Their problems are too, too big. Please, let's not speak of them again."

Alex blocked the stairs. Her face blotched with emotion, and tears filled her eyes and spilled over her cheeks. "You're going to leave them there? Just leave them on that island with a maniac?'"

"I'm sorry I dragged you into this. I'm sorry you will know earlier than most that you can't save the world. Hell, you're lucky if you can save yourself. I hope you're more successful than I."

Alex let me pass. She spoke to my back. "I thought you were different. I thought you cared. You're just like Mom. You only care about yourself. Maybe I should go home. What's the difference?" She pushed past me and stopped, took a breath. "If we had a GPS you wouldn't have to go to shore. You could float around for thirty minutes, take a reading of your location, and come home. Simple.

Easy. Then we could give Cal the exact location of Kuna."

"A good GPS is expensive. I know, I bought one for your grandfather."

A thousand-watt bulb lit in Alex. "Grandpa has a GPS? That's perfect!"

For a million reasons I would not innumerate for Alex, I could never borrow anything from Doug. "He never took it out of his underwear drawer. I doubt he still has it."

"He might," she said, hopefully.

"Whether he still has the GPS or not, is not the question. He's not here. And even if he does come up to the cabin, I absolutely and positively forbid you to ask him to borrow the thing. He would ask why, Alex, and then how are you going to answer him? Don't bring it up again."

Alex stomped up the stairs, across the deck, and flung the screen door open and disappeared into the cabin. I stood there, staring at the closed door, feeling her disappointment settle on me. I was in no shape to fling the weight off. Besides, I deserved her derision, didn't I?

Carolyn stood at the top of the stairs holding a bag of groceries. "Why are you crying?"

ALEX AND I LIVED in separate galaxies. We drifted together at the end of the day, but the silence magnified the distance that remained between us. I'm not proud of myself, but I gave up trying to talk to her.

My dreams of demons and a great swallowing darkness still tormented me. I would have preferred to forget all about Bimala, but she populated those dreams, too. Often, she lay in the grave and not the girl. During the day, I could concentrate on little else.

Carolyn—such a dear friend—continued to come to the cabin each day. She pushed the boxes away from the window and set two wicker chairs there. She served cups of honeyed orange spice tea. "You need something to distract you, a vacation for your brain. Let me take you somewhere. We could take a hike. Janice saw larkspur on the Lulu City Trail."

Getting out of the cabin was the only rational thing to do. The walls constricted with each passing day. Sadly, rationality had little power over me. "I can't."

"How did you sleep?"

I'd avoided looking at the clock through the night. I figured I would relax into sleep more readily if I wasn't anxious about the passing of time. "I finished that novel you loaned me."

"You only started that book yesterday."

"Are you sure?"

"I brought the fattest book on the shelf. I meant for you to be bored into oblivion and restful sleep."

"I hated the ending."

"Robin, sweetie, should you talk to someone?"

"As in a psychiatrist?"

"Could this be PTSD? I mean, you're showing the signs— insomnia, upsetting dreams when you do sleep, troubling memories. What worries me is that you're not getting better."

"Has it even been three days?"

"Four."

Really? "I'm not ready to commit myself. I saw something horrible, and it's taking time to process, that's all. I don't think that constitutes a trip to the loony bin."

"The last few years have been tough for you. There's been lots of loss. If you're like me, the ground beneath doesn't feel solid anymore. Adding a murdered child to all that ..." Carolyn took my hand. "Sweetie, this may be bigger than you want to admit."

"I'm so tired."

She rose to rummage through her purse for a pill bottle. "Listen, sharing drugs is never a good idea. At least that's what they say, but a good night's sleep could only help. My doc gave me these when Wayne first left. He insisted that everything looks better when you're rested. I'm not so sure waking up alone looked any better, but I managed his absence a bit better, I think."

I read the label but didn't recognize the drug.

Carolyn took the bottle from me. "Zolpidem? I think it's Ambien. I'm only leaving you one. Don't drink alcohol, or you might end up trying to walk on the lake, if you get my drift."

She poured a tiny white pill into my palm. I didn't have to ask her why she only gave me one. She wasn't being stingy; she was being cautious.

"You'll sleep like the dead," she said. "Don't take the pill until you're ready to be out for at least seven hours." Carolyn pulled her chair closer until our knees touched. "More importantly, you shouldn't dream, sweetie. This will give you the break you need."

I set the pill next to my teacup. "I'll take it tonight."

"There's no reason to wait. I can stay with Alex or take her back to my place."

"She's at the shop."

"I'll stop by and get her. Call when you wake up. You would be doing me a favor. I love her company."

When I was a girl, I feared getting too close to the edge of a cliff. A power lay in wait for those who dared to wander near and pulled careless girls over the edge. Looking down at the pill, I felt the pull of sleep as if it were a cliff. I popped the pill in my mouth and chased it down with what tea remained in my cup.

Carolyn helped me to the futon and tucked me under the covers. She closed the blinds, and I fell asleep without struggle.

16

My brain struggled to make sense of searing flesh and a dream of swimming in a tar pit. I don't know if the frustration of the dream or the pain woke me. But I was screaming. Although not fully awake, my brain somehow knew to hurry me off a griddle-hot tin roof. In the process I burned the bottoms of my feet and my palms. I landed in a heap on packed sand.

I squirmed to keep my burned parts from the irritating sand but failed. Too many scorched bits. However rudely I'd been transported, the landscape before me was familiar. The dock. The interminable sea. A shade pavilion.

Kuna.

Bimala ran around the corner of the hut. She put a finger to her lips and held up her hand to still me. Only then did I realize I was crying.

Out of sight, a man shouted angrily in accented English. "What is this screaming? What is this noise?"

Shaitaan? My throat seized.

Bimala wrapped the end of her scarf around her hand. She motioned for me to move back and around the end of the hut, then dodged around the corner and disappeared. I took a breath to call after her, to beg her to stay. That would have been a mistake. Instead, I looked longingly at the cool water, but did as Bimala said and stayed in place. Blisters rose on my palms, forearms, on my right elbow, and on the backs of my legs. The sand cut into my soles like glass.

"I am very sorry to disturb you, sir," Bimala said to the man. "The pan was too hot. I burned my hand. That is all. Please, please forgive me. All is fine now."

There was a hard slap and a sudden expulsion of breath. I pressed my back against the hut. She'd lied and received her punishment to protect me.

"I do not come here to be disturbed!" he said.

"It will not happen again," she said flatly.

Surely, Shaitaan could hear my beating heart. The urge to run pulled at me but running would gain me nothing. Any run on Kuna would be too short to keep Shaitaan far behind. I decided, though, that if Shaitaan found me, I would indeed run to make catching me harder, at least. I didn't want to think about what he would do with an uninvited visitor to the island.

"Where is the girl?" he commanded.

I stiffened.

There was a pause, a shuffling of cloth. "She is in the hut, sir. She cleans the vegetables for the evening meal. She has much to do, sir, to make the meal to your liking."

"Bring her out here."

Another pause followed by indecipherable whispers, Bimala and a small child. Was I to stand there and listen as Shaitaan brutalized another child? I couldn't.

"How is her English?" he asked.

"Her words are not so good, sir. She is a slow learner, I am afraid."

"If teaching her is too difficult, I can find others to teach her, and they will do as I ask. They will not make excuses." And then a silence more dreadful than his voice. Finally, "I am too good to you. You are here too much on your own. You think you are the queen of your kingdom. This will soon change; do you hear me?"

Only then did Bimala's voice reveal her fear. "I will increase her lessons, sir. Please forgive my laziness. We will do nothing but study English all the day."

"The foreigners do not come to my houses for conversation, but they want to be understood. She will bring more rupees to my pocket if she will do what she is told."

Bimala's voice quivered. "Sir, your daughter is still very, very young, only a baby."

I tried to make sense of what I'd just heard. The young girl—Pooja?—was Shaitaan's daughter? Bimala was to teach her English. Foreigners wanted young girls to understand them. Shaitaan would fill his pockets with rupees from selling his own daughter. Bimala must have assumed I knew this all along. No wonder she saw me as deliverance for her and the girl.

"She is to bring me tea," Shaitaan said.

I straightened and drew my feet under me, ignoring the pain.

"I will bring the tea to you, sir," Bimala said hurriedly. "I am faster and she is still very clumsy."

"I will teach her not to be clumsy."

Surely, Bimala would not send her daughter to that monster. Did she have a choice? Bile rose in my throat. All that lay within view was sand, sea, and shrubbery. Nothing remotely weaponlike.

I heard water pouring and the clanging of pots. Shaitaan had moved, most likely, to the pavilion, and Bimala was preparing the tea. The pause provided time to collect myself, steady my breathing, but I could do no more than look from one corner of the hut to the other, watching for Shaitaan.

Bimala hurried around the corner, pushing the girl—perhaps eight, maybe younger—before her. "Angel Lady, honored one, you must take my daughter with you. You must go, now."

I should have made the connection much sooner. Not only had Shaitaan fathered Pooja, the child Bimala carried was also his and doomed to face the same fate. My presence was such cruelty. I represented rescue to Bimala, but I could do nothing, not in time to truly deliver her and her daughter. Pooja's eyes held both fear and hope. Her gaze nearly crushed me.

I opened my palms to Bimala. "I … I can't."

A flash of understanding passed over Bimala's face. Her chin lifted and she pulled Pooja back around the corner and out of sight.

My mind swung between two urgent questions: How had I gotten here, at this horrendous moment in time, and what, if anything, could I do to help?

The burns drilled pain down to my bones. And I was so very thirsty.

All went silent except for the gurgle of the surf and the rattle of the palms overhead. I checked my pockets for tissue to wrap around my palms to perhaps quiet their screaming. Instead, I found a device like a smart phone, only bigger. It was the GPS I'd given to Doug for a recent birthday.

But how …?

A sticky note in Alex's loopy printing said to press and hold the power button. I obeyed her instructions, mostly because my brain could not form any sort of plan to save Pooja or to escape. The thing chimed, and I nearly fainted.

I held the GPS to my pounding chest to puzzle out how Alex had gotten it into my pocket. I remembered nothing after laying on the futon. For me to end up on Kuna meant she had slipped the GPS into my pocket and touched my hand to the map of Kuna as I slept.

But how had Alex gotten the GPS from Doug? I pictured her jimmying a window at his house and scrambling inside.

Oh, Alex.

The GPS's screen shone green with tiny icons. People with 20/20 vision would find icons helpful. Unfortunately, I didn't have cheaters on to read anything smaller than Alex's bold printing. I squinted down. The GPS coordinates were illuminated in the corner of the screen, but I couldn't read them. I pinched and spread my fingers on the screen, hoping to enlarge the numbers.

It worked!

I hadn't a clue how to save the coordinates, so I recited the latitude—18.90—and the longitude—17.31—over and over and over.

But that longitude was impossible. Each time I traveled to Kuna I stayed for thirty-one minutes, not seventeen minutes. Stupid, stupid magic! When had the rules changed?

Clinking china startled me back to alertness. I listened in on a conversation between Bimala and her daughter. "Pooja, my daughter, to defy Shaitaan is to die. We have talked of this often. Remember, *Bapa* God's favor is with us. He sent Angel Lady to us, and now he will make us strong.

"You must take this tea to Shaitaan. I will pray, and I will follow to be close. I will hide behind his *kutiya*. Do not be afraid. I will protect you." In the silence, I imagined kisses and forced smiles. "Go now. Be brave. Smile. I am right behind you."

Despite the burns that covered my body, I shivered, for Bimala was sending her daughter to that beast, fully intending to do whatever was necessary to protect her.

I peeked around the corner to where Bimala had instructed Pooja, the side away from the ocean and sheltered by the palms. Buckets and wooden spoons hung from hooks, and a fishing pole leaned against the hut. Not twenty feet away, the door of Shaitaan's hut yawned open. I watched for any movement, but there was none. I eased along the wall of Bimala's hut.

Bimala crouched behind a stand of shrubs, watching Shaitaan and Pooja. Under the shade pavilion, Shaitaan sat in partial profile as Pooja poured his tea.

He was not the man of my nightmares. His wavy hair lifted in the breeze, and the fabric of his golf shirt pulled defiantly over his belly. He had boobs. I would have pegged him as an accountant or engineer, someone mild and kind who brought gifts home to his children, until he poked at Pooja with his silver-handled cane.

I grabbed a stout log from Bimala's cooking fire and thrust the flaming tip into the sand to douse the fire. Pooja struggled to keep the tray level as she backed away with her head lowered. Shaitaan hooked her arm with the cane's handle and pulled her closer. Bimala tucked the hem of her skirt into her waistband.

Shaitaan ranted at Pooja. "What's the matter with you? Are you stupid? What use are you? Look at me!"

When Pooja looked toward her mother instead, Shaitaan brought the cane down on Pooja's shoulder. The girl slumped to the ground, the tray spilling on the sand. She made no sound. She tightened into a fetal position. Bimala drew a knife out of the folds of her dress.

I tightened my grip on the log, tearing open blisters.

Perhaps I allowed a gasp to escape because Bimala turned her attention to me. She took in the log in my hand and frowned. She shook her head and gestured me toward the trees and the sea beyond. My eagerness to obey sickened me, but I pushed off and ran as if a great hoary beast chased me, dodging around palm trees and pushing through thick growths of shrubs.

When I broke out of the forest, I ran into the sea full tilt until the water pressed against my thighs. I collapsed under the surface and pulled hard at the water until my lungs demanded a breath. The coolness doused the fire in my skin, but the relief was short-lived. Salt clawed at the burns. I put my face in the water and plowed on.

SALLY WOULD NOT LET me leave her cabin until she had washed all of my burns and applied an ointment that eased the pain. She wrapped my feet in gauze and loaned me a pair of Richard's slippers to wear for the trip home.

She looked up from her work. "You've always been my rough

and tumble girl. I can't tell you how many nights I lay awake praying for your safe return." She capped the ointment. "But you always came home to me. For that I'm profoundly grateful to God."

Richard smiled at me encouragingly.

"I hope I didn't make you worry too much," I said to Sally.

"I admired your spunk. You weren't afraid of anything. There were times when I wished you—well, I wished you liked reading more. Just to give me a breather." She patted my knee and gathered the first aid supplies back into its red case.

I promised myself to visit Sally when I wasn't transitioning from one reality to another. She deserved my full attention. My thoughts were snarling and snapping dogs. I was angry with Alex for sending me into such a dangerous situation and worried sick for Bimala and Pooja. In my absence, had Shaitaan asked too much of Pooja? Had Bimala been forced to protect her daughter? Did Pooja still live? Did Bimala? And why had I run so keenly away from two children in peril? I truly didn't want to know the answer.

I stood to leave the neat little bathroom. "Thank you for taking such good care of me."

Richard stood in the doorway, beseeching with his eyes for a longer visit. "You're not leaving already, are you?"

"I'll be back soon, I promise, when I'm not so preoccupied." I held up my bandaged hands.

Richard left to answer a knock on the door.

Sally leaned closer. "Richard doesn't think I understand what's happened, but I do. It's a small thing between a mother and a daughter for one of us to die. I knew if I was patient that you would come back to me ... or I would go to you."

We found Richard walking into the great room with Alex trailing sheepishly behind. I touched my forehead to Sally's. "Thanks for being patient with me."

I avoided making eye contact with Alex. Truthfully, I was angry at her for sending me to Kuna. Better to let the anger fade a bit before we talked.

Richard loaded the bicycle she'd ridden into the back of his SUV and took Alex and me home. We drove in silence. Richard glanced sideways at me and at Alex in the backseat. Thankfully, he had the good sense to keep his questions to himself.

At the cabin, Alex jumped out to help Richard unload the bicycle. I didn't relish walking on my burned feet, so I sat in the passenger seat, enjoying the chilled evening air against my fiery skin.

I shifted to heft myself out of the car. Richard put up a hand. "If I could talk to you for a minute?"

Alex disappeared inside. I straightened as best I could. "Could I come by in a few days? Things should quiet down."

"I've got something for you." He pulled a shiny key out of his pocket. "I wouldn't expect you to notice a new door, not with how bad you're feeling. I was finishing the trim when you—well, I'm not sure what to call what you do. I suppose you simply arrive, don't you?"

When I didn't answer, he continued.

"This key will let you in—if you ever want to visit the boat, that is. All I ask is that you lock the door on your way out."

"Richard ..."

"I don't pretend to understand what you do, where you go, and how you get there and back again. I like things neat and tidy. Math is my language of choice. Answers can be tested and proven. All I know is Sally is sleeping better. She can read and putter in the kitchen again. We played checkers last night."

I held up the key. "Thanks for this."

"I hope you'll keep coming," he said with a rueful grin. "Perhaps you could come over the normal way, you know, on your bike. Or you could call. I wouldn't mind coming to get you."

I looked toward the house. Alex had probably barricaded herself behind a book.

"That girl has a good heart," he said.

"She can be extremely careless."

"Yep, she's young, all right."

"She has to understand that her actions have consequences, sometimes dangerous consequences."

Richard rubbed his evening scruff. "I wish I'd done things differently with our daughter. We about drove each other crazy. She was an artist of sorts, liked things messy and kind of off-kilter, a little too out of control for my tastes. Honestly, I was angry all the time, and I took that anger out on her." Richard frowned on a thought. "There's not much difference between fear and anger. Have you ever noticed that?"

"I'm well acquainted with fear these days."

"That surprises me."

"Anger, too. I'm excellent with anger."

He looked toward the cabin door. "I kind of got that."

"I should talk to her."

"Kids need to know they'll always get another chance—as many chances as it takes—to get life right … if she's lucky. I wish I'd told my daughter that."

I shuffled to the sleeping porch where I found Alex. She jumped when I said her name. "We need to talk," I said.

Richard had been right. Alex knew exactly what she had done and felt terrible. "The GPS, though, Grandma, was a stroke of genius, right?"

I'D BEGGED ANOTHER SLEEPING pill off Carolyn but waited until Alex's breathing slowed and deepened. I felt robbed of the night's sleep Carolyn had promised me with the first pill. And, not surprisingly, I feared even worse dreams after actually seeing Shaitaan.

Although I tried not to speculate about what had happened to Bimala and Pooja after I'd left Kuna, my imagination went wild. Every time I closed my eyes, I saw Pooja looking up at me with eyes full of pleading and accusation. Even with the help of the little white pill, I woke through the night from the pain of my burns and to wonder what was happening on Kuna.

Shame kept my stomach roiling about. My only thought had been getting off the island with my life, not with trying to help those precious girls.

I WOKE TO POUNDING on the door. I waited, hoping Alex would meet whoever wanted to see me so badly. I couldn't imagine who. I slipped back into a shallow slumber.

Another round of door banging woke me again. Only this time, a voice called, "Robin! For heaven's sake, open the door! I know you're in there!"

Doug?

Doug!

"I'm coming!" I gathered the bedding from the futon and turned in a circle, looking for a place to stash the wad. My thoughts only made sucking noises.

Doug's sensible adult voice came through the door. "Robin, we really need to talk."

"I'm coming!" I ran to the bathroom and threw the bedding behind the shower curtain. The woman in the mirror looked homeless, startled, and about eighty years old.

I uttered an expletive. Splashing water on my face would saturate my bandages, so I squeezed toothpaste on my tongue and pulled a brush through my hair, instead. Now I only looked seventy-five, as well as homeless and startled. I spritzed cologne at my pulse points.

"Robin?"

Alex had stacked her bedding neatly against the wall, but she was no where in sight. She could have been at the library, inserting the GPS coordinates for Kuna into the Internet. My heart fluttered.

"Robin!"

I opened the door. Doug walked past me into the cabin. A wall of moving boxes thwarted his progress. "What the—?"

"Coffee?" I asked.

His eyes paused on my bandaged hands and slid down to my feet. His expression went distant when our eyes met. No surprise there. He'd avoided any show of interest or concern about me since the divorce. I supposed a show of empathy proved too contradictory for him since he'd already sliced my aorta open. Without a word spoken between us we agreed the bandages were none of his ding-dang business.

"It's a little late for coffee," he said.

My watch read two-thirty. The white pill had worked better than I'd thought. "Water then?"

"We were surprised to learn Alex has been staying with you."

The urge to punch him in the face burned in me, not for what he said but how he said it. Since he'd moved out, he'd developed the ability to be in the room, speaking and upending my world but remaining untouchable, emotionally or otherwise.

Having him in my living room was like being offered a tall glass of water after a trudge through a desert and having the glass snatched from my grasp. A good solid hit to the jaw would surprise him and probably make him mad, which would have been preferable because he would have to acknowledge my presence. True to form, I didn't hit him. I played along. I settled for being with Doug but not truly *with* him.

"Is there a problem?" I said.

"It would have been nice to know Alex has been here for a whole month. I *am* her grandfather, you know? We would have made the trip up sooner, spent some time with her on the water. It's way past time for her to get to know Tiffany. We could have avoided this whole incident."

"What incident?"

Doug loved the high moral ground. This used to be a source of admiration. After the betrayal, however, this moral superiority soured my stomach. I offered him a seat in a wicker chair and sat across from him. Once seated, he told me the whole story, how he had arrived in Grand Lake with *her* the day before. Not long after, Alex had come to their door.

"You can imagine my surprise," he said.

Doug had heard from Alex about Nicci rushing to finish her certificate program. I wondered what else Alex told him. Had he heard anything about Bimala and Pooja? Or Richard and Sally? Arrivals and departures? I sure hoped not.

"Alex stayed for lunch," he said and described an elaborate spread. Doug patted his stomach and licked his lips. "It's getting tough to keep my boyish figure."

After lunch, while *she* cleaned the kitchen and Doug made a few calls, Alex wandered around their house, getting the lay of the land, she told them. She made her way to their bedroom, found Doug's underwear drawer and the GPS that I had given him for a birthday. *She* walked in just as Alex plunged the GPS into the pocket of her hoodie.

"Alex practically knocked Tiffany over, running out of the house," he said.

"This was yesterday? And you're just telling me now?"

"Tiffany thought I should cool down first." He paused, waiting for my appreciation for *her* great wisdom.

Keep waiting, Dougie boy.

"You can see why we're concerned," he continued. "This sort of behavior is indicative of a bigger problem, as you well know. We should look through Alex's things. She's probably carrying a pharmacy in her backpack."

Doug ran a finger across a moving box and blew the dust off his finger.

"Tiffany is very upset. Having Alex rifling through our things was quite the intrusion. She wants this resolved today. The girl needs an intervention. We don't want this to get out of hand."

Where to begin? "Kids *are* intrusive, Doug. They're young and inexperienced. And they tend to be impulsive. They want to make a difference. That's your granddaughter, Doug. There is no bigger problem. If you knew Alex, you would know that. She simply got caught up in the moment."

At least, I hoped that was true. Alex had assured me she'd borrowed the GPS from her grandfather. I didn't appreciate being on the receiving end of a lie. Alex and I could work that out later.

"As I recall, you dragged your feet when it came to Nicci, too," he said, smug. "You need to put aside your affection for Alex, Robin. You must see this clearly. Alex very purposefully looked through our drawers and took the first thing of value she found. She was looking for a source of cash, Robin, and that can only mean one thing. In fact, what other reason could there be for taking a GPS?"

Alex was determined to save two young girls from a horrible fate. I wouldn't fault her for that, even though she did so in a reckless manner. "I won't have her grilled, not by you and certainly not by *her*." I looked around the room, hoping to find the GPS to hand back to Doug. No such luck. "The GPS will be in your hands by the end of the day. That's my promise. You'll also have an apology from Alex." I stood, pointed toward the door with a bandaged hand. "You should leave now."

After Doug left, I rested my forehead against the door for a good long while. I should have been looking for Alex. We had things to settle and understandings to establish, like no lying to your grandmother and no sending her to hinter parts of the earth while she's sleeping.

Standing there with my head to the door, I remembered Nicci at age fourteen, sitting on the end of our bed. Doug sat in a chair by the window with his head in his hands. Streams of mascara streaked Nicci's face. We'd found drugs in her purse for the first time. She'd been acting distant, dismissive, and angry. Everything I said caused fireworks, so I had committed the most heinous crime known to motherhood, I read her diary.

I learned things about my daughter from her musings that abraded my heart. The guys she'd given herself to, and their contempt of her afterward. How she had been afraid but wanted to be considered cool. The drugs started at her friend's house. The girl's mother kept a bottle of Xanax in her nightstand. I remembered being grateful there were no opioids in the house. That came later.

"Mom," she'd said, "there's something else."

I looked toward Doug, but he'd already slipped out of the room. His truck roared to life in the driveway.

"What is it, baby?" I asked Nicci.

"I'm probably pregnant."

Something drained out of me.

"I can't have a kid, Mom. You know that, right? For one, it wouldn't be normal, probably a freak with missing arms or something. They show us pictures of kids born to drug addicts."

"You're not a drug addict." *Are you?*

"No one knows how much it takes to mess a kid up."

I drove Nicci to the clinic the next day. Heaven went silent, and I realized without truly knowing that I had not been the mother I'd wanted to be. Nicci had slipped through my fingers, gone looking for what she craved from me and finding shortcuts and dead ends. I'd been too distracted with building our business, and about a gazillion other temporal and shallow pursuits.

I shook my head to release the memory and slid to the floor, where I indulged in a good cry that only managed to leave me feeling worse.

17

Alex took the posture of a supplicant before Doug and *her.* She handed the GPS to Doug. "I'm so sorry for the trouble I've caused. I thought the GPS was a smart phone. I've always wanted one. No one seemed to be using it. I've been working on controlling my impulsive behavior, Grandpa. If you could pray for me, that would be great."

She stood with her fingers entwined at her waist, relaxed and queenlike. Her eyebrows rose questioningly as Alex spoke. "I want you to feel completely comfortable here, Alexis," she said. "Your grandfather and I look forward to many happy memories with you. All I ask is honesty."

Alex took a step toward *her.* "I totally understand if you don't invite me to your house ever again."

I expected Doug to jump in with reassurances that Alex would always be welcome. He sat with his elbows to his knees, studying his hands. I'd promised Alex not to get hysterical, but I was finding that promise harder and harder to keep.

We stood in awkward silence for some moments. The great room of *her* cabin smelled of dryer sheets and expensive perfume. Every *tchotchke* stood its ground with perfect balance and precision. Someone had artfully arranged the sofa pillows. A picture window framed an identical view to mine: The same valley fenced by snow-dusted peaks and floored by a sapphire lake. But I couldn't see how *her* place qualified as a cabin. No plaids. No moose. And nary a pinecone. Had she ever fried bacon in the gourmet kitchen?

"Perhaps we should sit down." She gestured to the sofa and the chairs that faced the cumbrous fireplace.

A rush of heat coursed my veins, and I eyed the front door longingly.

Tiffany hooked a strand of Alex's hair behind her ear and glanced at me. "I can't help but think that all of this could have been avoided, if we'd had a chance to get to know you sooner, Alexis."

Alex took a step back. "Alex. My name is Alex."

"There's no better time than right now to get to know each other. Doug, go get those brownies I baked this morning. Robin, can I offer you a cup of coffee or tea? Perhaps you would prefer a glass of wine? Doug can make you a gin and tonic. That's your preference, isn't it?"

Doug scurried toward the kitchen.

How ironic that she dared to lecture me on keeping lines of communication open. There would be no need for open or closed lines of communication if she had kept her sticky fingers off of Doug. And how would *she* know what I liked to drink? Had their pillow talk been about my drinking habits?

She turned to me and became doubly earnest. "Robin, we've been friendly in the past. How long have we been neighbors? Ages! For the sake of dear Alexis, shouldn't we work our way back?"

To stay in that room with her meant biting through my tongue. To leave was to surrender the high ground, as I would be the hard-hearted bitch, *she* the conciliator. What a conniver!

Alex wrapped an arm around my shoulders. "Grandma and I have gotten really busy at the shop. Bidding has closed on a couple of maps. Turning the orders around quickly is super important, so we have to get going. Those high-percentage approval ratings are golden. Thanks so much for accepting my apology." Alex moved toward the door and dragged me along. The girl was brilliant.

Doug chased after us to the road with a plate of brownies. Alex questioned me with a look, and I nodded. She turned toward the cabin and walked briskly away. Doug looked over his shoulder toward the gaping door and back to me. "I'm sorry," he whispered. "I'll come by later and we can talk."

I caught up to Alex in front of the Cogdill's cabin. "Can you believe that woman? She is so full of herself."

"Don't worry about her, Grandma. There are more important things to think about." Her eyes sparkled. "My time at the library has paid off. I know exactly where Kuna is. It's off the coast of India."

"The Maldives, then?"

"But here's another surprise: The island goes by another name, *Sundar Maut*. That's why we had such a hard time finding it. I compared the satellite picture to Bimala's drawing, and the shape matches really well." Alex's face shone with intoxicating joy. She stopped suddenly and held my gaze. "We have to call Cal. We have to call him, right now."

"We still can't say how we know any of this. And if we can't tell him how we know about the island, he won't trust what I tell him. How can he? It all sounds so improbable."

"We'll *make* him do something, Grandma."

Young girls are so convinced of their power and the rightness of their causes. I wouldn't—more truthfully, couldn't—dissuade her about calling Cal. She would learn her limitations like we all did: She would run into a thick, hard wall. The wall would be too tall to climb and too long to run around. The wall, forever after, would remind her of her limits. I really hated that about life.

"And Grandma, I wasn't kidding about the maps. We sold two, one of the older ones and the one of that harbor fort in Canada. It's not tons of money, but that makes a $155 toward buying *Zella* back."

That much money wouldn't buy a bronze cleat for the gunwale, but beginnings—humble or extravagant—should be celebrated. "Let's make sundaes."

"Call Cal first." Alex gathered and knotted her ponytail like she did when she had a job to do. She skipped ahead of me and pushed through the cabin's door.

I stopped and looked down the road toward Doug's place. This was what kept echoing in my head: Doug's promise to come to the cabin later. I sniffed down my shirt and ran my hands through my hair. Could I find that dress I wore in Tahiti, the one that slipped off with a pull of a tie?

I should make some guacamole.

"Grandma, are you coming in?"

How long had Alex been standing there?

"It just dawned on me," she said, palms out. "We're being totally stupid. Cal doesn't have to know *how* you know about the island. We can tell him we finally found a match. I *did* find a match, right? Shouldn't you call him?"

I called Cal but his voicemail picked up on the first ring. My message rambled on about Alex working long hours in the library—which she had for something else—and how she had finally found an island, by chance really, that matched the map he had brought to me.

"I'm sorry for any misunderstanding we may have had earlier. I should have waited before saying anything. Well, I guess we finally found what we needed to help the girls on that island. If you want to ask me any questions, feel free to call. Thank you. And goodbye. I hope your trip proved successful. Goodbye. I'm hanging up. This is Robin Connelly."

Oh brother.

DOUG NEVER SHOWED UP. WAS I surprised? Not really. But I was sickened that an empty promise had tied me to a false hope for hours, days, and, well, decades. I was pathetic. In an effort to wrestle control of my destiny—for at least the rest of the day—I called Carolyn.

"Meet me for coffee?" I said.

She hesitated. "There are a million people out there."

I pulled the curtains back to take in the lake. Scows with bloated sails crisscrossed the lake. Rooster tails rose from speedboats pulling water skiers. A typical summer day. Jet fighters buzzed the lake. That was different. "Is this the Fourth of July already?"

"Afraid so."

True enough, people jammed the small public beach on the far side of the lake. Perhaps Bruce the Moose—our town mascot of sorts—would walk ashore for another visit this year. That would give the tourists something to tell their friends.

At any rate, no shopping for us. "I'll put a pot on," I said. "Do you have anything sweet to bring?"

CAROLYN FROWNED AT ME over her coffee cup. "How do you suppose Wayne replaced those signs so fast? I know for a fact that new signs take weeks to get back from the sign maker."

"Maybe he had extras in storage?"

"I can't drive anywhere in the county without seeing *her*."

I didn't relish another visit from Wayne. "You aren't thinking of taking the signs again, are you? You were pretty lucky he didn't file charges."

Carolyn avoided my eyes. "I've moved on."

"Why is that so hard to believe?"

"Maybe I haven't moved on to anything better. It's more like I've switched tactics. My goal now is to simply bring a touch of annoyance to their lives, without jeopardizing my friends with legal action. I thought you would appreciate that."

If I didn't ask her, I wouldn't be culpable. I added more water to the tea pot and rinsed out the French press.

"You can fidget with that pot all day. I'm going to tell you. What's the point of launching an attack if no one ever knows?"

Carolyn had honed her persistence by nose-to-nose confrontations with kindergartners. By my modest estimations, she had convinced over five hundred of the little darlings to sit on carpet squares and to be kind to hamsters. Nothing could protect me from that kind of training. I would hear all about her devilish schemes.

I glanced through the window at Alex on the deck. She sat curled in a chair with a fat book. Shouldn't she be swimming with friends or going to a picnic? Maybe a parade? She turned to me through the glass and smiled.

"Let's join Alex on the deck," I said.

"Should she hear this?"

"I have reason to believe she's heard worse." Once Alex knew the topic of conversation, her gaze dropped back to her book and stayed there.

"May I continue?" Carolyn said. She didn't wait for an answer. "I found out last week that I go to the same hair stylist *she* does. Josie—the stylist—is a fount of information. Evidently, *she* spills her guts to Josie on a regular basis. I can put up with my hair looking like a crop circle for such rich intelligence. Josie does a truly rotten job with my hair."

"You haven't told Josie about the signs, I hope."

Carolyn batted away my concern. "I taught Josie's daughter. She still thinks highly of me, so I wouldn't want to dissuade her of that. So no, I haven't told Josie about any of my exploits."

Alex showed no interest in knowing how old women dealt with their broken hearts, which was good. I urged Carolyn to spill everything.

"Josie's intel helped me plan a precision attack."

"Should I call a lawyer?"

"Remember, I only hope to annoy. From where I'm sitting, that's called personal growth."

We all turned toward the lake at the sound of revelry. A pontoon boat flying about three hundred U.S. flags crawled past the cabin. Men with sunburned paunches and women in patriotic T-shirts raised their glasses to us and wished us a happy Fourth of July.

"Who are those people?" Alex asked with disgust. "They're awfully close to the dock, don't you think?"

I waved back to the boat. "Tourists are the price we pay for living in such a beautiful place. Your great-granddad insisted we be polite to the visitors, but he never expected us to like the intrusion. He was very wise that way."

We sat in a companionable silence. The day's warmth released the soapy smell of pine and the smoke of a charcoal fire wafted overhead. Doug had always preferred grilling over charcoal. The memory of his fire-lighting ritual made me smile.

Carolyn cleared her throat. "There's more to my story, you know?"

Alex returned to her book.

Carolyn continued. "*She* hadn't been to see Josie in some time. When Josie asked after her health, she got an earful. It turns out she is very allergic to cats. She had to be transported to the hospital in Estes Park last week. Anaphylactic shock. According to Josie, she nearly died."

"You aren't thinking of putting a kitten in her bed, are you?"

"Nothing like that. I subscribed her to *Cat Lover* magazine." She smiled mischievously. "It won't be long before she'll start receiving oodles and oodles of mailers for cat toys, cat bookends, catnip fortune cookies—that's a real thing, by the way—cat teepees, cat jewelry, cat pillows, and my favorite, the hoodie with a kangaroo pouch for your cat. I signed her up for everything."

"And that's not mean?"

"What's mean is creating a profile for her on a dating service for cat lovers."

"You're going to hate yourself in the morning."

"I don't think so."

But she would hate herself. And when that day came, I would be a good friend and bite back my I told you so. "Can I show you the dock?"

Carolyn frowned. "The dock? I've seen the dock a million times."

I tilted my head toward the dock and mouthed the word *please*.

She followed me down the steps. "You know," she said, "we'll have to climb back up."

We dangled our feet in the lake. The cool water felt fabulous on my healing burns. A couple I recognized from HOA meetings glided by on paddle boards. They hadn't moved out of hearing when Carolyn said, "Do they know how ridiculous they look on those things?"

I truly studied Carolyn then. How had I missed the draw of her mouth, the smudges under her eyes, or the way her shoulders rolled under the weight of an unseen load. "What's going on?"

"My kids are going to Cancun with Wayne and *her*. They'll be gone for a week. A whole week."

I pulled her into my arms. "It will be hotter than hell in Cancun."

She cried into my shoulder. "Not hot enough."

Her kids and grandkids traveling with Wayne and the other woman meant a week of excruciating silence, or worse, pictures of her grandchildren playing in the surf with *her*. Smiling in front of the pool with *her*. Eating pineapple on the stick with *her*. That made me cry, too.

We blew our noses and cobbled together a Fourth of July dinner, complete with nitrates, saturated fats, obscene amounts of salt, and plenty of gluten. The decadence of the fare gave me a buzz. Carolyn insisted on doing the grilling since I still wore bandages on my hands, although the blisters had crusted and now itched.

When our stomachs could take no more insult, we snuggled into sleeping bags on the chaise lounges and watched the fireworks from the deck. Alex scored each explosion from one to ten. She'd seen lots of big-city Fourth of July firework displays. According to her, Grand Lake's show stood above even Denver's. How could it not? The lake redoubled every spark in its reflective waters.

I never slept well on the Fourth. I dipped into dreamland only to be awakened by yet another firecracker. *It's three in the morning, people!* I finally gave up and returned to the sleeping bag in the deck chair. My thoughts dosey-doed between Carolyn's Quixotic battle for dignity and Bimala, the girl imprisoned in paradise.

I truly believed Carolyn would eventually tire of her plots and find something to do that bolstered her soul, which begged me to ask if hope existed for my ravaged soul? To continue on with my heart in my hand, waiting for Doug to return, only meant more heartache to come. But to plot revenge didn't appeal either.

What was the opposite of waiting in the same old place of the heart?

Moving.

I needed to move somewhere, not in a pack-the-boxes kind of move. My heart needed to move. From Doug. But to what?

Not a man. Definitely not a man.

Eew.

What about the rest of my family?

I hadn't talked to Lauren in weeks, my very own daughter. Whether she meant for me to or not, I always felt like an intruder when I called. But isn't that what mothers do? We're killjoys and the askers of awkward questions. We have a level of discomfort and persistent love to maintain with our adult children. We're not really mommies anymore and too vested in our children's happiness to truly be friends.

And because Nicci sucked me into a black hole of regret and disappointment every time we talked, didn't mean I couldn't— although I would have to be much braver—inch my way closer to her.

And I'd neglected other relationships in my preoccupation with Doug. Carolyn deserved a more committed friend. I could make more of an effort.

Alex.

Above all others, she deserved my devotion. But she merited far more than me. The world is fraught with danger. Only an army of people charging blockades, protecting her flanks, and repelling onslaughts would do.

Doug flashed into my head, but instead of dismissing the thought, I let the idea of recruiting him on to Alex's team rumble around in my head. I liked someone with history stepping up for the cause. True, this required a step back when I was supposed to be moving on, but couldn't I move on *and* conscript Doug? I mean, he was still her grandfather, and I was her grandmother. Nothing had changed there. Loads of people have figured out trickier relationships.

I will move forward by reaching back.

I thought constantly of returning to Kuna but always talked myself out of doing so. What would I find? What could I accomplish? I was in no position to help those girls. I offered exactly nothing but false hope and crushing disappointment. My best chance at being any kind of hero was to be the best grandmother Alex had ever had.

18

I stood astride my bicycle near the boat launch. Across the parking lot, the Adams Falls trailhead lay in the chilling morning shadow of the mountains. Only a few cars had parked in the lot, most assuredly those that belonged to back-country hikers from days earlier. A gaggle of day hikers trudged up the trail, guided along by the log and limb fence, their heads down, all gripping coffee mugs.

At that distance, I watched Doug as he bent to pick trash from the long grass along the trail. He stuffed each scrap into one of the grocery bags he kept in his truck for this very purpose. An unreasonable happiness settled on me. Not everything about Doug had changed.

He turned at the sound of my tires on the gravel. "What's this about?" he asked, evenly.

I dismounted and leaned the bike against the railing. "I expected you to come by last night to talk about Alex."

"The day fell apart. Tiffany had invited some folks up from the city. She said she'd told me ..." He shrugged.

No, he hadn't changed so very much. He still tuned out what he didn't want to hear, now from her. I turned toward the lake, not eager to see him feign innocence. The sunrise cast a rosy glow on Shadow Mountain and birds rioted in the trees. I leaned against the fence. I couldn't remember the last time I'd watched day rise on the lake and mountains. In fact, I itched to join the day hikers.

Doug cleared his throat. "I promised to take Tiffany to breakfast before we leave for home."

"Do you remember our hikes up the inlet?"

"We should probably talk about Alex."

"Sure. You betcha. Let's see." He'd cut himself shaving that morning. I resisted the urge to wipe away the sticky blood from his throat. Instead, I reminded myself this conversation was all about supporting Alex and building a team.

"Just a couple of things, really. First, I appreciate your concern over Alex. I can see how taking the GPS looked. You have to believe me, though, when I say my affection for her hasn't blinded me.

"Perhaps, yes, I could have noticed things sooner with Nicci. And I really wish I had. But Alex is so not Nicci. She's clear-headed and, I will admit, a little impetuous, but she's a great help to me. Martha Stewart would envy her organizational skills. The Traveling Man has never looked better. That thing with the GPS, well, I'm asking you to forget it ever happened."

"Give her a pass?"

"You have the thing back; she's apologized. She really does deserve another chance. I promise you won't be disappointed."

"And the other thing?"

So like Doug to avoid committing until he knew every nuance of a decision. "Will you or won't you give her another chance? Anything else I have to say really doesn't matter unless you see her for the girl she is."

"Tiffany is still upset. She's more than willing to have Alex in our lives, but to let her off easy? I'll have to talk to Tiffany first."

When had he started consulting a wife before making a decision? "Can you tell me how you're leaning?"

"I probably shouldn't."

"Oh-kay."

"Your sarcasm doesn't help."

To think I'd conceived two daughters with this man. "I'm

sorry?"

"Are we almost done?"

I'm doing this for Alex. "I should have told you Alex was spending the summer with me. I'm being downright greedy with her, which is all wrong. She needs her grandfather."

"That's what I tried to tell you."

"You did, you surely did. I could try to explain myself, but that won't help either one of us. Let's simply agree that Alex is more important than any of that. We were pretty good parents, but we need to be even better grandparents, no matter what has passed between us.

"Alex will be a young woman before we know it. She needs a man in her life, and you're the best one for the job. And there is a chance, albeit slim, that we'll have other grandchildren. Lauren could find an Italian with ambitions to match hers, and they could have children. Those grandchildren will definitely need a safe place to land."

Doug nodded knowingly and turned serious. "Listen, you should know that Tiffany gets nervous around you. She gets all stiff, and then she says some pretty off-the-wall stuff."

"I'm not following you."

"You intimidate her."

"And the reason you're telling me this?"

"I want her included in anything we do for Alex."

"I sort of assumed ..."

"Could you tell Tiffany that?"

"Can't you?"

"It would be better coming from you."

"I'll send her a text." Or maybe I wouldn't.

Doug stretched, signaling the end of the conversation. "It's time to hit the road, but we'll be back next weekend. We'll rent a boat, maybe head over to Steamboat. Would Alex like that?"

"She's been bugging me to take her to Quackers."

Doug grimaced. "The rubber duck store?"

"In so many ways she's still a little girl ... until you underestimate her."

ALEX RIPPED THE TAPE off a moving box, and the flaps opened like a book. She lifted a pile of plates wrapped in craft paper and unwrapped each one. She dealt the plates out on the kitchen table like playing cards.

"None of them match," she said. Hand-painted flowers, the next more delicate than the last. "And what are they for? They're awfully small."

"They were my mother's." I ran my finger over a bouquet of forget-me-nots on a gold-rimmed plate. The brushstrokes were ripples under my touch. "She scoured antique shops whenever we traveled. They weren't expensive, maybe a buck or so. She hung them all over the house.

"Other kids brought home Tinker Bell dolls or T-shirts. We brought home maps and teeny-tiny plates. And Dad couldn't resist a mineral shop. One of these boxes holds a shoebox full of coprolites. Maps, plates, and fossilized dinosaur poo—such are the things my memories are made of."

Alex scanned the walls of the cabin. "Do you want to hang the plates?"

To hang the plates meant taking down the art, or what passed for art, from the walls. There was a moose-shaped cutting board and a ski poster from Winter Park, circa 1973, with tattered edges. A macramé wall hanging filled the wall above the futon. We'd stuck treasures from hikes—feathers, mistletoe, rocks—into the knots. A family of packrats would feel right at home in its tangled jute.

I rewrapped the forget-me-not plate. "Maybe we opened the wrong box."

"There's no turning back now," she said, unfurling the

wrapping and returning the plate to the table.

"Turning back is the wisest thing to do when the music goes spooky," I said.

"Grandma, this is like that television show I told you about. We're going to make three piles. One is for the things you want to keep. The second is for the things you want to sell or give away. The third is for stuff headed for the landfill. Easy."

My stomach clenched, and my heart raced.

"One box, Grandma. We're only emptying one box."

"We should have started with kitchen gadgets."

"We'll do gadgets tomorrow, I promise. Which plate is your favorite?"

The blowsy roses plate had hung behind the toilet in my childhood home. Looking at that plate made me queasy, all thanks to a bout of stomach flu and a can of chili con carne. The daffodils plate had hung with the daisies by Mom's dresser. I'd shaved Mom's head as she sat in front of the mirror. "I'm not sure I have a favorite."

"Then let's put them in the sell pile. I'll take pictures and post the lot on eBay this afternoon."

I rewrapped the daffodils in craft paper. "I'm not ready. I thought I was, but I'm definitely not. I'm sorry."

Alex stilled my hands with hers. "Then let's leave them out. At least you can enjoy them."

I'd never asked Mom why she'd collected dessert plates. I supposed, in the end, it didn't matter why she'd collected the tiny plates, only that she had simply enjoyed them. And now Alex and I could enjoy them.

That night, we ate white cake with white frosting off the plates. My chest ached the whole time. As much as I'd loved my mother, I hadn't bothered to ask her about a small thing that brought her pleasure.

I declared my days of settling for a distant knowledge of a

loved one over.

I hardly knew what fourteen-year-old girls cared about anymore, but I asked question after question in hopes of finding out. I started by asking her about her favorite candy bar. In the spirit of fairness, I confessed to preferring Kit Kat bars above all else. Soon, she asked the questions and the answers carved closer to the heart.

I feigned a yawn. "I'm getting sleepy."

"I'm trying to understand Mom. She does some pretty crazy stuff."

"Tomorrow."

I didn't fall asleep as fast as I'd hoped. I replayed my talk with Doug. While I wished the conversation had been easier, I believed he understood what was at stake. The whole thing about the plates with Alex made me feel positively stupid. Logically, I couldn't think of a reason to keep them, but my heart clung to them like a lifeline.

Alex snored softly. How I loved that girl.

In the thickening dark, I picked at the sloughing skin of my hands. My thoughts turned to Kuna, or as I now knew the island to be, Sundar Maut. No matter how busy I kept my days, the nights belonged to Bimala and Pooja. Had Shaitaan left the island yet? Did he leave the supplies they needed? Were they still alive?

The girl and her daughter lived under suffocating tyranny, their bodies not their own. And I could do nothing to help them. Even with the information I'd given Cal, he couldn't make plans to go to the island. He'd surely asked himself how I could know about two young girls on an island off the coast of India. Under normal circumstance, I wouldn't.

No, I couldn't deliver the girls, but I could straighten out some misconceptions I'd left with Bimala. As long as she believed me to be one of God's angels, I feared she would lose the faith that had buoyed her. I would return to Sundar Maut to explain my visits and to tell her I wasn't a divine creature. And to be a friend.

19

Bimala insisted on preparing a breakfast of rice and fish.

The girl simply did not understand time and the limitations it imposed. She noted the phases of the moon, felt the pull of the tides, and tracked the sun in its course across the sky. She didn't wear a watch. She didn't clock into a job. Being late for a dentist appointment was a foreign idea. And so, thirty-one minutes meant nothing to her. I made a ball of the sticky rice and popped it in my mouth. Pooja watched me with full-moon eyes as she fingered her breakfast.

"This island is known as Sundar Maut, not Kuna, to people who make maps," I told Bimala.

Her hands stilled. "Beautiful death," she whispered.

"What?" I said, but she simply covered the rice pot as if I hadn't spoken.

"Why do *you* call this place Kuna?"

Sometimes we don't know the weight of our questions. Bimala buried her face in her hands. It didn't really matter why she called the island one name and the rest of the world used another. I took a breath to withdraw the question, but Bimala spoke first.

"I do not remember very much from the Dalit school. I was very young, a girl away for the first time from *Mata's* skirts. My favorite subject was story. The teacher played all the parts. Some days she spoke with the deep voice of a giant. On other days she sang the words of a Persian queen or roared like a lion. I waited all through maths and letters for the time of the stories. I am very sad for forgetting the stories. I wish to tell Pooja, although I have only one voice.

"There is one story I do remember. I think because the man named Yusuf had so many brothers, and many brothers would have been a help to *Pita* and *Mata*.

"Of all the brothers, Yusuf's *pita* loved him best, but his brothers hated him. I do not remember why. Perhaps Yusuf brought his *pita* dates and grapes in the heat of the afternoon but none for his brothers.

"The brothers could not forgive the love *Pita* had for Yusuf, so they threw him in a deep well and left him there to die. One brother could not sleep for the terrible thing they had done. He convinced the other brothers to pull Yusuf out of the well and to sell him as a slave to a place far away from his home.

"Yusuf's *pita* wondered where the boy had gone. The brothers—because they had shame over what they had done—lied. They told their *pita* that the boy had been killed by a wild animal. *Pita* cried and tore his clothes." Bimala clenched the cloth of her dress. "The story makes the heart sick."

"You don't have to continue."

"You asked, so I must tell you. It is because of the story of Yusuf that I call this place Kuna. The brothers meant to kill Yusuf in the well, but the well was not so dark and not so deep that *Bapa* God did not see Yusuf. No, *Bapa* God saw Yusuf there. *Bapa* God would not let the brother sleep until he rescued Yusuf from the well.

"This, too, is a dark place, like a well. But *Bapa* God sees us here. That is the meaning of Kuna; it is *well*." She lifted her hands to the sky.

"Bimala ...?"

"We do not always see the work *Bapa* God is doing. He is good and he is strong to rescue from this place. But even if he does not, even if—" She looked to Pooja. "*Betee*, daughter, bring me a bottle of water from the shelter."

Pooja blinked, considered the last bite of fish in her bowl, and rose to do her mother's bidding.

Bimala opened palms to make a scale. "Shaitaan weighs the value of having Pooja for himself or to save her for the men of Main Land. He is hungry for her, but he is also greedy. I pray Pooja will not have to go to him, but if she does ..." Bimala touched her lips to staunch her emotion. "Her days as a child are not so many now."

The fish and rice sat in my stomach like a rock. I'd come to offer friendship, but the girl and her daughter needed something much more immediate and substantial, to be rescued from hell. Instead, I'd planned on explaining how I traveled to the island, and how I wasn't an angel but a woman with an odd genetic anomaly. In other words, rip all hope from their grasps.

I couldn't make eye contact with Bimala, so I watched Pooja, distracted from her errand, kicking at the water and catching the spray in her outstretched hands. My heart caught. A girl born to slavery could still capture a moment of wonderment.

Bimala grasped my forearm. "Angel Lady, please, look to the sky."

I followed her gaze. The blue made my eyes ache.

"You see there are no clouds to threaten us. The wind touches us with gentle fingers. Our bellies are full. There is no better day than today—there is no better time than now to leave this place, is that not so?"

An expansive stage of water and sky lay before me. I didn't belong there. "I won't come again unless I have a plan. I'm so sorry."

BACK IN RICHARD'S SHED, I fingered a flap of upholstery on the captain's seat and rested my head on the steering wheel. I allowed the memories *Zella* conjured to wash over me. The slap of water against the hull and the cold that bit my nose on early-morning fishing trips. The tug of the fish on my line. Dad's groan over bait lost to yet another winter-starved trout. The simplicity of being. The here and now of time on the water with Dad. To be loved and to love.

I gripped the steering wheel and let the tears come. My last sight of Bimala had been of a girl bereft of hope. I'd done that to her. Since my first visit to the island, my world had slipped many degrees off center. Nothing made sense.

Zella alone—in her cracking, peeling, landlocked state—remained true. She was the work of my hands and the platform for my purest moments. I vowed afresh to get her back. I'd run out of options for helping Bimala. Sure, I would call Cal again and leave yet another message that would make him roll his eyes, but I promised myself to plead her case and to be completely truthful with him.

I slipped out, careful to lock the door as Richard had shown. Sally called to me from the porch. I considered pretending I didn't hear her. I wasn't good company for anyone. But this was Sally.

She stood on the top step, her hands over her heart, a look of sublime pleasure lighting her face. "Hello," I said.

"Have you been to see Gloria?"

I ran my hands through my hair, already sticky from drying salt water and sweat. I picked my way over the flagstone path. "I keep forgetting to call."

We held hands while sitting in the porch swing. Shadow Mountain Lake was tetchy under a low ceiling of gray. Sally sat silently, gazing for long moments at the distressed lake and then to me, only to smile tightly as a mother does when she's worried.

She squeezed my hand. "I shouldn't tell you this, but you have always been my favorite. Your sister and brothers were all so self-contained. Nothing flapped them. They are like your father that way, don't you think?"

I nodded.

"You, my darling, are the child of my heart. I'm afraid I passed on to you an abundance of self-doubt. By the time you were in school, you were so much like me in this, second-guessing everything you said and did.

"I knew you would grow up and develop the ability to hide your angst, as I had done. We dither on the inside and act commanding on the outside, isn't that right? I often heard you coaching yourself to stick to your decisions."

She patted my hand. "A healthy portion of self-doubt can be a good thing, if it keeps us humble and ready to listen. We remain teachable. Your heart, dearest, is steadfast, and when you determine to do something, you accomplish beautiful things. I could always count on you."

Sally frowned and her eyes flitted to the porch ceiling. "I'm prattling on so. What was I saying, dear? I've completely lost what I meant to say. I'm a stupid old hag."

I looked through the window to where Richard sat with a cup of coffee and the paper. I willed him to look at me.

Sally put her hands to her head and rocked. "What day is this?"

"Thursday."

"No, that's not what I mean? You know that's not what I mean. Stop putting words in my mouth. Is this bridge day or isn't it?"

It took Richard an hour to calm Sally down. I insisted on walking home, but he wouldn't let me, so I waited for him on the porch. I reran all that Sally had said. She hadn't been speaking to me, Robin, but to her daughter who had sat on the edge of their family. What had Sally meant to say to her daughter? I would have wanted to hear that my mother noticed how brave I'd been and that I tackled the hard things of life with grace. Mostly, though, I wished I'd heard that I should never, not for one minute, accept anything as impossible.

WHEN RICHARD DROPPED ME off at the cabin, Alex was shifting boxes from the back bedroom to the living room.

"I thought we agreed on *one* box a day," I said.

Alex avoided looking at me. "Bimala and Pooja need a place to stay. We can't ask them to sleep on the floor." And then her green eyes drilled me. "Besides, they should have the best place."

I took a box from her hands. "Let's make something for dinner first." Now, I was avoiding *her* gaze.

"You aren't going back, are you? You're going to leave them with that awful man."

"I promised Bimala I would only go back if I had a plan. To drop by for a visit is cruel. The girl is fighting for her life and the lives of her children."

"Children? You've only mentioned Pooja. Are there more? Grandma, what's going on?"

I weighed the wisdom of telling Alex the true situation for Bimala and Pooja. How could knowing what Bimala faced make anything better? And yet, couldn't Bimala's story work as a warning for Alex, a way to say, This is what men can be like?

Proceed with caution!

I looked up when I heard her sniffing back snot. Alex wiped her face on the hem of her hoodie. "I've heard about trafficking. A sophomore disappeared last year. She ran away. She was only looking for a place to belong.

"Anyway, they found her in Las Vegas. She was pretty messed up. They said a guy offered to help her, to give her a safe place to sleep and something to eat. She's in some kind of treatment place now. She hasn't come back to school, so I'm not sure why. It's just what kids are saying."

She raised her gaze to mine. "This is what's happening to Bimala and Pooja, isn't that right, Grandma? That man is using them to make money."

I pulled her into my arms. "Pretty close."

Alex pushed back. She settled her green eyes on me. "We have to help them. I doubt her parents are looking for her. They probably think she's dead. We can't just leave them there."

We ate peanut butter and jelly sandwiches for dinner and tackled clearing the bedroom. To make room for all those boxes, we carried the kitchen table onto the deck. Miracle of miracles, we found a box labeled linens with the queen-size sheets for the bed inside. Alex volunteered one of her pillows, which shamed me into doing the same. We wiped down the nightstand and headboard with lemon oil, scrubbed the walls, and vacuumed the carpet. Alex hung two of Mom's plates by the dresser's mirror.

In the glow of our achievement, we settled onto the deck with bowls of ice cream. My muscles screamed for a hot bath, but I was too tired. Across the lake, the lights of Grand Lake shimmered.

A lemony light silhouetted the great hump of Green Mountain. Soon, an arc of light rose with unquenchable determination, and the fermented orb slid up to brighten the sky and dim the stars. A ribbon of yellow danced across the water to us.

I expected an exclamation from Alex. What could be more wondrous than a full moon rising over the Rocky Mountains? When she didn't speak, I thought she'd fallen asleep, but the moon's sheen lit her troubled face.

"We can't solve all the world's problems," I said, sounding as trite as I felt. "We can only do what we can do."

"I could be one of those girls."

"Bimala and Pooja? That's impossible. Those girls are nothing like you. Besides, you have me. You have your mother and your grandfather. We would never let anything like that happen to you."

"I ran away, Grandma, just like the girl at my school. I didn't know what else to do. Mom didn't believe me."

A pit opened in the bottom of my stomach. "Didn't believe you about what, sweetie?" A long silence followed my question, which I waited out against every intuition I'd ever honed.

"Grandma, you can't get mad. Mom is trying so hard. She has to study all the time, and she says the house is too noisy. I try to be quiet, but she needs it really, really quiet, so she goes to the coffee shop on the corner, which is way noisier than our house."

I reached for her hand. "I hate that you were on your own so much. I wish Nicci had said something. You could have stayed with me. I hear good things about the schools in Grand County."

"I thought about calling, but I worried Mom would quit school, and I didn't want her to blame me. She was so close. Only a few more months and she would graduate. But then things got harder."

"Harder? How did things get harder?"

The moon heaved higher into the inky blackness, growing smaller and whiter as it rose. I counted to one hundred and twenty-one before Alex spoke again.

"Mom will be pissed if I tell you."

"Does she have to know?"

"Grandma, I know you, you'll say something."

"Maybe saying something is what needs to happen for things to get better. That's a chance we should take, don't you think?"

A motor droned in the distance. I remembered full-moon *Zella* tours of the lake with Dad and Mom. He'd cut the engine when we reached the deep waters. We lay on the deck like sardines, bathed in the moon's luminous glow, marveling at the brightness. Receding into those memories pulled at me. Instead, I rubbed the back of Alex's hand with my thumb, coaxing her on.

"I don't think I can say it."

"Just tell me the beginning. You can stop whenever you like."

Only crickets chirruped. I chewed the end of a finger to occupy my mouth. This was no time to press for answers. "You have to know that Sean is really great. I mean, he helps Mom a lot. He's real good about taking care of stuff that worries her, like the car and just about everything else. He does all the cooking, and if I need a ride somewhere, he never complains, not ever. He sits through my play rehearsals, which are, honestly, pretty horrible. He's like a dad, at least how I dreamed about having a dad. Mom's other boyfriends were into her but not so much me."

"Something changed?"

We had a rhythm now. I asked a question and Alex agonized over what to say for a very long time.

"Sean works nights, so he's at the house when I get home from school. He's cool, he stops whatever he's doing to make me a snack. Coming home to an empty house was kind of scary before Sean, so having him there was nice, you know? We talked about school and stuff. He understood what I was going through."

"He sounds like he's trying to be a good guy, but sometimes he made you uncomfortable."

"Sometimes, I think, like, I just misunderstood him. I mean, Grandma, he told me I was pretty, and he sounded like he meant it. That was nice of him, right? Dads say that kind of stuff to their daughters all the time. But then he said I had a nice body, and he couldn't understand why the boys weren't lining up to take me out. I didn't believe that part so much, but I liked hearing it."

Doug and I had told Nicci—all right, *I'd* told Nicci—that having men around that weren't biologically related to Alex was a bad idea. I think I'd read an article. Anyway, she'd called me a pervert. We'd left Mimi's Restaurant—in opposite directions—without eating our lunches.

"Grandma?"

"Yes? Is this the hard part?"

"I was pretty stupid."

"Oh, baby, this isn't on you. Although you're amazing beyond your years, you're still a child. If adults act badly toward you, that's on them, not you." I swallowed hard, hoping she believed me enough to continue her story. But she sat in silence, the moon glinting off her trapped tears. When she didn't speak, I said, "I have to ask, Alex. Did he touch you?"

She groaned. "Grandma, can we stop now?"

More than anything, I wanted to honor her request. I couldn't. "No matter what happened, I love you, I respect you, and I will always, always believe you."

"Mom didn't. I told her everything. I'd never seen her so angry. She accused me of being a flirt, a slut, and a liar. She told me to stop showing off my boobs."

"Did he touch you?"

"Grandma, *please*."

I'd been traveling halfway around the world in hopes of rescuing two strangers from sexual tyranny, and my very own granddaughter had been violated within miles of the cabin. "You did the right thing telling your mother. Knowing Nicci, hearing about Sean scared her. She felt trapped. That's when she lashes out."

Alex continued. "I think maybe she saw something between me and Sean. I didn't ask what. Really, I couldn't. I mean, Sean's her boyfriend. I figured she hated me. She couldn't stand to look at me. That's why she brought me here."

"I'm so glad she did."

She sat straighter and swiped tears from her cheeks. "Grandma, I want you to know that, well, he didn't, like, go too far, if you know what I mean."

I didn't want Alex to think what she'd said shocked or disappointed me, but I was shocked and horribly disappointed by Nicci. And me. Disappointment morphed quickly to self-loathing. Distancing myself from Nicci had become much easier since the divorce. I lacked the fortitude to go toe to toe with her on things that mattered or even the things that didn't. But withdrawing from Nicci had meant withdrawing from Alex. If only I'd been more present. If only I'd picked Alex up after school to spend the afternoon with me, rather than leaving her to depend on Sean.

"I should have been there for you, Alex. I'm so very sorry I wasn't."

"Here's the problem, Grandma: I liked it. I liked how he looked at me and how loved I felt. But he wanted more. At first, he stopped when I asked him to. Then he got angry. He punched a hole in the wall. Maybe that's what he couldn't explain to Mom."

"I'm calling Nicci in the morning."

Alex voice came out squeezed. "You don't have to do that. Sometimes it takes Mom awhile to see things, but she eventually does."

I agreed to wait until Nicci graduated to talk to her. Alex believed that the associate degree in nursing would give Nicci a sense of mission and purpose, and their portion of the world would become a safe haven. I didn't have the heart to contradict her.

Alex said, "I could have been one of those girls who end up on the street, but I wasn't because Mom knew to bring me to you. Bimala and Pooja are facing Shaitaan alone. Who is there to help? Grandma, can't we do something?"

Cal was Bimala's only real hope, but he hadn't returned my calls. And I'd left many messages trying to explain the first call, and the second, and the third. My stuttering explanations hadn't helped. He could not risk his life to save Bimala and Pooja on the sketchy details I'd shared with him.

"I could try calling Cal again," I said.

Alex's eyes sparkled with moonlight. "We don't need him." She scooted to the edge of the chair. "I can't believe we haven't thought of this before. You can take stuff to the island and bring everything back. You do it all the time. I mean, anything you touch travels with you. Why can't you bring Bimala and Pooja home with you? If you're all holding hands when your departure time comes, they'll come too, won't they?"

Dad had never talked about traveling with people, but Alex

was right. Whatever I touched traveled with me. Even a bag of clothing tethered to my ankle traveled along and back again.

Still.

"It might be possible for Bimala and Pooja to travel with me, but they might return to the island after only a few minutes. They'd be right back where they started, no better off and maybe worse. I've seen what Shaitaan can do."

We talked until the moon was a spotlight suspended from the stars and formulated a plan based on an uncomfortable amount of *would*s, *could*s, and *should*s, with an important *if* thrown in. First, I would bring an item back with me from the island from my next visit, something that belonged there, a shell or flower. If the thing didn't return to the island in short order, I would risk raising Bimala's hopes that I could, indeed, save her and Pooja. We speculated about what we could do with the girls once they arrived here—with no passports or visas. In the end, we couldn't worry about that part yet. We had to get them to Grand Lake first. Satisfied with our plan, Alex went to bed.

Bathed in the moon's silvery light, I pulled the sleeping bag over my head and slouched deeper into the chair. If not for the occasional mosquito that buzzed in my ear, I would have slept on the deck. Who was I kidding? Every time I closed my eyes, they bounced open.

Every girl deserved a stalwart protector. Sadly for Alex, that job fell to me, and I had already failed miserably. Doug had a good heart, but new love and his worries about keeping that love distracted him. Nevertheless, I wouldn't let him off the hook.

As uncalculated as an exhale, a prayer formed on my lips. "You have to help Alex."

20

I was getting careless.

I touched the map with a bare finger and hadn't put my life vest on. Traveling to Sundar Maut had become familiar. No way would I drown in the shallow water off the island. But more truthfully, my cavalier behavior had more to do with a wildly buzzing mind than any level of comfort I'd managed. I'd woken several times throughout the night recounting all the ways I'd failed, well, everyone.

My sloppiness landed me in the indigo of deeper seas and farther east than usual. No matter, this was not a hurried trip. My plans, beginning to end, included slicing off a branch and maybe grabbing a shell to take back to Grand Lake for our experiment. My plans did not include seeing Bimala or Pooja. I couldn't bear disappointing Bimala again. Once I knew I could move things off the island permanently, only then would I make plans to evacuate the girls.

I swam toward the lagoon with lazy side strokes. I'd zipped Dad's pocketknife into the pocket of my board shorts to take samples. Alex awaited my return back in the Grisham's shed.

Under a low ceiling of clouds, the turquoise water lay dull and lifeless, but the clouds could not dull the sun's fiery handprint. The air was as thick as stew. One step on the rain-pocked sand and I checked my watch. I needed enough time to collect the samples and go. Departure was in 22.532 minutes.

I opened the pocketknife and sliced a clump of green berries strung together like pearls. There was fruit that looked like white tomatoes. They grew snuggly to a tree trunk, protected with swordlike fronds. Alex would think they were cool. I rejected a coconut lying in the sand. Bimala depended on the milk when Shaitaan forgot water. Instead, I pocketed a seashell with the markings of a giraffe.

A primal moan froze my movements.

I listened and swept the palm forest with my gaze. Bimala sat in the mottled shadows, her face a mask of anguish. Pooja lay across her lap.

Bimala startled when I greeted her. I knelt at her feet, keeping my eyes on Pooja's face, looking for signs of life. The girl's eyelids fluttered, and I released a long-held breath. Bimala looked at me with swollen and bloodshot eyes.

"He called for her in the night," she said. "I begged him to take me instead, but his hunger was too great."

My chest convulsed. Bimala put her fingers to my lips and shook her head sharply. "He will hear you."

I glanced toward the huts. Nothing moved, so I settled in the sand hip to hip with Bimala. I drew the mother and daughter into my arms—and mourned with them over all that had been lost. For many long minutes we sat there in a desperate embrace. Finally, Bimala relaxed into my arm; her tears wetted my shoulder.

This was no time for experiments with shells or seed pods. The time to take Bimala and Pooja off the island had long passed. By my watch only a few minutes remained until my departure. I shifted and worked away the cloth of Bimala's sleeve and Pooja's skirt to touch their bare skin, reasoning that touching their skin gave them the best chance of traveling with me.

"She is not ruined in God's eyes," I whispered to Bimala.

"No, but she is ruined in Shaitaan's. And he is the god of this island."

I drew them tighter. My back burned from the awkwardness of my position. I looked at my watch. Only seconds remained.

"Hang on," I whispered into Bimala's ear.

We turned our heads toward the snap of a twig. There stood Shaitaan. The whites of his eyes blazed against his dark skin, and he stumbled back from the three of us, landing on his bottom in shallow water.

The pulling nearly wrenched my arms from their sockets. I fought against the ripping of Bimala's arm from my grasp and the sliding of Pooja's ankle. I landed on *Zella* with a cavernous ache in my chest, alone.

I lay there until Alex knocked softly on the shed's door. "Are you in there, Grandma?"

We managed to slip away from the Grisham's shed without being seen, and, more importantly, without having to make any sort of small talk. We walked hand in hand in silence, all the way back to the cabin.

At the front door, Alex stepped into my embrace, finally crying. "I was so sure."

As magic went, mine sure was a sorry-assed version. I could travel to exotic places for free but only stay for an hour or less. I frequently floated in faraway oceans, seeing nothing of what other people traveled to see, like the Eiffel Tower or Notre Dame. No marvels of the world occupied the desert of the ocean. And when I met someone who needed my help, the magic proved utterly impotent.

I told Alex what I'd seen, minus the part about Pooja being raped by Shaitaan. "There was nothing to lose by trying to bring the girls home."

She settled her gaze on me for what seemed like an eternity. Finally, she said, "Now that Shaitaan has seen you, there's a chance he'll hurt Bimala. He's afraid. He can't explain who or what you are. When people are afraid, they feel powerless, and when they feel powerless, they'll do anything to feel that power again."

"Alex, honey, how do you know that?"

She averted her gaze. "I read a lot."

Doug would soon pick up Alex for the weekend as we'd planned. Alex didn't want to go, but I assured her I would do what I could for Bimala and Pooja in the meantime. I called Cal and he answered.

"Robin. I didn't think I would hear from you again."

I thanked him for picking up, and my mind went blank, all except for Bimala's vacant eyes.

"I don't have much time," he said. He admitted that he hadn't listened to all of my messages. "They were a little jumbled."

I'd been trying to help Bimala and Pooja without saying very much at all. That wasn't working. "Do you have five minutes?"

I held nothing back. I told him how one person from each generation in my family had been travelers. I made sure to tell him all about Dad—Cal's esteemed professor of geography—and how he had perfected traveling to warm oceans for a soak every Friday, packing a thermos of margaritas for the trip. "He never spoke of meeting people on his travels, but he had an unfortunate interaction with a barracuda that required thirty stitches. He had a terrible time explaining all those teeth marks to the doctor. Boulder isn't known for its barracuda population."

"That's quite a story," he said.

I told him all about traveling to Sundar Maut when I'd accidently touched the map he'd brought to me and what I'd found when I got there.

"You are an interesting woman, Robin."

"I'm really not. Everything else about my life is incredibly boring, even my family. Except for Nicci. She's exasperating but in a very normal way that's sad."

"Robin."

"Do you need proof? Give me your GPS coordinates. I'll travel to you right now. If you're inside, you'll have to step outside, and I would prefer if you were alone. Most importantly, I need something soft to land on."

"Robin."

"Don't you feel the least bit responsible for this? Your map sent me to that stupid island. Come on, give me a break."

"I have to go." His voice was flat but kind. "I will stop by the shop the next time I'm in the area. We can talk about this then. I have a meeting for another trip."

"Did I forget to tell you about Bimala and Pooja?"

"I'm hanging up now." *Click.*

21

Doug collected the crumbs of coffee cake on his fork tines. He'd appeared at my door, reporting for duty as a conscientious grandfather less than forty-eight hours from when I'd recruited his help. I probably had Tiffany to thank.

Not in this lifetime.

"I should probably get going. We're picking up the boat at ten." He pushed back from the table. "Is Alex ready?"

I took our plates and mugs to the sink. "You should know, Doug, that Alex is a little nervous about the weekend."

"What does she have to be nervous about?" he said, sounding offended.

"This isn't anything you've done. She's like all fourteen-year-old girls. She's pressing for independence, eager to show her stuff, but she really wants the approval of the people she loves. Plus, she thinks she's ruined her chances with Tiffany over the whole GPS incident."

Doug batted away my concern. "Oh that, she has nothing to worry about. Tiffany's a great gal. She knows kids mess up. Besides, she's really been looking forward to this. She's made one heck of a lunch, and she came home the other day with a new ski tube for Alex. It's shaped like a hot dog. Didn't we have one like that?"

Our eyes met and Doug winced. He hadn't meant to talk about us as *we*.

"Doesn't matter," he continued. "Tiffany's been working like a dog getting ready. She spent most of yesterday buying Alex everything she needs for a great time on the water. There are bags and bags of stuff. You can relax; we're going to have a great time."

I glanced toward Alex's suitcase sitting by the door. I hadn't even bought her a tube of sunscreen. Had she packed the shorts with the faulty elastic? This shortsightedness doomed me to also-ran in the grandma category.

Doug blinked, taking in the cleared living room. Not one moving box remained. He nodded approvingly. "The place looks great."

Alex and I had packed the Lakeview bedroom nearly to the ceiling with boxes, leaving the Pollywog room for what we hoped to be Bimala and Pooja'a sanctuary.

The boxes had nicely hidden the living-room carpet's true state. No matter how many times I vacuumed, it still looked dirty, especially near the doors where the canvas backing showed through. Now I longed to rip the carpet up and install something— anything—new and a lot less green. That wouldn't happen anytime soon. Expenses were higher with Alex living with me, which meant I wasn't saving much toward buying *Zella* from Richard, either.

Even with the shabby carpet, the cabin looked as it had when Doug joined my family for summer vacations. Did he remember the late-night games of Michigan Rummy that sometimes degraded into popcorn fights, or that he'd slept in the half-finished boat garage with my brother? Our tongues had touched for the very first time on that visit. My stomach fluttered at the memory.

"You're getting things together," he said. "I'm happy to see that, Robin. I hated seeing you flounder."

"Really?" I managed to sound pleasantly curious when I wanted to spit poison in his eye. I would never get used to the speed at which our conversations could turn injurious.

"It's good to see you taking my advice and listing the place."

"Listing the place? But I'm not. I mean, I wouldn't. Ever."

"This is no time to let your stubbornness override better judgment. Think about your future. The cabin is not sacred ground. The bones of your ancestors aren't buried under the floor. You would come out with a huge chunk of change that could launch you almost anywhere you wanted to go."

"Let me remind you that you absolved yourself of my well-being in quite a dramatic fashion two years ago. Remember that awkward meeting with the mediator? You don't have a vote in my life anymore."

"You don't have to be like that."

You have no idea. "I'm trying very, very hard not to be like that, honestly I am. Keep in mind that whatever decisions I make for my future will be made with the counsel of people whom I trust."

He lifted his hands in surrender. "Ouch. I'm just trying to be helpful"

"Can you be that oblivious? I'll tell you one more time: You nearly killed me by walking away from our marriage, and now you're acting like nothing happened. How am I supposed to trust someone like that?"

He shook his head and bit his lip, probably to keep from saying the wrong thing. "It doesn't help to rehash the past."

"You might be an amnesiac, Doug, but I am not. I remember everything, and there was a lot of amazing goodness between us. I expected that to continue to my grave, or yours. Whether you understand that or not, I can't receive advice from you as if you're some kind of favorite uncle. You're asking me to erase thirty-three years of my life. I can't do that."

"As usual, you're making much more of this than necessary."

"I need you to hear me on this. We have two daughters and one extremely worthy granddaughter we still get to share. Would you humor me? Would you remember who I am and what has passed between us—the good and the bad? Please extend to me the respect of our history. And unless you see me headed for a cliff, leave all concern for my future to me."

I'd only seen Doug's face caught in the netherworld between neutrality and queasiness once before, when I told him about a gynecological visit that hadn't gone well.

A muscle below my eye twitched. "Alex is probably lost in a book. I'll go get her."

AFTER DOUG AND ALEX left, I plopped into a chaise lounge on the deck. Already the sun had warmed the trees and the scent of pine filled each breath. No matter how deeply I breathed or commanded my shoulders to retreat from my ears, no hint of peace materialized. Instead, I analyzed every word that Doug and I had exchanged.

How Doug acted as if our marriage had never happened, I didn't know. And then it hit me. Doug had always been a champ at compartmentalizing. We often joked about his ability to leave the concerns of the business completely behind when we played golf, while my mind churned over a new hire or an untried supplier. How I'd envied Doug's single-track mind. He changed focus as easily as changing a hat.

Evidently, he had worn a lover hat, too, that he could exchange with his marriage hat without contradiction. When he slept with her, he was her lover. When he slept with me, he was my husband. And he didn't think about his deacon hat when he partied with plumbing manufacturer reps, either. How very convenient for him.

All this made me wonder what kind of hat he'd worn when he came to pick up Alex. Perhaps he had put on and taken off several until one felt comfortable. I hoped the advice-giving-uncle hat would be forever too tight. I had a hat for him: The ex-husband-who-regrets-his-behavior-but-is-now-stuck-and-yet-respectful hat. I would settle for a co-grandparent hat.

I only hoped that when he finally settled on what our future relationship would be, that I could live with his choice. Let me be perfectly honest here: It bugged the hell out of me that I was in no position to coach Doug on any choice he might make, ever.

I decided to write him a letter. He couldn't argue or twist my logic while reading. With carefully composed arguments, he would finally see the importance of taking a holistic view of our history. Why hadn't I thought of this before?

As I rose to gather paper and pen, the familiar sound of Carolyn's horn sounded. I changed quickly into my reception clothes and dashed out the door

BY THE TIME THE best man skewered the hapless groom in a rather mean-spirited toast, I'd given up on writing a letter to Doug. He'd never been a big reader. And I kept imagining him lighting the corner of said letter and tossing it into Tiffany's fireplace. Improving our post-divorce relationship rested fully on Doug's shoulders. I'd offered what help I could.

In truth, who could I help? I couldn't help Bimala or Pooja, that was painstakingly clear. And I wasn't much of a friend to Carolyn. I hadn't asked about her mission to annoy Wayne and the other woman in days.

Alex? Could I help Alex?

I had to try.

Nicci was still my daughter, and daughters listened—if the stars aligned correctly—to their mothers. After the reception, I borrowed Carolyn's car and drove the hundred miles to Denver. I met Nicci at The Roller Derby Diner.

Nicci slid into the booth and picked up the menu. "I'm starving. I forgot to eat this morning."

She hated nothing more than advice for healthy living, so I stifled a comment about skipping meals and said, "Get whatever you want."

She ordered French fries smothered with gravy and cheese. I marveled that Alex had been born with ten fingers and ten toes.

"So, what's up?" Nicci said, looking nervously around the diner.

"Are you expecting someone?"

"I don't have much time. I told my study group I would be late, but they'll be pissed if I'm too late. I have the advanced anatomy notes for the chapters we're covering tonight." The waitress plopped a mountain of fries and unnaturally dark brown gravy and a smear of orange topping in front of Nicci. She grabbed the ketchup, and I stifled a gag. "So what's up?" she asked again.

"Curious about Alex?"

"Let me guess, she's reading a book."

I ignored her sarcasm, but her dismissive attitude disappointed me. "You know your daughter."

"You drove all the way down here to watch me eat? I don't think so. Whatever you've got to say, you might as well spit it out."

"Let me start with how much I'm enjoying Alex. That girl is something else."

Nicci squeezed more ketchup over the fries. "Not like me, right?"

"I wish you wouldn't say things like that. You're my daughter. I've loved you since your days as a zygote."

"Even I wonder if Alex wasn't switched with my real baby at birth. There isn't much of a family resemblance."

"You're kidding, right? I see you in her all the time. She'll be talking away, and my heart will catch because I see you in her facial expressions or the way she chews on her hair. She's so smart and beautiful. Your noses are exactly the same."

Nicci exhaled an impatient breath. "So, why are you here again?"

"Alex is helping me post Grandpa's maps online. We've

actually sold a few. That girl is a whiz on a computer."

"Mom, please, I have someplace to be."

"Okay." I sucked in a breath meant to slow my heart rate. "Alex and I had an interesting conversation last night. She explained why she ran away so many times."

Nicci slapped her fork to the table. "Is this about Sean? She's fishing for your sympathy, that's all. Can't you see that? That little conniver, my god, she will say anything. I hope you don't believe her."

Her response didn't surprise me. This was Nicci's standard operating procedure. First, she acted impatient to get me to hurry through whatever I had to say, which meant I couldn't rely on what I'd rehearsed. Then she acted indignant and angry. The trick was to steer the conversation back on track. "That's why I'm here. I was hoping—"

"Listen, Mother, Sean is the best guy I've ever had. He's a total grownup. I have never seen him drunk, not once. He drives me crazy that way. He expects everyone to do the right thing, even me. He's forever helping someone with their car, or their lawnmower, or whatever. He can fix anything. Hell, last week he made dinner for the old lady next door.

"And I'm better with him, Mom." She spread out her arms. She had a new tattoo of a lion's face on her forearm I'd never seen. "Look at me, I'm going to be a college graduate. No one saw that coming. But Sean did. He, like, believed in me.

"I haven't had a drink in weeks. He hates how I get, and who can blame him? He forced me to choose between him and beer. I pretty much hated him for that, but Mom, I don't know what would happen to me without him." She shoveled a forkful into her mouth.

"He sounds great, and I'm so glad someone is loving you the way you deserve to be loved."

"But? *But*? Here it comes, the great big hairy, ass-kicking *but* to everything about me, isn't that right, Mommy dearest?" Nicci gathered her purse and books and made to leave.

I put out a hand to stop her, but her look warned me off. "Give me a minute, Nicci. Please."

She shook her head. "You have, maybe, thirty seconds."

"I don't have the advantage of knowing Sean, but I do know Alex. She's changed since I last saw her. Yes, she's older and smarter, but she also seems burdened, like she's carrying something too heavy. I didn't press her, I promise. We were talking about something else, and she told me how Sean had started asking for things."

She spoke through her teeth. "This is so bogus."

"Is it possible that Sean is your great guy *and* a man who has the potential to hurt Alex? Aren't both possible? Nicci, Alex is counting on you to protect her."

Nicci flipped her plate at me. The ceramic edge hit my collarbone and deposited gravy, cheese goo, and ketchup down the front of my shirt and into my lap. She slid out of the booth and made for the exit.

I followed, slipping on the puddle of slop. The waitress stepped toward me, her mouth ready with a question. I assured her I would be right back. Over my shoulder I said to her worry, "She's my daughter."

I caught up to Nicci in front of The Big Bunny motel. A girl in teeny tiny shorts and a potholder of a halter top swung a white towel over her head at passing cars. The time for words with Nicci had long passed, but I had one more very important message to deliver. "Alex will not go home with you until I'm convinced that Sean is no longer in your life."

Nicci threw her books at me. I dodged quickly enough to avoid a direct hit by an anatomy textbook. "You are such a frickin' bitch! Get the hell out of my face! Go!"

I turned and walked toward the diner with Nicci hurling

expletives at my back. Each step ripped my chest, renting places barely healed and those gone to stone. I thought of Alex, how the moon had reflected in her tears. I had checked with a family lawyer when Alex was only a baby, what I would need to gain custody. Without documentation of neglect and/or abuse the law would not help me keep her away from Nicci. Collecting that sort of data would mean a future without my youngest daughter.

God in heaven, help me.

I drove by Nicci as she collected her things under the sputtering motel sign. Seeing her down on all fours, a cigarette hanging from her mouth, split me open, but West Colfax Avenue—men standing on the street corners and music blaring from gap-mouthed bars—was no place to stop for a good cry. Through a blur of tears, I somehow navigated the cloverleaf at Federal Boulevard and continued under I-25 past the capitol building.

I was driving in the exact wrong direction to get back to Grand Lake. I needed a good cry, but I didn't want to have to explain myself to drug dealers or prostitutes. Colfax is the longest continuous street in the United States. I might have to drive its entire length to find a good crying spot, maybe in Omaha.

With Highway 225 looming, I pulled into the University of Colorado Medical Center. In the near-empty parking lot, I couldn't avoid the same old questions that had dogged me. How had I failed Nicci to bring us to this? Had I loved her too much? Been too permissive? Too rigid? Had I ignored warning flags? Should I have listened to my brother about a dairy-free diet or insisted on moving to a Montana wilderness area? Had I given in too much?

Will Nicci find her way?

As much as I wanted her to, Nicci would not turn to me for help, but I could not abandon the pulse of hope that longed for connection. I vowed, as I left the interstate at Highway 40, to keep the hope alive. In the meantime, I would do whatever I could to keep Alex safe, even if that meant defying the good-intentioned but misguided laws of Colorado. Nicci would never be my enemy, but I would fight her for Alex.

While declaring my devotion to Alex's safety, it only seemed right that I also work at softening the impact of my travel on Bimala and Pooja. Starting with my next trip.

POOJA LED ME THROUGH the palm forest. Her skin stretched over sharp bones like a grounded bird. When I realized she was leading me toward the huts, I dug my feet into the sand. She studied me with nigrescent eyes, "He is not here, Angel Lady. *Mata* needs you. Hurry quick, please."

The late-day sun penetrated Bimala's hut through a west-facing window. Bimala lay on her pallet along the wall. Her breathing came quick and shallow. Blood crusted her nostrils and a gash split her swollen lip. I fell to my knees, took her hand, and sent Pooja to fetch clean water.

Bimala winced under my touch, but I dipped and wrung the cloth until the water went red and then asked for Pooja to refill the bowl. When the girl left the hut, I unwrapped Bimala's *pallu*, propping her into a sitting position to do so. An angry bruise the size of a foot bloomed in shades of purple and red on the rise of her swollen belly. That explained her shallow breathing.

"You may have a broken rib," I said. "It will be difficult, but you must breathe as normally as possible. Otherwise, your lungs could fill with fluid." Or the rib had already pierced a lung. If so, I had nothing to offer her.

I washed her hands and arms, wiping the sweat from her forehead as I worked. Uniform bruises—about the size of an egg but rounder—covered her arms and legs. "What did he hit you with?"

Before Bimala could form the words, Pooja said, "His cane. He hit *Mata* with his cane. Many times."

Bimala put her hands on her swollen belly and asked, "Okay?"

I had no idea how to check the wellness of an unborn baby. "Is the baby moving?"

She shook her head tightly.

I put my hands over her stomach and pressed, hoping that the baby would shudder at my touch. Her stomach remained hard where I imagined the baby's fanny pressed against Bimala's uterus and soft like I remembered my own pregnant belly being, but all was still.

"I'll be going soon." Her hand grasped mine. I returned her grip. "I'll be back as soon as I can. I'll bring medicine and bandages. I'll try to find a stethoscope to listen for baby." I lowered my face to hers. "I am so sorry. This is because—"

I DIDN'T FINISH MY apology. I was on *Zella's* deck and then rushing to the Grisham's front door. I begged bandages and antibiotic cream from Sally, who studied me with a frown. She didn't ask one question, only offered everything in her medicine cabinet, including butterfly bandages left over from a fall the previous winter.

Getting most of what Bimala needed from Sally meant I wouldn't have to ride my bike all over Grand Lake before returning to Sundar Maut. At the door, she pushed my bangs to the side and kissed my cheek. I arrived back at The Traveling Man in less than thirty minutes.

I called Carolyn. She still hoarded boxes of materials from her classroom. Why not a stethoscope? "What are you doing?" she asked, her words squeezed by worry.

When I told her how I'd found Bimala, she said, "You aren't going back there, are you?"

"Wouldn't you?"

"I'll find a stethoscope. What else do you need?"

We arranged for her to pick me up at the Grisham's in thirty-one minutes. I touched the map.

22

I traveled back and forth, from Grand Lake to Sandar Maut, all through the island's night and Colorado's day. I smeared Bimala's wounds with antibiotic cream and pulled the edges of her gashes together with the butterfly bandages. I fanned her as she slept and woke her to give her water. I dosed her with anti-inflammatories every four hours.

Pooja slept on her pallet, rising to one elbow each time I stepped over the threshold. "*Mata* groans in her sleep."

Carolyn came through with the stethoscope and a container of homemade chicken soup as the horizon paled to the east in Bimala's world and the light sighed out of mine. My body ached for sleep.

When I arrived back at Bimala's hut, Pooja was stoking a fire in the gauzy light of dawn. The goat ripped at the sparse grass and chewed contentedly. "*Mata* is not hungry," she said.

I found Bimala leaning deep in the pillows I'd brought in the night, hoping she would breathe easier sitting up. "I have a stethoscope, but I think you should eat first. I brought some soup."

"I am not hungry."

"That's what Pooja tells me, but you must eat to get strong." Besides, I could do little else for her.

"Please, I must know about the child."

I touched my cheek to her forehead. Heat radiated off Bimala. "We have to get your fever down. Let's start there, and then I'll listen."

"And, please, Angel Lady, my back is very sore."

"Like a contraction?"

Bimala frowned at the word. She hadn't had any real help with her pregnancy or delivery when Pooja came into the world. She had been a child herself. That she hadn't died then was a sort of miracle. I took her hand. "Is it like the pains that came when Pooja was born?"

She shook her head. "It never stops."

I eased a rolled cloth under her lower back in hopes of relieving her discomfort, but she begged me to remove it. I spent the rest of that stay—the fifth? Sixth? Tenth?—bathing Bimala with cool water.

BACK IN GRAND LAKE, I emptied Carolyn's medicine cabinet. Bless her, she had penicillin, a nice broad-spectrum antibiotic that should help Bimala.

"You know you're supposed to take these until they're all gone, right?" I said, rattling the remaining pills in the bottle.

"I get horrible yeast infections whenever I take antibiotics. I eat yogurt like a Turk, but nothing helps. I've learned to take the least amount needed to feel better." Carolyn leveled a knowing look at me. "Bimala can use these more than I can."

I DOUBLE DOSED BIMALA with the antibiotics, hoping to get her blood levels up to fight the infection that coursed through her veins. Still, her fever raged. I removed all of her clothing and covered her with a cotton sheet.

She spoke, her hot breath on my face. "You are a terrible angel, but you are a good friend. That is what we need most, and I am grateful *Bapa* God sent you to us."

"When you're feeling better, I will argue with you about what you need most. For now, try to sleep." I promised to look after

Pooja, but the girl went about her day with no need of me.

Later, I offered Pooja the soup Carolyn had made. The girl dumped the contents when she thought I wasn't looking, but she must have been hungry. She prepared herself rice and cooked an egg for her evening meal.

CAROLYN PRESSED PRINTED PAGES from the Internet into my hands. "I did some research. Blunt force trauma to the abdomen is the most common non-medical reason for death in pregnant women. If the placenta becomes detached ... well, things will go horribly wrong. There won't be anything you can do for the girl. Are you prepared for that?"

I slumped into a kitchen chair. Antibiotics wouldn't keep a woman from bleeding to death. A picture of a fox on Carolyn's refrigerator reminded me of Alex. "What day is this?"

"It's Sunday, nearly noon."

"Alex will be home from Doug's soon. I may need you to get her and bring her here. Would that be okay?"

"I'll do whatever you need, sweetie."

I TOOK BIMALA'S TEMPERATURE when I got back to Sundar Maut. My fingers to her forehead confirmed that the fever had abated somewhat.

"Can we listen to the baby?" she asked.

I stalled, spreading lip balm on her cracked lips. I had little confidence I could find a baby's heartbeat, healthy or otherwise. And what could I do about a dead baby anyway?

She lowered the sheet to reveal her swollen abdomen. Before touching her skin, I breathed on the disk part of the stethoscope. I started low, just above her pubic bone, like I remembered my obstetrician doing. The sounds of outer space filled my ears— thrumming and whirling, a gurgle. Below her belly button, I heard the steady pumping of what could only be a heartbeat, a bass drum, slow and steady.

"I've found your heartbeat, I think."

Bimala blinked at me. "And the baby?"

I moved the disk to the left of her midline and back to the right, and then higher toward her belly button, pausing and listening, pausing and listening. A glub of stomach juice. A pop of gas. But no heartbeat.

"How far along are you?"

She frowned.

"How long has the baby been in you?"

Bimala shook her head and shrugged.

"It might be too early to hear," I said, although I put her at five or six months, plenty soon enough to hear a baby's heartbeat. "I'm not very good at this. Let me try again."

Bimala put her unnaturally hot hand to my arm. "You will be going soon?"

"I'll be back as soon as possible."

Bimala slid her gaze around the room. "Is Pooja outside? Is she occupied?"

I looked out the door. Pooja led the goat to where the grass grew lusher and tied him to a palm tree. "She's moving the goat."

"There is not much time. We must speak quickly before she returns." I sat beside her on the packed-sand floor. "We must make plans if the baby and I go to heaven."

"Bimala ..."

"Please, do not argue. I have been thinking. Shaitaan must not take Pooja to Main Land. You understand? If I die, this is what you must do: You must swim Pooja out to the deep, dark water and wait there for *Bapa* God to pull you away. It will be better for Pooja to sink into the sea than to live with all the other girls on Main Land. You will do this?"

How had we come to this? "I will get help, Bimala. Somehow, I will get help. You need a doctor. I will travel to the mainland, find a hospital. They must have helicopters."

"There is no time, Angel Lady."

She was right. There were too many uncertainties in the plan. Back in Grand Lake, I would have to find a Mumbai hospital online, but only if a computer was available at the library. If I printed out the satellite photo of the hospital and traveled directly to it, not too much time would pass. But what if the area around the hospital didn't have a lake or pond for my arrival?

A landing on terra firma was out of the question. First, arriving on land was painful, if not fatal. Second, a woman falling from the sky would attract too much attention. How would I explain myself? And how would I convince anyone to take action? There had to be another way.

I found Pooja sifting stones out of rice. She jumped at the sound of my voice. "Is there a radio? Does Shaitaan talk to people who are not on the island? How does he do that?"

She didn't answer my questions but rose and ran to Shaitaan's hut. Outside the locked door, she scanned the sea and looked over her shoulder to the hut where Bimala lay. A basket brimming with detritus stood by the door. She dug out ropes, old bottles, a flat soccer ball. She poured a key out of a Pringles cylinder and unlocked the door.

"Watch for him," I said, gesturing toward the sea.

I stepped into the suffocating air of Shaitaan's hut. A curtain hung limp over the one window. There was a mattress, neatly made with a cotton cloth and many pillows. A plastic table, the sort you see beside a lawn chair, served as a bar with liquor bottles and openers. An industrial electrical cord hung from the window.

A generator?

By the window, a fan sat on a shelf along with a Keurig and a tumble of Green Mountain coffee pods but nothing even remotely radiolike. Shaitaan must have brought a radio with him. Of course, a boat used to travel on the sea absolutely needed a radio, or perhaps a satellite phone.

It was Pooja's turn to startle me. "Angel Lady?"

I looked to the sea. The horizon remained unsullied by boats of any kind. I handed her the key and trotted back to Bimala. She slept as peacefully as she had since she'd been beaten. Possibly, we were gaining the upper hand.

I lay against the pillows with her and shut my eyes. I fell asleep without the usual tangled images of pre-sleep dreams. I woke up on *Zella*, now equipped with one of Carolyn's air mattresses she kept for her grandchildren's visits. I didn't want to move.

Carolyn stood over me, her e-reader in hand. "You look like death."

"I don't feel that good." I updated her on Bimala, reporting that she seemed more comfortable and that I'd left her sleeping.

"Then I'm going to insist you do the same," she said in her best do-as-I-say teacher voice. "You haven't slept for two days."

I lay in a strange soup of mixed realities. The now familiar interior of the Grisham's shed confirmed that I had traveled, but I still heard Bimala's shallow breathing and the rattle of the palms. I moved to sit up, but Carolyn put a hand to my shoulder. I didn't have the strength or the fortitude to resist her, so I let my muscles go soft. "What about Alex? Is she here?"

"She texted me looking for you. Doug and Tiffany want her to stay one more night. I told her that would be okay."

I closed my eyes. The oil and dust that had comforted me on my first visit to Richard's shed replayed its magic. Carolyn nudged me awake. "Don't get comfortable, not yet. I'm taking you home."

23

I don't know how long I'd slept, but hard rapping on the door woke me from a deep sleep. My head felt like concrete. I splashed water on my face and opened the door.

Cal stepped back. "I'm sorry for coming so late. I'm headed back to the city tomorrow, early."

I invited him in. He seemed uncomfortable in the tight quarters of the cabin, so I suggested we talk on the deck. The moon was a waning gibbous over the mountains, pushing long shadows across the deck with its golden light. From the moon's position, it wasn't quite midnight, but when had I fallen asleep, and how long had I slept? My mind would not do the math. From the way I felt, my sleep debt remained in arrears.

Once we settled into opposing chairs, I swallowed hard. "I've been, you know, traveling a lot to the island and back the last couple of days. My sleep schedule's wracked."

Cal shifted in his chair and turned his gaze to the lake. Rightly or wrongly, I interpreted his actions as disbelief. I didn't have the luxury to take offense. Bimala and Pooja needed immediate help, and Cal was my only lead.

"I don't know why you've come," I said, "but as long as you're here, you need to hear this: Bimala has been beaten very badly by the man holding her. I fear for her life and the life of her baby. Pooja is in great danger as well. There's no radio on the island to call for help. I thought about traveling to the mainland but doing so has its own problems. I left Bimala resting, but ... Cal, you have to help her."

Cal seemed to think carefully before he spoke. "Robin, I hear how worried you are about your friend."

I stood too abruptly and steadied myself against the chair. "I'm more than worried. You must listen to what I'm saying. I *can* prove that I travel. In fact, I'll show you. Do you have a minute? Wait here—"

"Sit down, Robin," he said with a little too much insistence, but I sat down, hating—yet again—the good girl in me. "I am trying to help. It's obvious you care deeply about girls caught in slavery. I thought it might help to hear about my most recent mission. I just got back from Mumbai."

"That's not far from the island," I said, scooting to the edge of the chair.

"Sure," he said, like I'd told him my mother was a fairy. He raised a rebuffing hand and continued. "The mission was very successful. We'd been watching the brothel for months."

My heart sank to my belly button. "Months? All that time? And the girls ...?"

"Yes, you're right, it was a tough situation." He closed his eyes, hung his head. When he looked at me again, he set his jaw. "Believe you me, we wanted to rush in, but to do so is very dangerous for the girls and for the rescuers. Timing matters. If we go in before we know the situation, the girls may be moved, and then we have to start over, building both local support and gathering intelligence. We want to get as many girls out as we can. Having good information makes the difference. In this case, we rescued thirteen girls."

"So you're saying that two girls on an island are too few for you to save?"

He ran his hands through his hair. "I'm not saying this well. I wanted to tell you what I saw to maybe bring you some peace of mind."

"Over my imaginary girls? You think I'm delusional enough to invent two girls enslaved on an island? For what? The attention?"

He looked to the deck planks.

"You come here as a sort of savior for captives, and yet you dangle an inaccessible hope in front of me. That's cruel, don't you think, to speak of missions and freedom and to refuse your help?" The sight of him, his little-boy sincerity and his false friendship sickened me. I stood. "I think you should go."

"Robin, please sit down. I'm sorry, I truly am. I didn't come to tease you with false hope." When I stood my ground, he continued, "Let me tell you what I saw on this trip, okay? Take what you can from my story, and then I'll go."

He gestured to the chair, and I sat down.

He rubbed his hands together and frowned over a memory. "The girls were in terrible shape. They sat like statues, wouldn't look at us or respond in anyway. I'm sure they believed they were headed someplace worse, even though the counselors reassured them over and over.

"I felt more hopeful for the girls who were crying, even though I couldn't tell if they were crying from fear or relief. Whichever, they could still feel, and that seemed right.

"When we got to Restoration House, a group of girls we'd rescued months ago met us. I don't know how to describe them but to say they had a light within them. They looked alive. Isn't that something?"

Bimala's sputtering flame had extinguished.

"The house mothers hung back, and the resident girls greeted those we'd rescued. They didn't say a word, but they knew each other's stories somehow, and the new girls stepped into their arms."

Cal leaned on his knees and shook his head. "It's not hard to put your life on the line for the innocent. When we leave them at the house, though, they're a long way from being okay. They're out of immediate danger, but their souls have been violated. The rescue is only half of the job, maybe less.

"Seeing the girls who had been at Restoration House for a while—Robin, that felt good, really, really good." He stood. "That's what I came to tell you. Whoever your girls—"

"My *imaginary* girls?"

"Whoever they are and whatever has happened to them, there is hope."

As I watched Cal drive away, a plan to help Bimala and Pooja started to form

THE NEXT MORNING, DOUG'S F-150 was parked in his driveway, so I knocked on the door of the cabin. "I have some things I need to get done. Would it be possible for Alex to stay with you again?"

"Big plans?" he said, with raised eyebrows.

Oh brother. "Not really."

Doug narrowed his eyes at me, but I wasn't telling him anything more. Finally, he shifted his weight and sighed. "We're headed for Breckinridge tonight," he said. "Tiffany's son is having a birthday. We would take Alex along, but the kids have a tiny condo. We'll be back by noon tomorrow. Does that give you the time you need?"

"If having her is too much—"

"Are you kidding? We had a great time together. I put her on the tube behind the ski boat. She took one pass, and man, that girl hung on. She needed a bigger challenge, so I put her on a wakeboard. She got right up and didn't crash once, not once. That girl is a Connelly—up, down, and sideways."

"Doug?"

"Yeah?"

"Alex needs our help."

Doug stepped onto the stoop and closed the door behind him.

"What has Nicci done?"

I recounted my conversation with Alex and then my visit with Nicci on Colfax. The retelling of the stories kindled a sort of despair.

Doug stood like Superman. "I'll call Clint the second I get home." Clint was our lawyer. He specialized in business law, but he would know a good family lawyer by reputation. Something melted in my core. Sharing this load with Doug felt absolutely wonderful, but immediately the weight of what could happen hit me; such was the tyranny of Nicci.

I reached across the space between us to touch Doug's arm. "You know we may never get past this with Nicci? She won't forgive us. In her eyes she's doing her best for Alex."

Doug dropped his chin to his chest. His shoulders shuddered with each breath. He looked up and our eyes met. "This would be a lot easier to understand if I knew what I'd done wrong with Nicci. I wasn't a perfect dad, but I've known guys who screwed up a lot worse—I mean, they were drunks or knocked their kids around—and their kids love them anyway. They have Sunday dinners together; they share vacations. Have I been blind? What did I miss?"

I'd never suspected that Doug had asked the same questions as me. "You're a good dad, Doug. And I'm a pretty good mom, definitely not the worst. As tempting as giving up on Nicci—"

"Really? You too?"

I continued, "Nicci is a harsh reminder that I'm not in control of very much, but I can—*we* can—still do the right thing for Alex. She deserves to be safe. I pray that Nicci will someday appreciate what we're trying to do, but she may not, and that breaks my heart. In helping Alex, we may be saying goodbye to Nicci."

As I left, we shared a hug as if we were posts, but I celebrated that we were united in this one thing.

IN THE SLEEPING PORCH, ALEX stood in front of her new suitcase, an explosion of Caribbean colors. She deserved a vote of confidence and sleeping in the porch did that. At the squeak of the screen door's hinges, Alex turned to me and held up a bathing suit. Her cheeks and nose blazed pink from her time in the sun. "Don't you love it?"

"So, you had a good time?"

I heard all about wakeboarding and the places they'd eaten around town. Also, how Tiffany had taken her shopping to buy new bedding and accessories for her bedroom at their cabin. They'd driven all the way to Winter Park to go down the alpine slide and saw a movie afterward.

"I was getting pretty sunburned, so a movie seemed like a good idea," she said.

I wanted Alex to answer the next question with an emphatic no. "Were you comfortable with Tiffany?"

"You get that you'll always be my favorite grandma, don't you?"

I loved that girl. "Having a good relationship with Grandpa and Tif—"

"She wants me to call her Gigi."

Gigi? Gigi was a French waif with the waist of a wasp. "Oh."

"She thinks grandma is old sounding. But you're not old, not by a long shot."

I helped Alex fold her new clothes and informed her about Bimala's injuries. Speaking of Bimala reminded me to check my watch. She needed another dose of antibiotics. But first, since Doug was off for a weekend with his new wife, I had to get Alex settled with Carolyn.

"Is the baby okay?" she asked.

I'd planned on being vague about what Bimala and Pooja had endured at Shaitaan's hand, but I wanted to be honest, too. "I don't know. That's why I have to go back. She needs medicine and a change of bandages. Carolyn is on her way here. You'll be staying with her tonight. Grandpa will pick you up from her house about lunchtime tomorrow."

"I wish I could go with you."

The thought of Alex on Sundar Maut sluiced ice water down my spine. I expected Shaitaan to return to assess the damage he'd inflicted on Bimala. And with each of my visits the chances of running into him increased. I remembered that much from statistics. I had no plan for that eventuality, but I wouldn't want to be worrying about Alex's safety, too. That was the one good thing about travel magic—no passengers allowed. No amount of cajoling from Alex could wear me down. She would stay in good ol' Grand Lake.

"When Bimala is feeling better, we'll focus on getting her and Pooja off the island."

24

Bimala grasped my arm. "The pains are coming faster, harder. This is much, much earlier than Pooja."

"I must get help."

"There is no one." She clenched tighter and pinched my skin. "You will stay? You will help me?"

I had refused the mirror when I gave birth to both of my daughters. I'd had no desire to have that vision stuck in my head for all of my days. And I had opted for a spinal with Nicci. I wasn't overly qualified to help anyone with a birth, least of all a young girl on an island with no running water, telephone service, or an obstetrician. "Yes. Of course. I will be here as much as I can."

Bimala motioned me closer. "You may want to dig a grave while there is still time," she whispered. "The baby has not moved for a long time."

Delivering a healthy child held its own hazards. The cord could tangle and would definitely need to be cut, all that mucous, a head that couldn't fit through the pelvis. All of these things presented themselves in turn and kept my pulse racing. Delivering a stillborn child? I hadn't a clue.

"Bimala, let's focus on delivering a healthy baby, shall we?"

Her eyes filled with tears. "Yes."

I ordered Pooja to boil a large kettle of water. I had no idea why, but clean water would come in handy for clean up. Besides, stoking the fire and carrying water to the kettle gave Pooja something to do other than fret over her mother. Even by the lantern's tarnished light, I could see the girl's hands were raw from rubbing together.

Bimala managed her contractions well, so I gathered supplies. I sharpened a knife on a stone and collected a pile of linens, but the pile was skimpy. I reminded myself to bring towels back from Grand Lake to collect the birth fluids. I ripped lengths of cloth from the curtains to tie the cord. Last, I carried an armful of water bottles from the pavilion to keep Bimala hydrated.

Orange light reflected off the sweat collecting at her hairline and on her lip. I wiped her face with a cool cloth. "I'll be leaving soon. I won't return immediately. I have more supplies to gather." I would also be reading articles on the Internet to learn about emergency deliveries.

Bimala gave me a wan smile and her face contorted into a grimace.

"Don't stop breathing," I told her as the familiar pull landed me on *Zella*.

CAROLYN STOOD ON THE swim ladder, her face a map of worry. "I can't find Alex. She wasn't in the sleeping porch—she wasn't anywhere—when I went to get her."

I sat up and bile burned the back of my throat. I rested my forehead on my knees. There couldn't have been a worse time for Alex to wander off. "Bimala's in labor. This is too early. She hasn't felt the baby move in a couple days. The poor girl. I'm all she has."

I leaned heavily against the aft bench. "Alex seemed good when she got back from the weekend with Doug and Tif—" Our eyes met. "Doug and *her,* I mean. I wouldn't worry yet." Nursing Bimala and worrying about Alex threatened to topple me. I weirdly longed for the singular focus of grieving the loss of my marriage, my good ol' days. How pathetic was that?

Miss Carolyn, the vigilant kindergarten teacher and counter of heads, pressed. "Has Alex made any friends in town? I could call around if you have numbers."

"She may have forgotten something at the shop. She's probably preparing a map for shipment." Did I believe that?

The more I speculated over where Alex might be, the more my heart raced. Only the best sort of people lived in Grand Lake, but over four million tourists visited Rocky Mountain National Park each year. Many of them streamed through our small town. Some of them didn't look all that friendly or kind. Criminals enjoyed the outdoors, too.

"Do you suppose Richard could look for her?" I asked. "I need your help gathering supplies."

"I'll talk to him."

As much as Alex wandering off panicked me, I had to get back to Bimala. "Could you get on the Internet, too? Gather some emergency birthing info?" I climbed down the swim ladder. "So much can go wrong."

"I learned how to rewire a lamp on YouTube. Surely—"

"Take notes and meet me back here in thirty minutes."

I reached for the map of Sundar Maut that now remained tacked to the shed's wall. Carolyn put her hand to my arm. "Robin? What if that man shows up?"

I'd formulated a very simple plan if I met up with Shaitaan: after I messed my pants, I would tell him to go to hell. I also hoped that the very female occupation of giving birth would disgust him into keeping his distance. Beyond that, I hadn't a clue.

"I need a lantern, one of those ridiculously bright LED things," I said.

BIMALA'S CONDITION REMAINED THE same. We timed her contractions at seven minutes, only varying by a few seconds each time. I inventoried yet again the birth kit I'd assembled. I would ask Sally if she had a ball syringe for cleaning the mucous out of the baby's mouth and nose on my next trip to Grand Lake. With each contraction, Bimala clenched my hand. The arthritis in my knuckles howled.

"Are you breathing?" I asked.

"It hurts," her voice squeezed.

"When you feel the next pain, take a deep breath. Fill your tummy with air and let your arms and legs go heavy." I remembered this part of birth training because I still used the relaxation breathing whenever I visited the dentist.

"Will the pain stop?"

Absolutely not. Those natural types who claimed childbirth was painless came off as sweetness and light, but they lied shamelessly to sell books. "I can't make the pain go away. But the more relaxed you are, the faster the delivery will go." Was that true?

She frowned at me.

"Try it."

Her breath caught. Another contraction pinched her face. She was fighting her body.

"Okay, take a deep, deep breath in, in, in. Fill that tummy." Bimala followed my instructions. "Now, let the breath out slowly. Very slowly. Let your arms and legs get heavier and heavier. Again. This time, breathe in and in and in. Now, as you breathe out, let your face go slack."

Bimala slung her words at me, red and hot. "Slack? What is slack?"

My heart thumped. Bimala was expressing the anger of transition. Delivery wasn't far off.

I put my hands on her cheeks. "Breathe with me." We took three more breaths together.

Her head fell back and she closed her eyes. "I cannot."

"You're doing great." Which was a kind lie at best.

"Angel Lady, come right back."

"What?"

Bimala had anticipated my departure before I had.

CAROLYN SAT ON THE aft bench, the flickering blue light of a laptop illuminating her face in the shed. "If the head presents during a contraction, it's time to push."

"Has Richard found Alex?"

"He's out looking, but he isn't back yet." She toed a stuffed garbage bag. "Sally filled this with towels. You'll be taking the bag with you."

"And the lantern?"

"Richard has one you can see from space. It's in there."

It was then that I noticed Sally, standing against the wall, watchful and expectant. I couldn't help but smile, and she wiggled her fingers at me. I mouthed, *thank you.*

Carolyn ran her finger down a clipboard and stopped. "The video said to put lots of absorbent material under the mother. Doing so makes cleanup easier afterward. There's also a pair of examination gloves and some hand sanitizer. How you use those is up to you."

"I'll need a bulb syringe, too."

Sally raised a finger. "I should have thought of that. I'll be right back."

Carolyn scribbled notes and leafed through pages until she got to what she wanted. "Listen up: Do not pull on the baby or the cord. The baby will deliver himself."

"Are you sure?"

"That's what the midwife in the video said. She looked—how do I say this?—authoritarian. She had a mustache."

"What else?"

"Do not touch the anal opening of the mother but put your hand just above there to catch the baby."

I repeated all of that back to Carolyn.

"There's dental floss in the bag, too. Evidently, it's excellent for tying the cord. Do you know where to tie it?"

I did not. "I need to get back. Bimala's pretty anxious."

"I wish that woman from the video could travel with you. She oozed confidence. That's what Bimala needs. If you're confident, she'll relax."

Sally rushed in with the ball syringe and handed it over the gunwale. "I'm so proud of you. You're doing something very brave."

"I don't feel brave."

"The brave never do. They're too busy doing what needs doing."

I poised my finger over the map and tried breathing into my tummy as I'd told Bimala. My stomach was a concrete block.

"One more thing," Carolyn said. "A lot of blood comes out with the placenta."

POOJA HELD A COOL cloth to Bimala's forehead. I gathered a blanket from Pooja's pallet. "I'll take very good care of your mother, and I'll check on you each time I come." Pooja looked to Bimala who nodded. "Your mother needs you strong and alert. There will be a lot to do when the baby comes. She would also want you to pray. Can you do that?"

Pooja nodded quickly and left the hut.

With contrived confidence, I positioned the towels under Bimala and watched for the baby's head during the next contraction. There was some movement, a pulsing of the opening, but I didn't see a head.

I knew another contraction had come when Bimala inhaled deeply and let out a slow breath. She moaned deep in her throat and clenched her teeth. "Slack face," I reminded her.

EACH TIME I RETURNED to Grand Lake, Carolyn fed me another bit of information. My head swam with the dos and don'ts of baby delivery. My legs quivered from swimming ashore and running repeatedly through the sand from the lagoon to the hut. The temptation to surrender to the bench cushions nearly claimed me.

"I need you to concentrate, Robin." Carolyn sounded like an overly confident midwife with a mustache. "Compress the bulb of the syringe *before* you put it in the baby's mouth. That bit is very important. Keep aspirating until his breaths are clear, no stickiness. Got that?"

I nodded.

"Also, wait until the cord stops pulsing and goes limp to tie it. Some people say to wait a whole minute. Others don't. I'll leave that to you."

Cord stops pulsing.

"Okay, so this is also very, very important because getting the baby to suckle helps with bleeding." Carolyn shot me a knowing look. "As soon as his airway is clear and you've dried him off, put him to the breast."

I fought dizziness. I'd never moved between two places so quickly and so many times. I now knew what a yo-yo felt like. Carolyn insisted that I take a minute to drink some juice and eat some yogurt. I thought to argue with her, but my stomach gurgled loudly.

"You won't be any good to her if you faint," she said.

As I finished the yogurt, the shed's door opened and in walked Sally with Alex. Even in the dim light of twilight, Alex's eyes showed red and splotchy.

I stood too quickly and almost swooned. Carolyn braced me with an arm about my waist. "What's happened?" I asked Alex.

"I'm sorry I made you worry, Grandma. I'm totally okay. How's Bimala? Is the baby here?"

Sally put a protective arm around Alex. "The girl's fine," she said to me. "We'll fix her supper and give her a place to sleep. She can stay as long as you need her to. You do what you have to do, Becky."

I raised my eyebrows to ask Alex if she agreed with Sally's plan.

"Absolutely," she answered. "Richard is firing up the grill, and Sally is going to teach me how to make biscuits. You've tasted her apricot jelly, right? Don't worry about me. Take care of Bimala."

Something had happened. Clearly, Alex was hurting. She noticed my hesitation.

"Grandma, honest, I'm good. We'll talk when you get back."

I looked from Sally to Carolyn and back to Alex. "You'll stay put?"

"You'll find me right here, I promise."

Carolyn handed me a sealed plastic bag.

"What's this?"

"Sandwiches and some fruit. And a camera. We want to see the baby."

THE SKY WHISPERED BLUE when I returned to Sundar Maut, but the birds had already started to party. They called as if to say, *Hurry up! Hurry up!* I kicked through the soft sand to the hut.

I offered Bimala a drink. Her head lay heavily in my hands. It dawned on me belatedly that I should have brought a blood pressure cuff. Would I know what to do if her blood pressure was high or low? Absolutely not, so I checked her cervix. This time the head pulsed into the opening with the contraction.

"Do you have the urge to push?" I asked, not hiding my panic.

"I'm so tired."

Already depleted by her injuries and her body's struggle to birth her baby, Bimala lay deep in the pillows. Dark circles had bloomed under her eyes. Her skin was the color of cream.

"This is the hard work of women," I said. "There is no rest for now, and I'm sorry for that truth. There will be rest later, I promise. Your baby will come, Bimala, very soon. When all is well, I'll look after Pooja and the baby, and you will rest. Right now, you have to give your baby everything you have and some that you don't."

25

I carried the baby's body through the palm forest to the clearing where Bimala and I had buried the little girl. I'd left Pooja to watch her mother as she slept.

I'd never seen a baby so small. His hands perfect but more fitting of a doll. He was nearly weightless in my arms, even wrapped in one of Sally's plush towels.

I laid him down to dig the hole. Such an insignificant end to a barely lived life. Before I placed him in the moist hole, I carried him to the lagoon, where clouds mushroomed on the horizon and the sky spread broad and blue and endless.

I was a tiny woman holding a tiny baby on a tiny island in the big, broad blue. "A baby has died," I explained to the hugeness. To God? "His father killed him. What will you do? Is there justice for this life?"

When the choking emotion passed, I said, "You saw that I tried, didn't you? That the mother didn't give up? That the sister doesn't know what to do with her grief?"

The weight of the baby grew unbearable. I took him back to the clearing and the hole I'd dug.

"I'm sorry," I said to the blanketed boy. "I will do what I can for your mother and sister."

BACK AT SALLY AND Richard's cabin, I showered and fell into the bed where Alex had slept the night before. Sally sat in a chair in the corner, watching. Her lips moved as she clenched her hands in prayer.

Although I'd slept for eleven hours, my head still hummed.

"Coffee?" Sally said. "I can reheat a cup."

My tongue felt like sandpaper. "I need to check on Bimala first."

POOJA SAT LIKE A loyal dog at her mother's head. Only the flitting of the girl's eyes in my direction acknowledged my arrival. But when I sat down, Pooja crawled into my lap and rested her head to my chest. I pulled her closer and breathed in the scent of her hair— salt, smoke, and sweat. I noted to bring some of Alex's fruity shampoo for the girl. Soon, Pooja fell asleep, and my heart surrendered to an exquisite ache.

Bimala's eyes fluttered open and blinked against the brightness of the day.

"Have you eaten anything?" I asked.

Her lips stuck together at the corners. "Pooja cooked eggs, but I could not eat."

I passed a water bottle. "You need to drink." Bimala closed her eyes against the bliss of the cool water.

Although the girl's ease against my chest soothed like the surest balm, I lifted her to a pallet, cursing the tyranny of minutes that pulled at me. I attended Bimala and helped her void her bladder and changed the towels we'd torn into pads. Such intimacy was the prize of women.

I left mother and daughter with a promise to return before their night fell.

BACK AT THE CABIN, I stood in the middle of the living room, considering my options. Dust lay like a blanket on every surface. I couldn't remember the last time I'd bought groceries. In the corner the philodendron gasped for water. My pillow beckoned my heavy head to lay down for a few brief moments.

I'd barely sat on the futon and shifted my weight toward the pillow when Alex entered from the deck. She took the whistling kettle off the flame and poured water into the French press. As the coffee steeped, she tidied her breakfast dishes, watching me surreptitiously.

"Grandma, I need you to come to the sleeping porch. I have something to show you." She stood over me, coffee in hand, waiting. Thinking Tiffany had lavished her with more swimwear, I asked her to bring whatever she had to me.

She presented the steaming coffee. "It would be better for you to come to the porch."

There was no resisting the girl. I sat on her bed and leaned into the wall. With the shutters open, a breeze swept through the room and goose bumps rose on my arms. The lake flickered, joyously. Alex stood before me, looking earnest and eager. The silly girl wore a life vest, but I was in no mood for adolescent games.

"What is this, Alex?" I said, trying to modulate my irritation, and failing.

She pulled a folded tourist brochure—available at every retail store in Grand Lake—out of her pocket and gingerly opened it. "You should probably sit someplace else. I'll land right there in fourteen minutes."

She touched a finger to the map of the lake. Before my mind could register what I saw, the ragged ridge of the Never Summer Range became dimly recognizable through Alex. And then she disappeared altogether. I stared at the spot where she'd stood only a moment earlier for an embarrassingly long time.

Alex is a traveler.

I straightened, instantly alert. How could that be? She was too young, too innocent, too much my granddaughter to be traipsing all over the world at the touch of a map. Oceans were deep and the ground was hard. Most sobering: She didn't know enough to be afraid.

I rushed to the dock, hoping to spot her floating among the waves and chastising myself for not paying better attention to where she'd touched the map. Ski boats sliced through the blue water. I clamped my eyes shut against an involuntary vision of a boat crossing paths with Alex. I ran up the twenty-three steps to the cabin, my legs screaming with complaint the whole way.

Where are the binoculars?!

Back on the dock, I scanned the lake surface, searching for Alex's head bobbing in the waves, concentrating my attention on the paths of boats. I lowered the binoculars, unwilling to observe such a collision.

The girl was too careless to be a traveler. Precautions had to be taken. "You do not purposely put yourself in danger!" I called out to the lake as I drooped to the dock.

"Grandma!" Alex called from behind.

There she stood at the landing to the sleeping porch, dripping water and grinning like a beauty queen. "I landed on the bed! How great is that?" She trotted down the stairs, wrapped in a towel, and sat beside me. "I can go with you to Sundar Maut," she said through shivering teeth.

"You most certainly cannot. You can't go anywhere."

Alex sobered. "I went to see Mom when you were helping Bimala."

"You traveled there? You touched a map?" That explained her red-rimmed eyes. "What's happened?"

Alex studied the lake, or something beyond and distant, for a long moment. "Mom's marrying Sean. I begged her not to. Actually, I got pretty hysterical, which set her off. It got messy after that."

Alex bent over her folded arms, hiding her face in her hair. She clearly understood that by choosing Sean, Nicci had not chosen her. I grabbed for the only consolation I could think of. "She hasn't married him yet. You know your mother changes her mind all the time."

"She bought a dress."

"A dress?" Nicci had not worn a dress since the third grade, and only then when I'd threatened to impound her bike. I opened my arms and Alex rushed in. Soon her wet clothes dampened mine. Even though I couldn't assure her of anything, I promised I would keep her safe.

My granddaughter is a traveler.

My daughter is marrying a man who abused my granddaughter.

How did we all get here?

"When?" I asked. "When are they getting married?"

"She said she would let me know, but I'm not so sure. Grandma, I said some pretty harsh things. I don't see her getting over what I said for a long time."

Where to begin?

First, we had the problem of Nicci seeing Alex travel. Not everyone handles such a spectacle well. It's best to be selective about who sees you and who you tell. Nicci would not be my first choice. Second, Alex had a lot to learn about traveling, some that would keep her safe or, at least safer. Other things that would make traveling more comfortable. Even more pressing, Nicci had betrayed Alex. Could such a violation be fixed?

"Where did great-grandpa land?" Alex asked.

Of course Alex considered traveling the hot topic. "Your great-granddad was smart enough to arrive someplace soft, which was the barn behind our house in Loveland. Keeping the stall clear and freshly plumped with straw fell to me."

Dad had loved that barn. Even before we started building *Zella*, we spent most of our time together there. When he came home from teaching, he tinkered with his father's old truck. We listened to ancient radio shows on his cassette player.

"He chose to arrive in the barn?" she asked. "I sure didn't choose the sleeping porch, it just happened. Did I miss something?"

And I hadn't chosen *Zella*.

The barn made sense as an arrival spot for Dad. The place anchored his memories. After a long day of teaching and advising students, he'd retreated to his workbench under the hayloft, just as his father had done.

"Travelers don't have control over very much, I'm sorry to say. Basically, we can try to avoid traveling when we don't want to, and we can take precautions about where we land. We have absolutely no control over where we return. I've suspected that we're entwined emotionally to our arrival spots, but I'm not sure about that."

Alex lifted her gaze to the treetops and back to me. "I love the porch. Sleeping with the cousins made me feel like I was really a part of the family. That sounds pretty stupid, right? I mean, sure, I was part of the family the whole time, but that time was different. I'm not sure why, but I sure liked the feeling."

And *Zella* was my last artifact of anything resembling equilibrium. "I think you're on to something."

Alex admitted she'd been feeling homesick, so she went to the library to chat with her friends online. She looked up her house on a satellite image, just to feel close. The house sat on the other side of South Platte Canyon Road from a reservoir, something she'd never bothered to notice before.

To center the image before printing the map, she'd touched the screen. She felt as if someone had hooked her around the waist to yank her from earth and thrown her into the reservoir.

"I lost my good flip-flops, Grandma."

Since Alex didn't know how much time she got to spend at her house, she stepped through the door, saw Nicci in her wedding dress, and demanded that Nicci not marry Sean. Her command infuriated Nicci, so much so that she didn't ask Alex why her hair and clothes dripped water on the floor. Neither did she show any curiosity over how Alex had gotten to Lakewood from Grand Lake. Knowing her mother wouldn't calm down soon, Alex stomped off to her room. Before her head hit the pillow, she was wrenched back to Grand Lake.

"I'm gonna need a package of oyster crackers," she said. "I nearly spewed."

We didn't talk anymore of Nicci, and I didn't tell Alex of Doug's promise to contact the lawyer. As usual, Nicci remained the unsettled question. As much as I hated the idea of losing my daughter, I could not and would not send Alex back to a house where Nicci's husband preyed on her.

When Alex came to say goodnight, I took her hand. "Darling, you have to be really careful about who you tell about traveling. Folks don't like the unexplainable. I suggest you wait to tell someone until you're very sure you can trust that person."

"I can disappear right in front of someone's eyes. How cool is that? I don't even need a magician to say magic words or step into a curtained booth or anything. People would spend good money to see that, right?"

I hadn't thought of that.

I worried how Nicci must have reacted to Alex's sudden disappearance. This traveling stuff could be a messy business. I texted Nicci, saying Alex was safe with me. She didn't respond.

IT'S A CRUEL THING for a woman's body to make milk for a child who never filled her arms. I returned to the island every few hours to help Bimala change breast pads and to bind her breasts.

No light remained in Bimala. Although her bruises had faded to purple and yellow, she shuffled around her hut and sat by the lagoon, watching the clouds gather on the horizon. Mostly she slept. Her temperature remained elevated but not high, which was good because I only had one more antibiotic tablet. I reminded her to breathe as deeply as she could, but she winced from the pain of trying. I could only guess how the rigors of childbirth had inflamed her already injured ribs.

I often found Pooja watching her mother sleep. I'd brought one of Lauren's dolls for her to play with in the lonely hours of her mother's recovery and grief, but on my next visit the doll lay in the crook of Bimala's arm as she slept. Before she woke again, I packed the doll into my duffel.

"Have you eaten anything today?" I asked Pooja.

She frowned at the question. Bits of egg collected at the corners of her mouth. A streak of soot smeared her cheek.

"What sounds good? I'll bring you something. Do you like sandwiches?"

"We have not much water."

Without her saying so, I knew this meant Shaitaan would soon return to the island. He would arrive to find Bimala bereft of her baby and Pooja dimmed by his abuse. They would be useless to him. In one way or another, he would dispose of them.

On another trip, I found Bimala squatting near the dead embers of her cooking fire. She didn't look up as I stepped into the clearing. I sat next to her, out of words.

"I am sorry that I did not die with the child," she said. "Heaven seemed close, Angel Lady, but then the image moved far, far away."

"You'll see things differently when you're feeling better. And you will feel better, Bimala. Healing takes time."

"We do not have the time," she said flatly.

I carried water on my next visit, rebuilt the fire, and warmed the kettle. I bathed Pooja, always keeping an eye to the sea for an approaching boat. The girl responded to my prodding to present an arm or a foot, but a tickle to her tummy brought no smile. When my own daughters were young, to redirect their anguish over much lesser heartaches, I'd told them stories. Would Pooja respond to a story?

Pooja settled into my lap and rested her head on my shoulder. I dismissed the story of "Goldilocks and the Three Bears." Pooja had no concept of bears or girls with golden curls. Trolls under bridges were too creepy. And I wouldn't add to Pooja's anxiety with a tale of a witch enticing children into a house of candy, only to eat them. Maybe she had a favorite.

"Would you like to hear a story?" I said.

"Do you know of Yusuf?"

"Not as well as your mother, but I know another story from the same book." Bimala would approve of a Bible story.

I rocked Pooja as I told the story of a Jewish man beaten, robbed, and left for dead on the road to Jericho. Two religious men saw the man lying near death in the dirt, but they crossed to the other side of the road to continue their journeys undisturbed. Then a man hated by the Jews took care of the man.

"The man who treated the beaten man kindly is a true neighbor," I said, finishing the story.

Pooja scanned the broad ocean. "What is a neighbor, Angel Lady?"

"Some say that a neighbor is someone who lives near you, but the man who first told this story said that a neighbor is the one who treats people with kindness."

Pooja looked over her shoulder to Shaitaan's hut. "When Shaitaan is here, he lives close to us, but he is not kind."

"Then he isn't your neighbor"

"You are our neighbor, Angel Lady."

My watch warned that my departure time neared. I lifted Pooja from my lap and took the girl by the shoulders. Her face shone pink from scrubbing. "I will try to be a much better neighbor, from now on."

I touched the map of Sundar Maut as soon as I landed on *Zella* because I had not yet bathed Bimala or changed her binding. I heated more water and sent Pooja to keep watch. Milk had leaked around the pads and dried to stiffen Bimala's binding. Above the binding, her breasts rose hard and lumpy, engorged with unspent milk. A fine thread of milk sprayed from Bimala's nipples as I removed the binding.

"I've brought cabbage leaves. Women swear by them to dry up milk. It's worth a try."

Bimala blinked, submitting to the insult of vegetables on her breasts. I snugged the elastic bandage against her skin and secured it with two safety pins. As the island's day faded, I informed Bimala that I would not be back until her morning and gave her the last antibiotic tablet.

I DREAMED OF SHAITAAN and woke with a racing heart. In my dream, Shaitaan had been choking me. I put my hands to my throat, expecting the skin to be tender. I'd slept only four hours. That would have to do.

A note by the stove told me Alex had gone to The Traveling Man to package up the maps we'd sold on eBay. I started a flame under the teapot and spooned an extra scoop of coffee into the French press. A buzz of activity on the lake drew me to open the door. The gleam of light off the water seared my eyes. I grabbed for my sunglasses and settled into the wicker chair still weighted by sleep.

As I waited for the teapot to whistle, I played with the eternity ring on its chain, sliding it this way and that, back and forth, the links of the chain purring against the gold. And I knew exactly how to help Bimala and Pooja.

26

Richard rubbed his chin. "I don't know anything about jewelry. This could be a piece of junk, for all I know."

Sally shook her head and sighed deeply.

I flashed a reassuring smile at her and spoke to Richard. "I understand your dilemma. Under normal circumstances, I would never ask, but you can see by the certificate that the diamonds are genuine, of the highest clarity and color. It's all right there," I said, pointing to the paper in his hand. "Take the ring to the window. Those diamonds glimmer. I turned heads whenever I wore that thing, which was all the time." The diamonds winked in the light, but Richard seemed unmoved. "As I said, I don't know what my husband paid for the ring, but a similar ring is worth more than what you paid for *Zella*. A lot more. And I don't expect change. You could get a much better boat."

Richard leveled his gaze at me. "What's the rush?"

I needed *Zella* to evacuate Bimala and Pooja from Sundar Maut. "It's hard to explain."

His face reddened. "You better try."

Sally put a hand to Richard's arm. "Well now, if Becky needs that boat, I think we should let her have it."

Richard turned his glower on Sally. I put a protective arm around her shoulders. "I don't like being rushed into things either. But time is precious, and it would take days to find a buyer for the ring in Denver. I don't even know where to start."

Besides, the logistics of a trip to Denver were daunting. I would have to borrow Carolyn's car, which meant she would have to find another way to work on Saturday. That seemed like too much to ask after all she'd done to help me already. I could rent a car, but I'd missed work again, so my wallet was nearly empty. No, I wasn't going to Denver anytime soon to sell the ring.

Only the most direct means of acquiring a boat would suffice, and *Zella* fit the bill. My thoughts turned constantly to Sundar Maut, wondering how Bimala and Pooja fared. If that last antibiotic didn't kill whatever plagued Bimala, she would require constant care to regain her health. Meaning, she needed more help than I could offer, which necessitated a trip to the mainland.

"I need your decision now," I said. "I'm sorry. That's the way it has to be."

Richard threw up his hands. "I've just finished sanding the hull. You can't put that thing in the water. I'm sorry, whatever your friends need, you're going to have to find another way to help them." Richard flipped a dismissive hand and stomped out of the shed.

Sally hooked my waist and pulled me close. We followed Richard out of the shed and watched him until he slammed the cabin door closed. "Your father has his pride."

"How is this about his pride?"

"I've never known a man who liked his plans better than your father. He gets his mind made up on something and considers anything less a failure. He's promised Uncle Mike a day on the lake this September. Richard doesn't like breaking promises."

"He could buy a different boat."

"That would be completely out of character, but he could, I suppose. And I suppose you could find another boat to buy."

In her way, Sally convinced me I was being as stubborn as Richard. I spent the rest of the day calling people with boats for sale. I learned quickly to ask if the boat was running, and right after that if they would take a diamond ring in exchange. Evidently, boat people preferred cash.

Morning would soon come to Sundar Maut. After the long night, Bimala would need fresh breast pads and help with her binding. The day had been a waste. I was no closer to rescuing Bimala and Pooja, which made me a stewpot of boiling resentment.

I resented Doug for landing me in a place where I couldn't contemplate a two-hundred-mile round trip—I needed a car! I couldn't burden Carolyn every time I went somewhere. I resented Shaitaan. That animal! He took what he wanted with no regard of the cost to others, even death. Women were no better than bugs to him. Richard made my list too, for not exchanging *Zella* for a ring that held tons of emotional collateral. And while I was making a list, why not throw in Cal? Would it have killed him to believe me? I am not a man-hater, but good golly, could someone with a penis please step up and do the right thing?

I could not drum up the faith to believe a man like that existed. There would be no knight in shining armor, so I mounted my bike and headed for the shop to round up Alex and let her know my plan, and, of course, to check on her. The girl had promised not to travel without me, but at fourteen, the cause-and-effect center in her brain hadn't fully developed.

At Rainbow Bridge that spanned the channel between the two lakes, I skidded to a stop. An empty speedboat idled at a dock not forty feet away. I waited for someone to race out of the cabin, cast off, and speed away. No one came. Perhaps the owner had forgotten he left the boat running. Perhaps a long-distance call full of distress had come from many time zones away. Perhaps he was talking the person on the phone through an intricate surgical procedure. I played with the idea of taking that boat off his hands. Who would know? There certainly wouldn't be any evidence once the boat bobbed in the Arabian Sea. Why not?

Get a grip!

Before me, the lake mirrored the cerulean sky, glinting in the afternoon sun. Beyond the lake, Mt. Baldy swelled above the surrounding peaks, monstrous and proud.

I'm so small.

With stunning clarity, I realized that rescuing Bimala and Pooja required many Mt. Baldy-like mountains to move. Wasn't God famous for moving mountains? I remembered something like that from my days in the pew. It wouldn't hurt to ask.

Hello, God, some sweet girls in the Arabian Sea think I'm one of your angels. It's a truly outrageous idea, I know, but they could use some help. Why not me? As it turns out, I'm available. But to get them off that island, I need a boat. The owner won't see the boat again, which could be a problem. You'll have to work that out, too. Please make sure the boat has a powerful engine and a solid hull. Many thanks. Could you hurry? Amen.

The thought of pedaling all the way to the shop and then walking back to the cabin with Alex filleted me. My legs shook with fatigue. Alex was a very smart and thoughtful fourteen-year-old girl. I decided to trust her.

I dismounted and turned the bike back toward the cabin.

I pedaled around a curve to find Nicci's Rubicon parked in front of the cabin. She'd heaped the cargo area with clothes, a bicycle, boxes, and plastic bins aplenty.

What now?

I looked over my shoulder, seeing in my mind's eye Alex working over the maps at The Traveling Man. Perhaps Nicci and I could settle whatever business she'd brought with her, and she could be on her way—with Sean?—before Alex returned.

I parked the bike beside Nicci's car and went inside. Nicci stood with her arms heavily laden in front of the Lakeview Room, where the boxes stood stacked as high as her shoulders. "Mom, really? Have you unpacked one frickin' box?"

No Sean in sight. "I'm surprised to see you, Nicci."

"That's a nice greeting," she said dryly and moved to the Pollywog Room. She took the room in. "Just to be clear, I've always hated how you decorated. Way too many patterns in one room. But this is your worst ever. Lauren threw up on that bedspread, like, what, thirty years ago? The Smurfs want their quilt back." She dropped her clothes on the bed.

"So, are you staying awhile?" I asked.

Her shoulders fell and her eyes got soupy. "I left Sean. Some really crazy shit has been happening. You wouldn't believe the dream I had of Alex. Man, it felt so real. She was right in front of me, and then she was gone. In my dream, I mean. At least, I thought it was a dream. She practically spit venom at me. The whole thing left my blood cold."

"You left Sean, really?"

She threw up her hands and marched out the front door. Per my usual, I followed. She spoke over her shoulder. "Is there a man on this planet who isn't a prick? Answer me that, Mother." She gathered another armload of clothes, mostly black, from the cargo area of her Jeep. "Sean's an asshole of the grandest scale."

I blocked her way, nodded toward her burdened arms. "Maybe we should sit down and talk. I'll make coffee."

Nicci sidestepped me and headed back into the cabin. I grabbed a plastic bin of shoes and followed. She dropped the clothes on the bed. "Alex tried to tell me, Mom, just like you. But I didn't want to believe her. I mean, the things she told me were pretty damn horrible. But the truly horrible thing is that I did believe her. How could I not? The way he looked at her, how he was always grabbing her. He couldn't keep his goddam hands off of her. That's why I brought her here, to you.

"Oh, he denies everything. He, like, begged me for the chance to be a good father to her. Can you believe that?" Nicci rubbed at the rash rising in the crooks of her arms. "He was messing with her, Mom, and I was too goddam scared of being alone to kick his ass out. I don't do alone so good."

Nicci stood before me, basically saying that I'd been right, that she should have believed Alex from the beginning, but she'd chosen not to. Wouldn't any mother brighten at hearing her daughter say this? And yet, I felt nothing. No compassion or relief, and certainly no hope for better days of connection with my daughter. If anything, I felt resigned. Hadn't we been here many times before? Hadn't she promised me hundreds—*thousands*—of times that things would be different?

This is what I knew would happen: She would toe the line for a week—maybe ten days. She would work hard at being a good mom and a somewhat pleasant daughter, and then she would call Sean. He would convince her that she'd imagined the whole thing, and she would run to him.

That was the pattern.

I hated the pattern.

Something had to change.

With a straight arm I directed her to the wicker chair. In the kitchen, I saturated two towels with cold water and wrapped the hot rash at her elbows. She sighed.

"Coffee?" I asked.

"I couldn't."

I sat knee to knee with her. "What has changed, Nicci, between us seeing each other in Denver and now? You had me pretty well convinced that Sean was the one and only for you … and Alex. Think before you say anything. I don't want histrionics. I don't want a story you've been rehearsing. I want what's true."

Nicci closed her eyes and slumped until her head rested on the chair back. A tear slid down her cheek. "I don't remember falling asleep, but I dreamed of Alex. She walked in when I was trying on the wedding dress." She opened her eyes. "Did I tell you Sean and I were going to get married?"

I couldn't tell her, at least not yet, that Alex had already told me about Nicci's wedding plans. "No, you didn't."

"I bought a really pretty dress. You would have liked it. Anyway, Alex stormed into the bedroom. Her hair was soaking wet and so were her clothes, which was totally weird—you know, dreams—but she started in on me before I could ask her why.

"She kept asking me why, like why I loved Sean more than her." Nicci moved the damp cloths to the back of her neck. "I'd never seen her like that. She looked at me, you know, like a pile of dog shit but also like her heart was broken in a million pieces. I reached out for her, but she didn't want anything to do with me."

I would never have wished that sort of rejection on Nicci, not from her own daughter.

"She stomped up the stairs, and I followed. I had to make her understand that Sean was good for us."

I should have challenged Nicci on this but couldn't. Her daughter—her most familiar reference point in the universe—had acted completely out of character.

"By the time I got to her room, Alex wasn't there. The room was as she'd left it in June." She scooted forward. "Mom, I honestly do not remember falling asleep or waking up. It kind of freaks me out."

I could not let Nicci's confusion distract me from protecting Alex. "So, I ask you again, what happened? What has changed? Nothing you've said explains why I should take you seriously, Nicci. Help me out here."

Nicci glared at me, and I prepared to be excoriated. But her face softened, and tears welled in her eyes. "I'm so tired, Mom."

"Should we talk later?"

"No, I can do this. I *need* to do this." She stood and paced in front of the coffee table. "Part of my lab work was helping out in a family physician's office. I've been at Dr. Mohler's office for almost a month. We see everything from newborns to old people, although I'm supposed to say elderly.

"A few days ago, a girl came in with her mother. I weighed her and took her blood pressure. You could have cut the tension between them with a knife, so I started asking the girl questions to lighten the mood. You know, the usual: Where do you go to school? What's your favorite music? Doing anything great this summer?

"The girl was a few months younger than Alex but a lot like her. Same hair. Same height but a little heavier and really sad. And she wore this blue polish that looked like shit. Alex's polish lasts about fifteen minutes. I'm not sure what she does."

Our eyes met. "Yeah," I said, "I've seen her pick at the polish, too."

"Anyway, this girl, I could not get her to smile. I gave up. I was leaving to check in another patient, and she threw up in the trashcan and started to cry. The mom stood up, but she didn't help the girl. She looked like she wanted to run. She sorta inched away from her daughter. I wanted to hold the girl so bad."

Nicci?

"I tried to assure her—the girl—that people get sick in the exam room all the time, and it didn't bother me one bit. 'You can't help it,' I said. 'You're sick.'

"She said, 'I'm not sick, I'm pregnant.' The mother, like, rushed from the room, leaving her daughter alone with me, a stranger. I didn't know what to do. I had other patients. Things get really backed up if I don't keep moving, and then there's hell to pay. But the girl seemed so very alone, so I washed her hands and face."

I blinked and rubbed my eyes. *Nicci?*

"I told her how I had Alex when I was sixteen, and that she turned out great. And then I asked her about her boyfriend."

"The girl spills everything then. There's no boyfriend. The baby's father is an older cousin—like in his twenties—that's been living with her, her seven-year-old twin brothers, and her mother.

The guy helped the mom, especially with the boys."

Nicci fought to still her shuddering lips. "That could have been Alex, Mom. Alex could have been the one trying to hold everything together because her mom had been stupid and lazy and selfish." Nicci's face crumpled into her hands. I squeezed into the chair with her and held her close.

I felt something then, something cracking open and spilling out in a rush of anguish and ecstasy. When her cries slowed, I said, "That girl isn't Alex. Alex is okay, doing great, in fact, because you made sure she was in a safe place."

"But, Mom, come on, it could have turned out all so different."

"You'll drive yourself mad thinking about what could have happened. The Connelly women are done with that kind of thinking. Instead, we're grateful for unexpected grace, and we're going to expect good stuff to happen. Are you with me?"

"Dr. Mohler says I have to clean up my mouth to make it in medicine."

"That should be a piece of cake for a medical assistant."

"I'm an ADN, Mom, an Associate Degree Nurse. Everything counts toward a BSN."

With that clarified, we worked together to move her into the Pollywog Room. I felt like we were truly together in something as we hefted the heavy loads. I fought to keep my tears behind my lids.

When she drove to the shop to bring Alex home for dinner, I traveled to Sundar Maut to change Bimala's pads. Her skin burned under my hands. I dosed her with the acetaminophen I'd brought and encouraged her to drink as much as she could. I made a mental note to bring ginger ale on my next visit. She needed calories.

I spent the few minutes I had on the island, showing Pooja how to work against the fever. "Keep cool cloths on her forehead and chest. Also, drizzle water on her arms and legs. This will cool her off. Do you understand? This is very important."

Pooja's eyes enlarged with fear.

"I'll be back as soon as I can."

I leaned near Bimala's face. "Miracles are in the air. Keep praying. Don't give up."

27

Richard stood with his arms crossed over his chest and his jaw set. In my driveway, *Zella* sat on a trailer hitched to his idling truck. "It seems Sally's been wanting an eternity ring longer than she can remember. I would be much obliged if you would trade that ring for the boat," he said flatly.

"Richard?"

His gaze narrowed. "I will regret this, I know I will. I don't appreciate acting the fool, except for Sally. You better go get that ring, or I'm liable to back on out of here and take the boat with me."

I lifted the chain off my neck and placed the ring in his palm. The better part of me—the part that found pressing others to act against their best interests unimaginable—wanted to refuse the trade, but getting *Zella* back meant I could help Bimala and Pooja in a way that mattered: I could get them off that island. So I pressed Richard for more. "I need your help getting her in the water."

"I figured you would. I sprayed a coat of polyurethane on that hull, which isn't near enough, but you can get her to your boat garage. I assume you have a lift to get her out of the water?"

I did. "Thank you for the work you've done on her. She looks really great." I stroked her hull. The new finish was rough under my hand. Dad would have been appalled.

"I hate to ask—" I started.

"The new Bimini came yesterday. It's on the deck."

"A new Bimini?" I couldn't have hoped for such a bonus. The cover would make the trip to the mainland more comfortable for Bimala. "The value of the ring should cover the cost, but I'll pay whatever difference there is. What I need are two fuel cans. Two ten gallons will be enough."

Richard squinted down. "That's a lot of fuel to carry onboard. In fact, ten gallons of fuel weigh over sixty pounds. I don't mean to be insulting, but that's awfully heavy for a gal like you. I would suggest four five-gallon cans, if you're bound and determined to carry that much."

Grand Lake wasn't Lake Superior, so boaters didn't carry that kind of backup fuel for a day of fishing. The Arabian Sea, however, dwarfed even the largest lakes. I needed those extra gallons to get to the coast of India from Sundar Maut. I couldn't exactly tell Richard that.

"I have a trip planned," I said through tight lips, hoping he wouldn't press for details.

"I can see that's about all I'm going to discover about your plans. Well, I hope you've thought everything through. If there isn't much boat traffic where you'll be traveling, you might want to carry some oil with you, too. Maybe a fuel pump and a set of spark plugs. You have jumper cables, don't you?"

I'd helped Dad rebuild the engine, twice. I'd changed the oil and switched out the ignition switch referring to a book from the library. I felt good about my abilities to keep *Zella* running, but the thought of being dead in the water—the Arabian Sea!—with a sick woman and a young girl popped a bubble of panic. "How's she running?"

"Like a top, but she's not a filly anymore. Be prepared is all I'm saying."

I rode with Richard to the East Inlet boat launch with *Zella* bouncing along behind. Not one speck of dust sullied the cab of his truck. Richard only spoke once. "I'll bring the fuel cans to the cabin later."

I felt like a spoiled brat, but I didn't turn down his offer. "Thanks."

Trucks with boat trailers clogged the parking lot, which was typical for a Saturday in Summer. The sun dipped toward Shadow Mountain in the west. I wished I'd brought my sunglasses.

The boat launch had its established order. Those coming off the lake went first, and a flotilla of boats waited their turn. The serious business of getting the boats off the lake without damage gave all of the boat owners grim faces. Orders were barked out truck windows and skippers coaxed boats toward trailers.

A couple yelled back and forth. "I can't back in any deeper," said the woman driving the truck.

"Just do it!" bellowed the man from the helm of his boat.

"The man said—!"

"I don't care what the man said! Back 'er up!"

Richard stepped up and spoke quietly to the woman before he moved to the water's edge. He motioned her deeper into the water until his extended palm signaled her to brake. The man eased the boat's throttle to slide into the trailer. On shore, boaters bungeed propellers in place and snapped covers closed. Such was the dance of the homeward-bound boaters.

With only one boat left to come off the lake, I unplugged *Zella's* trailer lights and screwed the drain plug into place. Richard lowered his tailgate as my father always had for better visibility for backing into the lake. And then he stood, hands deep in pockets and no small amount of disgust written on his face, watching the mini dramas of day's end at the lake. When our turn came to launch, I climbed into *Zella*, and Richard handed me the keys.

"Put your life vest on," he said.

Launching *Zella* awakened a competence that had slumbered long in me. I did my part without any second-guessing or doubt. It was like finding my skin again. I could hear Dad reminding me to check the moor lines, so I did. And then the fenders. All was ship-shape.

Richard backed us in with deliberation, slowly lowering the trailer and boat into the water. When he stopped, I turned on the bilge blower and cranked the engine. *Zella* purred to life. My eyes burned with tears at the sound of her. Richard undid the winch hook and gave me a push. He raised a hand in farewell and turned unceremoniously toward his truck.

I steered *Zella's* bow toward the center of the lake and slid the throttle to a low growl. She responded like a cat being stroked. Once past the few paddleboards and into the deeper water, I pushed her to a roar. Her bow bounced over wakes. I kept one eye on the gauges. Oil pressure, fine. Tachometer, humming right along at 3000 rpm. Fuel gauge, full.

A wash of lake scents and spray covered my face. The deck pulsed under my feet. The sheer power of the engine set my bones to singing. I steered into the wakes of large boats and opened up the throttle across the smooth water. I swung wide of a rock outcrop hidden under the surface and headed for the dock.

Nicci and Alex welcomed me with waving arms and hoots.

NICCI AND I SAT on the deck, eating the ice cream and strawberries she'd brought home from the market. The treat hit my stomach with a thud. *Zella* sat suspended over the water in the boat garage, and, hopefully, Bimala slept a healing sleep in faraway Sundar Maut. My knees bounced, and I looked at my watch again. Dawn would arrive in Sundar Maut in two hours. My goal was to be there when the sun rose over the horizon.

Traveling with *Zella* presented one big mystery. I had no idea what would happen when my thirty-one minutes passed. Would I travel back to *Zella*, even if I was on *Zella*? In the best scenario I imagined, I would feel a mild jerk as I steered her toward the mainland. And that would be the end of my traveling. We would continue the journey to the coast together.

Or I could be pulled off *Zella*, only to land somewhere else. Where, I did not know.

Alex and I had decided that our landing places drew us with emotion. In that case, I could end up almost anywhere. Perhaps the church where Doug and I had married. Or the delivery room where Lauren was born. The Villa Syrene on Lake Como? That had been quite the night. The gym at East High School? Oh man, I hoped humiliation wasn't the right kind of emotion to draw me there. Landing anywhere but *Zella's* deck would strand Bimala and Pooja in the middle of the Arabian Sea.

Nicci threw her wadded napkin at me. "Mom, you're like a million miles away, and remember, you can't bullshit me."

No, I couldn't. "I have two friends—they're children really—in a horrific place. They have no one to help them, and one is very ill." The truth of those words overwhelmed me. The lake sparkled. The trees whispered above us. The mountains sheltered us within a comforting rim. What business did I have sitting there, eating ice cream? I stood. "I need to get packing."

"What the hell? Mother, what is this about? Sit down, tell me what's going on, please." So rare was an entreaty from Nicci that I obeyed.

Nicci leaned forward, patted my knee. "Where are these kids? How long will you be gone?"

"India. Actually, an island off the coast of India, about 125 miles west. I honestly don't know how long I'll be gone. There are logistical questions."

"India?" Alex and I shared a furtive glance that made Nicci frown. "How do you know these kids, Mom?"

In spite of my preoccupation with getting back to Bimala and Pooja, I drank in the softness of Nicci's face. This expression melted me every time, especially at bedtime when a very young

Nicci had begged for one more story. We'd sat on her bed, bolstered by a mountain of pillows, encased in the yellow light of her bedside lamp. Nicci had leaned into me, content. I needed that Nicci to hear and believe one more story.

"Do you remember the bedtime stories I told you about the traveling man?"

"The guy who traveled by touching a map? The one who looked like Grandpa? I loved those stories. I couldn't get to sleep afterward because I was imagining all the places I would travel if I had that magic. I can't tell you how many times I snuck down to the den in the middle of the night. I opened Dad's atlas and poked all the maps, wanting to find a place where I could disappear to."

My heart snagged. "You were so young."

"I fantasized about moving to Orlando. I figured I would have tons of friends if I lived across the street from the Magic Kingdom," she said wistfully.

Such gentle longing from Nicci warmed me. She had never spoken of fresh starts to me. Had she? Her honesty was an opened door I longed to walk through. But Bimala waited for me.

"Nicci, listen, this might be hard to swallow, but those weren't made-up stories. Your grandpa actually was the traveling man, and I was the little girl who waited for him in the barn."

Nicci stared, slack-jawed, speechless. I'd never seen her like that either.

I stood again. "There's more: I inherited his ability. I'm a traveler, too."

"Mom, this is getting weird."

"I would love to sit here and answer your questions, explain how traveling works, but my sick friend is waiting for me. She needs care. The island is twelve hours ahead of us, so it's almost morning, and there's lots to do to get ready. The thing is, to get her to the doctor, I'll be taking *Zella*. And that's where things get a little fuzzy. I've never traveled with *Zella* before. I'm not sure what will happen."

Nicci set her bowl down with a thud. "So now you're telling me *Zella* is a magic boat? Mom, are you alright?"

"I'm sorry to dump all of this on you, especially when I need to take off so soon. If I had the luxury of time to explain everything to you, I promise I would. As it is, Bimala is very ill. I'm her only hope."

"I've heard of shit like this happening to people."

"You have?"

"Sure. We did a psych rotation." Nicci's eyes glistened with tears. "Listen, Mom, you need to get checked out with a doctor real soon. There are things they can do. To help."

I should not have been surprised Nicci jumped to dementia to explain such a delusion, but I was disappointed. I didn't have the time to present an airtight case for traveling.

I donned a life vest and found Alex's map of Grand Lake under the mattress. I handed the binoculars to Nicci. "Do you remember that deep hole in the lake?" I said, pointing down the shoreline.

"The one in front of the Brownsons' cabin?"

"The Brownsons don't own it anymore, but yes. This is how traveling goes: I touch the map and then I will disappear before your eyes—and I should warn you that it's a little unnerving the first time around, and then you'll see me bobbing around out there." I pointed toward the lake where I intended to land. Like a pedestrian checking both ways for traffic, I scanned the lake for boats and jet skis.

"This is totally screwed up, Mom."

"Truly, now watch that spot."

I touched the map with Nicci's eyes trained on my face. My vision got fuzzy, and she stumbled backward with her hand over her mouth. "Mom?"

28

Nicci and I made a list of supplies for the trip to the mainland of India I would soon take—God willing—with Bimala and Pooja. She chewed on the end of the pencil as she drew her finger down the paper. "This is totally doable. We'll have this stuff ready by the time you get back."

I couldn't help myself. I threw my arms around her and squeezed her tight to my chest. Nicci went stiff before she softened. "Holy crap, Mother."

I held her at arm's length. "If you're going to make it in medicine ..."

"Yeah, I get it, clean up my mouth. Right."

THE SODDEN AIR OF Bimala's hut smelled of blood and sweat.

Pooja watched me with red, unblinking eyes from where she squatted at her mother's head. Bimala's lips bled where they had cracked at the corners. I pulled the girl to standing and held her head to my belly.

"I'm here to take care of your *mata*. Go cool yourself in the sea and wash your face. You'll feel much better. There's a sandwich for you in my pack, along with some fruit. Eat all of it, even if you're not hungry, and drink all of the water. When you're done, bring your *mata* more water."

The girl stepped away to look at Bimala and back to me. "*Mata* is close to the angels, is she not?"

Each breath escaped Bimala with a moan. "She's sleeping, which is good. Her body is working hard to fight a sickness." I clasped Pooja's hand to my heart. Could she feel its frantic rhythm? "We'll be taking her to the doctor soon." I turned her toward the door. "Now, go take care of yourself."

I felt Bimala's pulse below her jaw. Her heart raced and her eyelids twitched. She moaned from a deep place. Was this the sleep of the recovering or the sleep of the dying? I had to be careful about what I promised the child.

Only repeated calls of her name woke Bimala. Her eyelids stuck together, making square windows of her eyes. She needed water. I pulled her to sitting and struggled to arrange the pillows, now damp with sweat, to support her. It was early for more acetaminophen, but I poured two capsules into my hand. We could worry about her organs when we got her to a mainland hospital. I opened her mouth with my fingers, slipped in the pills, and poured water through her lips. After a few tries, she swallowed the tablets.

A sort of desperation sat on my shoulders. I fought against its weight to do what I could for Bimala. I removed her breast pads. Her breasts now lay flat against her chest, so I didn't bother replacing the binding. Her blood smelled sour in her flow pad.

Once she was clean, I sat between her and the pillows, straddling her with her back against my chest. I wanted to support her, to feel the life still in her. I tipped her head back and poured tiny sips of water into her mouth. The heat of her bled through my damp clothes.

"Bimala, I have a boat," I whispered in her ear, not sure she heard me. "I will be back today to get you and Pooja. Your prayers have been answered. You have to be ready. Bring only what you can carry."

"You will take only Pooja," she said through three shallow exhales.

I cradled her head in my arms, like an infant, to look into her eyes. "We will go together, all three of us," I said with as much confidence as I could muster. "The boat is big enough. I am not leaving you here."

She closed her eyes. "I can't."

"I'll carry you, Bimala. I'm stronger than I look. And Pooja will help me."

Her eyes opened to slits. "Be her mother."

"You are her mother. She doesn't need another."

"Promise me."

"I promise I will get you to a doctor." I dripped water down my finger between Bimala's lips. With the minutes ticking by, I left the hut to look for Pooja. I found her digging a long, narrow hole in the clearing where we had buried the young girl and Bimala's stillborn infant.

"What are you doing?" I said, ripping the shovel from her hands.

"*Mata* told me."

I dropped to my knees before the girl and took her hands in mine. "*Mata* has a fever. She's probably dehydrated."

Pooja frowned, but her gaze drilled me.

"The fever is drying her up," I said. "When people get like that, they say things that don't make sense. She's dreaming when she's awake. Do you understand?"

"She hears the angels sing. She says the song is beautiful to her ears."

I fought the urge to slap her. I stood, kicked sand back into the hole. "I'll hear no more of this. I'll be gone soon, but you must listen to me. You must put singing angels out of your mind. The sun will not set before I return, Pooja, and I'm bringing a boat. We'll take your mother to a hospital where they can help her. You are to sit with your mother. Wet your finger and let the drop fall into her mouth." I watched Pooja walk resolutely toward the hut, and I prayed that her mother would still be alive when she got there.

I landed on *Zella's* deck in my very own boat garage.

I PREPARED *ZELLA* FOR travel. If I left by three AM our time, we could reach the mainland of India before their midnight. There was no time to spare.

I opened the refrigerator and tossed cheese, apples, grapes, oranges, lunchmeat, condiments, and lettuce—and the ginger ale I'd forgotten on my last trip—into a cooler. We weren't exactly going on a picnic, but Bimala and Pooja needed their strength. Plus, I didn't love Indian food. Curry upset my stomach. I grabbed the energy bars Nicci had left on the counter, gathered life vests, tethered the rowboat to *Zella*, and attached the Bimini. Finally, I loaded the four fuel cans and secured them to cleats.

In my pack, I stashed the rupees I'd ordered from the bank, my passport, driver's license, and a debit card I hadn't tried to use yet. Would I need a change of clothes? I sat heavily on the futon. By traveling with my landing place—the lovely *Zella Francine*—I would mess with the order of things. There was a chance I would be stuck in India with no way to get home. I stuffed a couple of skirts and tops, along with a good pair of walking shoes, into the duffel and called the job done.

The doors of the boat garage opened to the lake. I stood on *Zella's* deck, riding the rocking motion of the lake. Only a waning crescent stood watch, so the sky sagged toward earth under the weight of the stars.

I double-checked the security of the fuel tanks. Was twenty gallons enough fuel? Sundar Maut lay 123.7 miles from the coast of India at Kaup Beach. *Zella* had a range of 114 miles, but we'd only measured her range on a lake. Theoretically, those numbers gave me plenty of breathing room. Ocean currents, wind, and swells could subtract miles from that number. I had no way to know. The extra fuel cans added a margin for safety, I hoped.

As for getting Bimala from the shore to the hospital, I counted on the rupees to buy our way. That was the extent of my plan.

I couldn't know how *Zella* would fare as a traveler. I rechecked the map of Sundar Maut. Landing on the shallow coral shelf of the lagoon would splinter the hull, so I'd drawn a red X where the water deepened to mark the most favorable landing place. Still, a landing was like cannonballing into water from a twenty-foot platform. The relatively flat bottom of the boat would absorb tremendous force.

In a perfect world, I would wait until the next Sundar Maut morning to start for the mainland and a hospital. That would give us nearly thirteen hours of daylight for travel. Daylight held fewer surprises, but Pooja's words about singing angels troubled me.

I counted off the hours: If I left now, I would arrive on Sundar Maut at 2:00 PM their time. Once there, I must row to shore, help Bimala to the lagoon and into the rowboat. The trickiest part would be hefting her onto *Zella*. I estimated twenty minutes. Just to be safe, I added ten minutes, which wasn't all that generous considering Bimala's condition. But I didn't have any more time to add.

I put a bottle of water in the cup holder by the captain's seat and applied a thick layer of lip balm, cleaned my sunglasses, and smeared a streak of titanium oxide over my nose and cheeks. I considered leaving a note for Nicci and Alex, but we'd talked about all they might face in my absence, and I'd already written three pages of instructions.

I was stalling.

I'D GOTTEN FAIRLY COMFORTABLE with the uncertainty of traveling to Sundar Maut, but never had the stakes for failure been greater. *Zella's* engine could fail. I may find lifting Bimala into the boat impossible. What if Shaitaan had chosen this very day to visit?

I gripped *Zella's* steering wheel with one hand—praying my

touch would bring her with me—and poised my pointer finger above the red X. "Here we go."

"Stop!"

Alex stood in the doorway. She rushed *Zella* and grasped the windshield. Her knuckles bleached from the effort. "You can't go without me, Grandma!" She put a foot on the gunwale to board. Dressed in shorts and a T-shirt, she carried the beach bag Tiffany had bought for her.

"I surely *can* and I *will* go without you. I have no idea what I'll find when I get there. Bimala may be too sick to travel. Shaitaan might be there." My throat tightened at the mention of his name. "Oh no, baby girl, you are staying here with your mother, where you belong. We talked about this."

"How will you get Bimala onto *Zella*? Moving from one boat to another is hard, and you said she's incredibly weak. How will you do it?"

I didn't have an answer for her.

"And what if *Zella* floats away from shore, or worse? She might come ashore, get stuck in the sand. How would you get her out? Wouldn't that be bad for the propeller? Grandpa got nervous whenever the rental boat got close to shore."

"Alex, *dearest*—"

"You need me! I can pull Bimala into the boat while you push. You know, Grandma, what I'm saying is true. This is a two-woman job. And I'm the only one in the world who can travel with you."

She was right, of course. The anchor wouldn't hold against the coral bottom. *Zella* could slip away with the current. If she did, I could swim to her, but the bigger problem was Bimala. She had to board *Zella* to travel to the mainland. That task did require two women. But Alex was a child, not a woman. The island exposed her to terrible danger. Landing near the dock and mooring *Zella* eliminated all those risks, but doing so was like knocking of Shaitaan's door.

She continued, and from her tone, she believed I was weakening. "I won't get off *Zella*. I'll keep her idling in the deeper water and help you pull Bimala on board. Grandpa let me drive the rental boat. I wasn't supposed to tell you, but I'm sure you can see how great it is that I can drive *Zella*. And, Grandma, I'll travel back to the boat garage after thirty-one minutes. There won't be time to get into trouble. If Shaitaan is there, I'll hide or jump into the water. I'm a real good swimmer."

I *was* weakening. "You *have* to stay in the boat."

Alex made to enter the boat.

"Wait!"

"Grandma, I'll be careful."

"I've never traveled with anything as big as *Zella*. The landing will be rough. I would rather you didn't travel with me. What if you fall out and get squished under the boat?"

Her eyes widened.

"Wait five minutes." I showed her the map. "Aim for this side of the X. And board *Zella* immediately. Start her how Grandpa showed you because I will already be on the island. Turn her to the east and stay there, only giving her enough throttle to keep her off the coral shelf and pointed in the right direction."

"I wish Mom were a traveler."

"If you're scared—"

"I'm not! You know Mom would love—you know—being with us."

I'd searched and failed over the years to find something Nicci and I could share. Traveling would have been perfect. "There's still a chance." I took a deep breath to calm my nerves and held the map with Alex. "Baby, if I don't come back to the boat by the time you depart, do not return to the island under any circumstances. I can take care of myself. Can you promise me you won't do anything heroic?"

Alex hesitated but finally nodded. I didn't feel good about

taking her with me, but I didn't like my chances of getting Bimala on the boat without her.

"I'll see you in a few minutes."

29

Zella landed in the turquoise waters with a cracking of wood. Her gunwales plunged under the surface, and water flooded over her sides before she popped onto the surface. The force of the landing knocked me off my feet. I lay stunned in water that covered my ears, coughing to fill my lungs with air. I rose to my hands and knees and stood. I'd landed as I'd hoped, about seventy-five yards off the shore. The rowboat was still tethered to *Zella's* stern. Upright. A miracle.

I waited. Listened. No glugging signaled a leak, and the water level remained constant. Still, I jumped into the water to inspect *Zella's* keel and hull. I wouldn't start a journey that couldn't be finished. I ran my hands along the keel—it remained straight and true, and the hull seemed solid, although my hand caught the sharp edge of a crack near the port bow. With steady baling, we should be okay. Such was my expert assessment of the situation.

The engine hummed to life when I turned the key, but the noise shot like a cannon in the stillness, so I shut her down. I dug the baling bucket out of the aft bench and left it floating on the deck. I prayed Alex would get the message.

A gray veil of rain fell some miles off, stirring up whitecaps in the deeper water. I strained against the wind as I rowed to shore.

Just as I tied the rowboat to a palm, I heard a splash. When I turned, I saw Alex rise from the sea, sputtering and wiping hair from her eyes. The girl didn't estimate time well, but she'd landed right on her mark. We exchanged waves, and I ran into the cover of the palms toward Bimala's hut.

Pooja squatted outside the doorway, her head in her arms. Sand encrusted her arms and feet. She looked up with red and swollen eyes as I stepped into the cooking yard. "I cannot move her, Angel Lady. I tried, but I could not move her."

I took her hands and pulled her to my chest. The girl was a rag doll. I brushed sand from her face and told her to go to the lagoon and wait for me there. She didn't move. "We're leaving as soon as I get your mother on the boat."

"I dug a grave for her, Angel Lady."

I forced my words around a hard knot in my throat. "Go now. I'll check her."

Bimala lay twisted with her arms reaching and empty, her head off the pillows, her eyes staring without seeing. I fell to my knees at her head, my hands poised over her chest. I knew without searching for a pulse that the time for helping had passed.

God. In. Heaven.

Her eyelids wouldn't stay closed. I swallowed down a sob and lifted her back onto her pallet. My hands ached for something to do, so I washed her face, hands, and feet. "I will take Pooja to a safe place. I heard about a safe house in Mumbai. She will grow up whole, Bimala. No one will own her."

Pooja had not gone to the lagoon as I'd told her. I found her stoking the cook fire. "Do you need to say goodbye?" I asked.

She shook her head without looking at me. I didn't blame her for thinking I'd failed her mother. I could have done more, pushed harder, insisted.

"Come." I led her through the trees to the lagoon. She stopped short when she saw *Zella* rocking on the waves. Alex had the boat positioned perfectly, the bow nosed toward the unseen mainland and the engine idling almost noiselessly. She straightened from her baling and waved. "That's my granddaughter, Alex," I told the girl.

Once I had Pooja safely aboard and stern instructions had been repeated to Alex not to return once she left for Grand Lake, I pulled Alex aside. "I have something else to do on shore. I'll only be gone a few minutes."

"Where's Bimala?"

If Alex knew Bimala was dead, she might eat up time with more questions. "I'll be right back." I climbed down the swim ladder to the rowboat. "I've lost track of time. Chances are I'll arrive back on *Zella* before long. If I'm not done, I'll have to return to the island but not for long." I dug into the water with the oars. "Sit together at the helm! I don't want to hit you when I arrive! And don't raise the Bimini!"

"I'M SORRY FOR THIS indignity, Bimala. You deserve so much better." I pulled her body toward the door by her hands. I'd never felt anything heavier. I stumbled but caught myself when I stepped into the soft sand under the trees. Her body left a channel in the sand. I kept expecting her to return my grip. Of course, she didn't.

The grave Pooja had dug proved much too shallow and short. I set to digging the hole big enough. The scritch of the shovel against the sand insisted I release my grief. It rose and pressed, grew hard and white, demanding release. *Not now. Not now. Not now.* I would drink that fire later.

I swooned. At first, I blamed the heat. My vision faded, the unseen arm hooked my waist, and pulled me to *Zella*. Alex held Pooja on her lap at the helm.

"Grandma, I only have five minutes until I go."

I looked to Pooja. "You've seen me travel, right? Alex is a traveler, too."

She looked to Alex with wide-eyed wonder. "A traveling angel?"

"She is here to help you," I said. "After she goes, I will return to you here. I won't be traveling anymore, only with you on *Zella*, and we will go to the mainland to find a safe place for you to live. Stay low and out of sight. No matter what you hear, stay out of sight." I scanned the horizon. Nothing but shades of blue. "Stay right here and wait for me. Understand?"

"Grandma—?"

"Bimala won't be going with us, Alex. I'll explain when I get home."

Alex's face crumpled.

"We must save our sorrow for later, sweetie. For as long as you're here, stay with Pooja. Remind her what she must do. I'm not sure how long I will be. Turn off the engine. We'll take our chances. We need to save fuel."

Pooja leaned over the starboard gunwale as I lowered myself into the water to swim ashore. "The Bible! Mata's Bible! We cannot leave without her Bible. She told me to take it, and I forgot."

THE SHOULDER I'D INJURED against the coral throbbed with each shovelful, and blisters rose on my hands. Looking into the shallow grave, my heart sagged under the weight of my failure. If I had gotten back to her sooner, or stolen a boat, or insisted that Cal watch me travel, would Bimala still be alive?

Yes she would.

I dragged Bimala into the grave, straightened her skirts, and adjusted the drape of fabric over her shoulder. Then I folded her hands over her chest and whispered a prayer as she would have insisted.

"God in heaven ... God in heaven ... God in heaven. Amen."

I leveled the sand and brushed the area with a palm frond to erase my footprints. There should be something more to memorialize a life. Perhaps delivering Pooja to Restoration House would do that. Only God could judge if that was enough.

I headed for *Zella*. Sweat flowed in rivulets down my face. As the blue sea became visible through the trees, I remembered Bimala's Bible and my promise to retrieve it. But I was so very tired.

What was my hurry? Pooja could return to shore with me, to honor her mother and rest for the journey ahead.

And yet.

And yet the clap of the palms grated, and the white sand stung my eyes. I'd dug yet another grave—the third!—and left Bimala to molder under the sand.

Find the Bible and get off this island of death.

I turned for the hut. The Bible lay where Bimala had always kept it on a table by her pallet. I wrapped my blistered palms in the bandages we'd used to bind Bimala's breasts and took one last look around the hut. I gathered leftover medical supplies—a bottle of acetaminophen, extra bandages, antibiotic cream—and stuffed them into the duffel draped across my chest.

I can only explain what I did next as habit. Each time I'd visited Sundar Maut, I checked the dock to be sure Shaitaan had not arrived and moored his boat there. When I looked this time, a sleek speedboat was indeed moored to the dock, rocking in the agitated water.

I dodged around the corner of the hut and pressed my back to the wall—out of sight of the speedboat and Shaitaan's hut. My heart pounded the breath right out of me, and I coughed noiselessly into my hand.

He's here!

But how had I not heard the speedboat arriving? Had I been too focused on burying Bimala? I couldn't afford to get that distracted again.

I peered around the corner. The speedboat was designed for open water, a cigar boat valued for its machismo and streamlined design. And its speed. We never saw such boats on Grand Lake. They were too noisy and created distressing wakes. *Zella*, on the other hand, was built for fishing and occasional water skiing. She could never outrun such a beast.

Someone—Shaitaan?—had snapped the boat's cover into place, which meant he planned to stay for a while. Had he noticed Bimala and Pooja were missing? The curtain over the door of his hut billowed in the breeze.

How many men were in there? *Oh God, only one. Please, only one.* Would they stay in the hut long enough for me to return to *Zella*, get her started, and then travel far enough toward the horizon to be out of sight?

Impossible.

I slipped into Bimala's hut. From her worktable, I took the knife I'd seen her use to cut vegetables. The blade was a good eight inches long. I tested its sharpness against my thumb and felt the sting of its blade. This would get the job done.

Outside, crouched behind the hut, I watched Shaitaan's door through a few breaths. When he didn't come out, I tightened my grip on the knife and ran across the narrow beach and onto the dock to his boat, pumping my arms and running on tiptoe, looking over my shoulder every few steps.

The knife sliced easily through the boat's fabric cover, and I climbed through the crescent-shaped slit. Not one breath of air stirred under the canvas. Tiny spots popped and sizzled in my vision. I would swelter if I stayed too long.

I snapped open the engine cover latches. A wave of heat rolled off the engine. I managed to lift the lid only six inches in the tight space. With my cheek to the deck's carpet, I swiped sweat from my face and waited for my eyes to adjust to the dim light. Although I listened for footsteps on the dock, I would not have heard an elephant stampede over my pounding heart.

I had two options for sabotaging the engine. I could cut the fuel line or remove the electrical line that came out of the distributor, a trick Dad had pulled on me numerous times when he suspected

I planned on taking *Zella* out with friends. Since the fuel line was wrapped in a stainless-steel mesh, I opted for the distributor thingamabob. I thanked Dad under my breath for—in his own way—teaching me how to disable a boat. In two tugs I held the line in my hand.

It wasn't enough to cripple Shaitaan's boat. I couldn't let him call in his goons to chase us to the mainland. I cut the radio's mic cord and crawled back out of the slit. I squatted on the dock behind the boat. The distributor cord made a soft plop when it hit the water.

Disabling his speedboat stranded Shaitaan on the island as Bimala and Pooja had been. I liked the irony of him marooned, rationing his water, and wondering if he had been completely forgotten. I congratulated myself on meting out an appropriate punishment without even trying.

I couldn't hide behind the boat forever. I counted down from five several times, before I took one final look toward Shaitaan's hut and ran toward shore. If I reached the cover of the forest, there would be no need to worry about Shaitaan catching me. But if he saw me ...

As I pushed off the dock and landed in sand, Shaitaan stepped from his hut, not five yards from me. I skidded to a stop, looked behind him. He was alone. I should have run. I should have told him to go to hell, then run for the lagoon and *Zella*. I should have done something—*anything*—and run, but my brain stuttered and popped. My feet sunk into the damp sand.

God in heaven!

Shaitaan moved toward me, one hand clenching his cane like a club, the other holding a satellite phone. He stopped when he eyed the knife in my hand.

"Who are you? What do you want?" he said, raising the cane.

This close, I saw the man for what he was—not huge. Not scaly or taloned. He stood only two or three inches taller than me. But he had killed three people—that I knew of. A child. An unborn baby. A mother who was also a child. The heat of my anger turned my heart to stone.

I fingered the handle of the knife. It would slice through the skin of a snake. I considered my target. His fat stomach for a slow death? Or straight through the heart?

He took a step closer, moving his gaze from the knife to my face. No fear registered in his eyes. I raised the knife and tightened my grip.

The cane hammered my arm, and the knife fell to the sand. He kicked the knife into the damp sand. His lips curled into a smug grin. My heart beat like a cornered rabbit as I rubbed my forearm.

"I have seen you here before. What do you want?"

Bimala had told me his rage fed on fear. I swallowed hard and lifted my chin. "I came to bury Bimala and your newborn son."

His eyes measured no reaction to the news of their deaths. "And what will you do now?" he said, flitting his gaze to where the knife had landed.

"I'm taking Pooja away from here."

"The girl belongs to me," he bellowed.

"I'm taking Pooja away from here," I said again, because I couldn't think of anything else to say. And it was the one thing I must do.

"You do see the impossibility of taking the girl anywhere, don't you? You are nothing but an old woman, and now you are injured. There is room, I am sure, for one more grave on the island."

Running to Pooja meant turning my back on Shaitaan, and he still held the cane and the satellite phone.

He looked behind me and down the long dock. The sourness of his flesh reached me.

"You are alone?" he said, flexing his grip on the cane.

I was more alone than I had ever been.

He lunged and brought the cane down on my bad shoulder

with a crack I felt down my spine. I fell to my knees, fighting for breath.

"You are an idiot! You thought you could come here and walk away with my property? You thought I would stand by and let you take her?"

My bad arm hung stunned at my side. "You are very good at using a stick to get young girls to do your bidding, but I am not a child." I struggled to my feet with a fistful of sand and threw it in his face.

As he coughed and sputtered, I dug in my feet and rammed his chest with my head. The impact sent another shock through my body. He toppled and landed on his back, dropping the satellite phone. I stumbled past him and grabbed it and ran for the lagoon and Pooja. I hoped the cane was more than an object of torture, that the man was truly disabled.

My thighs burned, but I ran. My lungs were coals, but I ran. I tripped over a fallen palm and scrambled to my feet. And ran.

Behind me, he yelled. "Woman!"

I ran for the blue through the trees.

"Woman!"

The rowboat waited for me on the shore, and *Zella* rocked gently in the waves. I pitched the phone into the rowboat and pushed the bow from the sandy shore. My fingers still tingled from Shaitaan's cane, but my arm did my bidding.

Pooja's head popped over *Zella's* gunwale. I gestured her to squat, and she obeyed. I was relieved not to see Alex. When the water neared my waist, I heaved myself into the rowboat, landing with my belly across the hot seat. Seated, I thrashed the oars wildly, missing the water completely with the first two strokes.

I heard my dad, *Bend into your stroke, Robin. Oars in water. Pull! Bend into it. Oars in the water. Pull!*

But the storm that had stirred the waters now pressed at my back, slapping small waves against the bow. I barely moved.

Pull. Pull. Pull.

Shaitaan's white shirt flashed through the trees. "Woman!"

Pull. Pull. Pull.

A razor of pain cut across my palms.

God in heaven!

The wind calmed. The palm fronds hung limp. The sea settled to glass. I made purchase with each stroke.

Shaitaan broke out of the trees. He raised a handgun and took aim. I stood in the small boat, holding the satellite phone over the water. "I've disabled your boat—"

"Liar!"

"—and the radio. There's no way off this island except this phone."

He waded into the water to his knees, the gun still aimed at my chest, only cab-hailing distance away.

"Is the girl on the boat?" he said with a nod toward *Zella.*

The rowboat rocked. I eyed the seat with longing. "Pooja is somewhere safe."

"She belongs to me!"

"She belongs only to God."

"Nonsense!" He waded closer. "She is mine!"

I sat slowly and held the satellite phone inches above the water. "If you drop the gun, I'll call someone to get you when I'm away from here."

"You are a fool! I don't need you or the phone." He lifted his chin to *Zella.* "I have your boat." The gun sounded—like a monstrous metallic cough—and a hot knife sliced my arm above the elbow. I dropped the phone into the water and collected the oars.

God in heaven!

Another cough and I prepared for more pain, but none came. Shaitaan held the gun with two hands. Another cough. A shot shuddered through the rowboat. I dug into the water with the oars—pulling, pulling, pulling.

A click. Another click and another. And another. Shaitaan muttered angrily, studying the gun and releasing the clip before he slapped it back into place.

Another report and I turned to the sound of cracking wood. A splintered hole gaped in *Zella's* hull, just where Pooja hid.

The rowboat's bow bumped *Zella*, and I clambered aboard. Pooja squatted like a cat on the starboard side—not the port, but I squatted before her and ran my hands over her body. "Are you all right?"

She slunk back into the corner, watchful. Unmoving.

I touched her shoulders. "Stay." And crawled to the helm. I had planned on towing the rowboat as insurance, but tying the line made me too vulnerable. I provided quite the target in my baggy white shorts.

The key turned. The engine sputtered and died. I adjusted the choke and tried again. She rumbled to life. I pushed the throttle forward and *Zella* leaped ahead, her bow bouncing over the small waves.

I turned to see Shaitaan siting the gun on me. I instinctively cowered, although I enjoyed no real cover. No report. No crack or splintering wood. He spiked the gun into the sand and waded to where I'd dropped the satellite phone.

"God in heaven."

I beckoned Pooja to my side and eased into the captain's chair.

"You are hurt," she said, nodding toward my arm.

My arm, the very same arm with the insulted shoulder and blow from Shaitaan's cane, burned like fire. Blood streamed over my elbow and dripped onto the deck. There would be time to fashion a bandage when we put more sea between us and Sundar Maut.

Over my shoulder, the island revealed none of its terror. The palms shimmied in the breeze. The lagoon's white sand glimmered. Turquoise water lapped the shore. And Shaitaan was no where to be seen. Perhaps he had another satellite phone or a longer-range gun.

Oh God.

I shook my head to clear my thoughts and checked the compass. The heading needed adjusting but only by a few degrees. I eased back on the throttle to save on fuel and lashed the steering wheel in place.

Pooja helped tie a bandage torn from a T-shirt because my shaking fingers wouldn't cooperate. I retook the helm with my good arm.

We had several hours of travel ahead of us, so I opened the cooler. Pooja's eyes widened at what I'd brought. I invited her to eat whatever she wanted, and she selected an orange and some grapes. I handed her a bottle of water. "Drink every last drop."

The immensity of all that blue and the hum of *Zella's* engine underscored my self-doubt. I regretted not holding onto the satellite phone. All good sailors valued a lifeline, and *Zella's* radio was old. I had no idea of its range. We'd only used *Zella* on Grand Lake, nothing as vast as the Arabian Sea. I set the radio to channel sixteen, the international distress channel, and hoped I didn't have to make a call.

And there was the beach landing, illuminated only by a weak moon, to make in the dark. I'd only made a beach landing once before—many years earlier—in Mexico in broad daylight. The night would hide obstacles in the shallows and lining up the bow to the shore would be nearly impossible.

Pooja settled in my lap, her head against my chest, closed her eyes, and fell asleep. The warmth of her body worked like a starting gun for my tears. I feared I would wake her, but she slept on as my tears flowed—for Bimala, the baby, and utter relief at being off that island.

The horizon lay undisturbed in every direction. Many miles

separated us from Shaitaan, but I couldn't stop watching for him. What if the satellite phone had been waterproof after all, or he had kept a spare distributor thingmabob in his hut? What would I do if I saw him gaining on us? I hadn't wet my pants yet that day. I could start with that.

Without land to orient our progress, my eyes flitted often to the compass, making course corrections with a nudge of the steering wheel. A mistake of only a few degrees could land us far from the intended destination. I lamented not begging to borrow Doug's GPS.

Zella seemed awfully small to be in such a big ocean. The swells loomed large. I eased back on the throttle even more and cut into the swells at an angle to ease the pounding against the cracked hull. We would definitely miss Kaup Beach.

When Pooja woke, she stood with her hands braced on the windshield and the wind blowing through her hair. The girl had just lost her mother, but she savored the rush of wind and the bouncing of *Zella*. She had never been off the island. Of course, the freedom was intoxicating.

Twice I stopped *Zella* to refill her tank and to check the water level in the engine compartment. While water sloshed inside, I couldn't be sure of its source—our odd landing or the cracked hull. I bailed what I could and continued.

I'd expected to see land much sooner, but only blue lay before me. Behind us, the sun slipped closer to the horizon. *Zella* sputtered, but the gauges looked good. I worried that the compass wasn't working but chided myself. The sun was at our back, clearly west, so we were headed east toward India.

I hefted the last fuel can onto the swim deck and added all but the last quarter to the tank. Three more inches of water filled the engine compartment. I considered baling but decided to race for the shore instead. I restarted *Zella* for the last push, or so I hoped.

Finally, the coast was a ribbon of green on the horizon. I

allowed myself to breathe easier. White sails bulged in the wind closer to shore, and we passed fishing boats lolling in the swells. I estimated we were about ten miles from land.

The sun flared and settled into the sea. Dusk deepened to blackness, and lights winked on up and down the coast. My skin vibrated with weariness and apprehension.

I eased *Zella* to a crawl as we approached the coast. By the light of a flashlight, I read the fuel gauge. It hovered near empty. The moon paused below the horizon but brightened the eastern sky, outlining a level coastal plain.

Zella idled beyond the breakers, where we waited for the full light of the moon to guide us ashore. When the slivered moon illuminated the white sand coast and the breakers' foam, we were much closer than I'd thought.

I pointed *Zella* toward the beach and pushed the throttle forward. Too little momentum and the waves could turn us parallel to the beach, a landing that could prove disastrous. To achieve a dry, solid landing, I needed enough push to stick *Zella's* bow into the sand, perfectly perpendicular to the breakers.

I asked *Zella* for more and she delivered. We rode a breaker to the shore and made purchase in the sand. Her bow lifted proudly in the moonlight. In the shadow of *Zella's* bow, I changed my clothes to look like a western tourist, not a castaway. Pooja held the flashlight while I shifted the contents of the duffels, jettisoning clothes Bimala had been meant to wear.

I settled Pooja in front of a hedge that would shield her from the view of houses lining the beach. The sand was soft for sleeping. "Wait here for me. Don't move," I said.

Back on *Zella*, I slid into the captain's chair and gripped the steering wheel. Beached on the sand, *Zella* no longer belonged to me. If asked, I couldn't explain her or my presence in India without drawing uncomfortable attention. If left stranded, someone would claim her as their own.

Now that she'd delivered us safely to the mainland, I could live with that eventuality. But what if I touched a map? Wouldn't I land on her deck again—among strangers? That was a risk I couldn't take.

"I wouldn't do this if it weren't absolutely necessary," I said to the night, thinking of my father.

On the swim deck, I loosened the last fuel can and unscrewed the cap, patting my skirt pocket for the matches. Fumes bit my nostrils as I tipped the can and poured the fuel onto the deck. The next bit proved tricky. The wind kept blowing out the matches.

I climbed back onto *Zella* and crawled along the gunwale, careful not to touch the gasoline-flooded deck. I found Dad's logbook in a compartment below the steering wheel. Shielded from the wind, the pages took flame. I threw the burning book toward the fuel-saturated deck as I dropped to the sand.

Whump!

Red and yellow flames shot up from *Zella*. I raced to where Pooja waited for me. We lay like two spoons in a drawer as *Zella* burned. A few curious people stepped onto the beach from the homes beyond the high-tide line. They nudged one another, shrugged, and turned back to their beds. I meant to watch *Zella* burn until the last ember glowed, but I sank into a deep, dreamless sleep.

The next morning, Pooja and I ate a breakfast of apples, cheese, and ginger ale. When finished, we brushed the fine sand from our clothes. A bruise bloomed angrily on my forearm, where Shaitaan had struck me with his cane. My shoulder was hot to my touch, but no fresh blood seeped through the bandage on my arm. All that remained of *Zella* was ash and the charred remnants of her frame.

Her destruction meant more than losing a boat. Had my traveling days gone up in smoke with the cedar of her deck and hull? Without her as my consistent destination, it was possible I wouldn't travel at all, or perhaps the powers that be would reassign a destination. Until I summoned the courage to test those hypotheses, I would avoid maps at all costs.

I pulled Pooja toward the concrete steps that rose to a busy street with glass-fronted stores, some recognizable by their designer names. Cars, mostly taxis, sped by. Opportunity and ambition determined their paths, certainly not traffic signals or right-of-way laws.

In an act of desperation, I stepped to the curb and raised my good arm. A taxi screeched to a halt not two inches from my toes. With Pooja seated beside me, I handed the driver the paper where I'd written the address of Restoration House, and the tires fought to find purchase on the sandy pavement as we dodged into traffic. I pulled Pooja into my side, to reassure her and to still my shaking hands.

She gaped at the world as people and cars and shops blurred past the window. Too fascinated by the sights of a city to notice our harrowing journey, she pressed her palms to the glass to take it all in.

I gripped the door handle until the blood squeezed from my knuckles. Soon, my hand cramped, so I followed Pooja's example: I fixed my gaze on the passing scene. The relics, the colonials, and the gleaming glass of Mumbai's new prosperity jarred my sense of place and reality.

I finally closed my eyes and rested my head on the back of the seat. The taxi accelerated, jerked right and left, and thudded through potholes. Horns honked. All of them. At once. All the time. The cacophony reminded me of greedy seagulls calling dibs on a lone herring. The taxi driver hit the steering wheel repeatedly and cursed in what I took to be Hindi.

A sudden turn pushed me into the door, and the taxi stopped abruptly. Before us, an iron gate blocked entrance to a deeply shaded garden with a saffron yellow house at the end of the drive.

Girls of all ages, dressed in saris, danced on the lawn or talked—heads together—in clusters. Even over the rattle of the taxi's engine, the girls' laughter reached me.

The sign on the gate read, "Restoration House."

30

After a brief interview to assure our health, we were welcomed to the house by the director, Mrs. Sita Chawla. Once I got Pooja settled into our dormitory room, I followed Mrs. Chawla back to her office and offered to provide more information.

She declined, saying, "We do things a little differently at Restoration House. First, we embrace, we welcome, we build trust. We accept each girl's starting place. Then, when the time is right, we talk. There isn't too much we haven't heard, so we have learned to love first, before the words."

I released a long-held breath.

"I will send the nurse to look at your arm," Mrs. Chawla said and bent to kiss Pooja's forehead.

For the first three days, Pooja and I rose and ate breakfast in a room alive with chatting girls. We sat at a long table with the residents but remained separate. We were watchers. After a breakfast of *roti*—India's version of the pancake—and roasted veggies, the youngest girls headed off for school in the far wing of the house. Pooja and I settled under a bahava tree in the courtyard, a wide, paved yard where the dramas of Restoration House unfolded.

On their breaks from schoolbooks, the younger girls ran into the courtyard. They pushed each other in the swings and flew down the slide. They were followed by the girls teetering on either side of adolescence. The long-legged girls jumped rope and whispered secrets. Those whose saris rose over budding breasts braided one another's hair in the shade of the tree. They reminded me of the sparrows that roosted in the cottonwood trees at home, chitting and chirping raucously when something struck them as funny.

Next, a mixed-aged group filtered in with a boom box of enviable proportions. These were the dancers. I recited a prayer after the first day that they would skip dancing to the traditional Indian music—such disjointed melodies—and go straight to the hymn of the day. My prayers were not answered. Each dancer stepped into the center to perform for the others. Only then did they switch out the CD for something more melodious and familiar to my ears.

On the fourth day, Pooja sat on my lap and rested her head on my shoulder, watching without wanting to be seen. By the time we returned to the dining room for the midday meal, the shoulder clobbered on Sundar Maut complained hotly, and my clothes were damp from our combined sweat.

After lunch, when the sun drilled the courtyard, girls in their late teens swept the pavement before laying out lengths of cloth they'd dyed and block printed, creating runways of red and blue and yellow. All the while talking and laughing. This wasn't what I'd expected of Restoration House. Not the joy, anyway.

When my stomach gurgled over the scents of our evening meal wafting from the kitchen, about fifty girls filled the courtyard. Dressed in white pajamas—and yes, I know there is a proper term for martial arts garb—they formed straight lines and, miracle of miracles, they wiped the smiles from their faces and stopped talking.

The participants ranged in age from Kindergarten to early college. They copied the precise and bold movements of their black-belted teacher, filling their lungs and shouting with each pose. At first, Pooja jumped and buried her face in my neck. Then, she stood beside me, watching. Always watching.

A girl about Pooja's age, took her by the hand and pulled her gently to join the exercises. "Come," she said. And Pooja followed. The girl with a braid down her back coached Pooja through the poses, encouraging her to say her words with power. At the end of the lesson, the two girls held hands and walked to dinner.

Bimala would have loved to see her daughter connecting with the outside world. The thought was a knife and a balm. Bimala should have been sitting with me, under the tree, watching Pooja step from fear to friendship.

Mrs. Chawla pulled a plastic lawn chair close to mine and sat. Beyond her initial welcome and invitation to stay, I hadn't talked with her beyond salutations in the halls, where she moved with efficient grace in her royal blue sari and pearls.

She watched as the two girls disappeared into the school. "This is the moment I live for—when a girl steps from the shadows into the light. This is only a first step, but now she has a friend to walk with her."

Since arriving at Restoration House, I'd worried that Mrs. Chawla would decide that a woman and a girl, arriving at her gate with stories of a tiny island and a cruel master would, in the end, strike her as improbable. And we would be escorted back to the gate and kindly asked to leave. I could not let that happen to Pooja.

"Mrs. Chawla, what must I do to arrange Pooja's stay here? Is there a fee? Are there papers to fill out? She has nowhere else to go."

She flipped a dismissive hand. "We are supported by benefactors who have charged us to welcome girls with open arms. Funds are always a concern for me, but never for the girls. Yes, there are some administrative duties to look after but nothing urgent. Pooja is most welcome to join us and stay as long as she needs us."

I blinked against the burn of tears. "She's seen a lot for a girl her age."

Mrs. Chawla nodded. We sat in what passed for silence at Restoration House. Even though the courtyard had emptied of all but the two of us, the chatter and laughter of the girls drifted on the weighted air of the coming evening.

She sat with fingers laced over her matronly middle, looking into a far distance. Whatever she saw there brought a hint of a smile to her lips. She had to know that I was studying her, but she remained content to shelter in her thoughts.

She wore her gray-streaked hair in a demure bun that exposed her broad forehead. As women do, I looked for evidence of her age. Her skin retained the strength of youth—both taut and smooth— but a pucker of skin at the base of her neck told me she was also in her fifties, a sister in chronology. The neck doesn't lie.

Our eyes met, and this time I smiled.

She said, "I heard from our team in the States this morning. A man I know on the rescue team vouched for you. It seems you have a reputation for caring."

She had to mean Cal. "I'm sure Mr. Branigan doesn't know quite what to think about me."

"Women with power and passion always confound men, is that not so?"

How much had he told her? "I wouldn't want you to overrate my abilities."

"You have loving hands, Robin. Pooja was deeply wounded and at a loss when you arrived. You've provided a safe place for her to observe the world, and to decide if she wants to take part. From what I have seen, I would say your abilities are extraordinary. I would also wager that your abilities are the fruit of pain." She studied me with knowing eyes. "Am I correct in this?"

"Yes." To say more, to lay out the story of Doug's betrayal seemed trite next to what the girls of Restoration House had suffered.

"And so it is that not everyone in captivity wears chains. The heart is a cruel jailer." Mrs. Chawla raised her eyebrows as if considering her own wisdom.

A pair of the horrible, rasping birds I'd come to know on Sundar Maut created a ruckus in the branches above, and a shower of leaves fell on us when the birds took wing. Mrs. Chawla looked into the branches and smiled to herself and then settled her gaze back on me.

"Mr. Branigan has talked to the American Embassy here in Mumbai," she said. "He says it would be best if you could find a way to lose your passport and apply for a new one. That is the only way for you to get your passport stamped with an exit visa to return to your home. You should know that the men in immigration are very partial to their stamps for coming *and* going. Do you understand?"

She shifted her gaze to the dining room. "Mr. Branigan also warned against asking too many questions of you. Fortunately, my work here has prepared me to accept what is past and move toward what is better, so I'm agreeable to this limitation."

She patted my knee. "It is my experience, Robin, that rushing into matters of immigration and passports can only bring headaches. I hope you know that you are welcome to stay as long as you like. You could be a great benefit to the girls. Tell me, what sort of job experience do you have?"

I told her about the plumbing supply business and the work I did there to keep it afloat during the recession.

She beamed. "Oh my goodness, this is fabulous news. The girls need bookkeeping fundamentals for their businesses."

She expected me to stay? "I haven't talked to my family since I arrived. I'm sure they're terribly—"

"I assumed ... I'm so sorry. You should call them right now." She slipped her arm through mine, and we stood together. I must have stiffened at her touch because she said, "We do a lot of touching at Restoration House. The girls have been emotionally and physically disconnected from caring for a long time." She tilted her head toward the door where Pooja had disappeared, and we walked arm in arm.

"Each year, four hundred—sometimes five hundred—girls come to Restoration House. We don't have the funds, the staffing, or the time to do clinical work with the girls. But we have love. We love the girls as God the Father loves the girls. He doesn't see a damaged person. He only sees His creation. He is totally enthralled by each girl's beauty. Every one of these girls is a treasured member of His royal household, just as you are."

I stopped, stunned by her words. "I don't know about that."

"Robin, you must stay at Restoration House until you believe this of your Father and yourself. Will you?"

I wasn't comfortable expecting anything for myself. "I will stay to help Pooja settle in."

"All kinds of things can happen by then."

31

"What the hell, Mom? Why haven't you called? We've been worried sick about you. Are you off that terrible island? I nearly had to tie Alex to a chair to keep her from returning to you. I've burned the map in the barbeque."

"I'm sorry for worrying you. A lot has happened, Nicci. But I'm okay. Really."

"What happened? When are you coming home?"

Mrs. Chawla sat on the other side of her desk, listening without looking like she was listening.

"Nicci, I'm using someone's phone. I can't talk long."

Mrs. Chawla raised her gaze to mine. She whispered, "Take the time you need. I have to check on the girls in the workshop. Simply close the door when you're finished."

I told Nicci the whole grim story of Bimala and finally coming face to face with Shaitaan.

"Holy shit, Mom. He could have killed you."

He almost did.

She raced on. "So, what's next? How do you get home? *When do you come home?*"

Leave it to Nicci to ask the impossible questions. When I laid out the hurdles that needed clearing with the immigration office, she surprised me with her suggestion. "I know you worry about me, and I've given you pretty good reason to mistrust me when it comes to Alex, but maybe this is a chance—without you here to rescue me. It's time to get my shit together.

"I've put some applications in around the county. One office seemed pretty interested. They said they would call within a few days to set up an interview." She inhaled deeply. "Mom, don't worry about us, please. I can do this. Alex is good and so am I. Besides, your friend Carolyn stops by every day. She says she's worried about you, but she's checking on me and Alex. I'm good with that. You're doing something pretty amazing there. You should see it through."

In all of our days as mother and daughter, Nicci had never asked me for room to succeed at being a grown up. Tears stung my eyes. "I believe in you, Nicci."

I WAS NEVER QUITE alone at Restoration House. I slept on the lower bunk in a room with twenty girls about Pooja's age. She made a pallet on the floor beside my bed, and most nights crawled under the cotton blanket to join me, her heart beating against my back, her arm draped over mine. The bathroom was a communal affair, like I'd shared with a floor of girls in college, only much smaller.

Even after class, when I sat with a cup of Darjeeling tea in front of the air conditioner, grading the girls' classwork, the girls' voices rang through the halls. But more insistent than their voices were their hammers, pounding silver to make lighter-than-air earrings and their saws rasping through gold to make pendants as they trained as metalsmiths. Always, there was cacophonous music and laughter.

The days collected like pennies in a dish that became weeks that gathered into months. Today, in the bookkeeping class, I taught the girls how to determine the cost of goods sold. I worked with an interpreter—one of the older girls—but most of the girls spoke passable English.

The girls fidgeted in their seats. They preferred being in their workshops, making gold and silver jewelry to sell on the Internet, but most saw the value of tracking their income and expenditures. If their attention wandered, we danced the Macarena, truly my most valued contribution to their education.

"Mrs. Angel?"

I looked up from papers to find Ahana, half in and half out of the classroom door.

I stood, beckoned her closer. "I'm so happy to see you." I pushed two chairs together and directed her to sit next to me. "How was your day?"

She smoothed the fabric of her skirt, adjusted the pleats of her *pallu*, and pulled an errant thread from her sleeve. I hadn't seen her smile in the weeks since she arrived at Restoration House. Her face, still young and plump, resisted the light. Espresso eyes never rested. Her right eyebrow had been plucked bare except for a few strands at the bridge of her nose.

I captured her hand, bent into her gaze, and willed love to reach her through my touch. "Ahana, I've been waiting for you to come."

Her eyes widened.

"This is the moment I live for—when a girl trusts me enough to pay a visit." She frowned, and I worried that I had pulled the curtain back too far. In the early days of their stay at the house, the girls preferred to remain hidden. "Why have you come to me today?"

"I do not understand the lesson you taught on costing goods."

I flipped a wrist at her concern. "Sometimes, when girls first arrive, the numbers don't behave themselves. I want you to know, there's no hurry to learn bookkeeping. Let's take our time, shall we?"

She pulled at what remained of her eyebrow.

I stilled her hand with a touch, and she released her brow. "Ahana, it takes time to feel safe, even at Restoration House. Your precious, beautiful brain is still busy looking for trouble. Your eyes flit to every corner and look under every desk, even now." She lowered her head. I rubbed small circles on her shoulder. "Darling girl, you've had to be vigilant for a long time, and it's very good that you were. But soon—maybe in a few days or a week, maybe longer, but not too long, I promise—your heartbeat will slow, your breaths will come easier, and the numbers will behave themselves."

"They told me I'm stupid."

"Really? That's odd because I don't see a stupid girl when I look at you. I see someone wondrous. I see a girl who has survived what has killed others. I see strength in you that will help you achieve your dreams." I was parroting what I'd heard Mrs. Chawla and the other aunties say. I hoped Ahana believed me.

Her eyes welled with tears, and I knew she had finally heard me. I took her hands in mine. "It's okay, for now, that you don't see the same girl I see. It takes faith to see ourselves as *Bapa* God sees us, and faith is something that grows over time. Until you have the faith you need, I will believe for you. I don't have as much experience as Mrs. Chawla, but I've been watching her and learning. We'll learn together, all right?"

"Can I do the assignment again, please, Mrs. Angel?"

Or maybe she hadn't heard me. "The numbers can wait, *betee*. Your new assignment is to spend as much time as possible with the other girls."

Ahana hugged herself and chewed on her lip. Clearly, the thought of joining strangers—even girls who shared her experiences—terrified her.

I'd listened in when Mrs. Chawla talked to girls who were hesitant to join in. She never allowed their excuses or their fear to hold them back. She found the strength in each girl and built on that. So much of living by faith, she'd told me, was to see what was possible long before what we hope for happens.

I draped an arm around Ahana's shoulders and pulled her

close. "Coming to me about your schoolwork shows that you are a determined young woman. And determination helps us make friends, something infinitely more important than the cost of goods sold."

We walked to the dining room, where the tables had been pushed to the walls and Jackson Five music played at an ear-splitting level. The roomful of girls sang along and danced. I was tempted to join them.

I leaned in to whisper into Ahana's ear, "It's good to stand back and watch but only for a short while. I promise there is a girl more uncomfortable than you in this room. Do you see her?"

She surveyed the room, looking intently at the faces of each girl. She lifted a hesitant finger toward a girl pressed into a corner, watching with eyes wide with apprehension. "That girl? She looks like she's going to be sick. Do I look like that?"

I lied. "Absolutely not."

Pooja stood before us, hands on hips, eyes drilling me. "Mrs. Angel, we're going to be late."

I frowned at the clock. "She's not coming tonight. This is—"

"This is the first Wednesday of the month. Alex *is* coming. We have to go. Now." She leveled her gaze. "I have called for the taxi."

IN THE BACK OF the taxi, I closed my eyes. Pooja slipped her hand in mine and patted my knee. "It will be all right, Mrs. Angel Lady. Keep your eyes closed. I will tell you when we get there."

I measured our progress toward Marve Beach—where we would catch a ferry to Manori Beach—by the scents and sounds of the streets. The curry that hung on the air started my stomach gurgling as we sped down Jigamata Street. On Aarey Road the human scents of waste and decay assaulted me, so I breathed through my mouth. I opened one eye to confirm that we'd stopped for a traffic light—a miracle!—beside a cow, chewing her cud at the curb.

We arrived at Marve Beach, and I paid the driver, only to be pressed by the crowd to the Manori Beach ferry, the cleanest and safest beach in Mumbai, which wasn't saying as much as I wished it did.

We stood shoulder to shoulder with about fifty people on the ferry as it lumbered its way across the mouth of Manori Creek, coughing and sputtering. We disembarked ten long minutes later on a sagging gangplank onto saturated sand. Pooja hailed a *tuk-tuk* for the last leg of our journey to the shore.

We paused in the dry sand to savor our safe arrival at Manori Beach. Across the Gorai Creek, the Global Vipassana Pagoda glinted the setting sun off its golden spire. The scene quieted my breathing, and I rolled my shoulders to loosen the tension stored there.

"Should we not hurry?" Pooja asked, tugging on my hand. We trudged hand in hand through the sand to the northern end of the crescent-shaped beach. I'd picked this beach because no rocks hidden by the surf would turn Alex's arrival into a catastrophe.

The sun had just dipped its toes into the sea and slipped wordlessly into the deep. A heathered haze rose from the horizon and graduated to pink and gold. I sat in the sand with my forehead to my knees and prayed: *Lord, give darling Alex a safe landing, and banish all the bacteria from the Arabian Sea. Thank you and amen.*

Pooja watched expectantly where the waves covered her feet with its every sigh. When a horse-drawn cart passed us, she returned to me. "The good Father will answer your prayers, Mrs. Angel Lady."

I squeezed her hand for knowing me so well and for the faith she loaned me regularly. We sat hip to hip in the white sand, watching the beach fill with couples and groups of walkers hoping to be cooled by the offshore breeze.

I hadn't wanted Alex to visit me in Mumbai, but she'd raised arguments and evidence against all my concerns until I finally relented. That girl was persistent and a little too smart.

Choosing the perfect beach in Mumbai for Alex's arrival had been an exercise in frustration. Pollution is a serious problem along the city's shores, and the currents of the west coast are treacherous. Her arrival place also required enough busyness to cover her landing but not so busy that she would land on someone. Manori Beach, while not perfect, came closest to meeting these requirements. I texted Alex. "Come now."

BY THE TIME ALEX swam to shore, dried off, and gargled with the hydrogen peroxide I'd brought, we had little more than sixteen minutes left in our visit. We shared a towel, facing the fading colors of twilight over the sea. Pooja collected sticks and pieces of shells to decorate the sandcastles she liked to build. I sometimes forgot how young she was.

"Tell me everything," I said, taking Alex in. She'd cut her long hair to shoulder length and added bangs. "You've cut your hair."

"A little incident in chem lab," she said, rolling her eyes. "My lab partner is forbidden to use a Bunsen burner for the rest of the year, which is totally okay with me."

"Are you all right?"

"Grandma, I'm okay." She dug in her pack and pulled out an envelope and handed it over. "You should see the changes Gloria's made to the shop. It's a totally different place. She says business has been much better with the salon close to Main Street." Alex combed her wet bangs into place with her fingers. "She talked me into bangs, and I really like them."

I peeked in the envelope. I didn't have to count the money. Gloria was Johnny-on-the-spot when it came to paying the rent. Making income through rental property seemed like cheating, especially since Carolyn was the one Gloria called about clogged drains and invading rodents.

I hadn't gotten used to the idea of The Traveling Man now

being Gloria's Glory Station Off Main. Dad's maps had, however, found a good home at the Where's Waldo Map Company—a funky shop in Old Colorado City. I knew we'd found the right buyer when the owner told me he'd been one of Dad's students.

"Alex, you won't have to visit anymore." I waggled the envelope. "This will get me home."

"But you love working with the girls."

"You're right, I do, and I'll come back, but only when the time is right." A couple walked into earshot, so I tucked the envelope into a zippered pocket of my tote. Once the man and woman passed, I said, "I can't say that I love India. Mumbai is like an anthill. But I've come to love the girls. I've learned more from them than I could ever teach them."

Looking into Alex's fresh and expectant face, I was overcome with love for the girl. I lifted her hand to my lips. "I've really missed you. Seeing you makes me incredibly homesick. I can't wait to get home to you and Nicci."

Alex's face turned unreadable, and I feared my return to Grand Lake might be an intrusion. I tried to reassure her. "I promise not to bug you too much. Cal has asked me to help him with fundraising for Restoration House. He wants me to talk about the girls I've met and how their lives have changed. I'll be traveling to—"

Alex's eyes widened.

"Not like that. I'll buy a ticket, pack a bag, and board a plane, just like everyone else—present company excluded. We're heading to an event in Santa Barbara next month."

"You'll be great."

"I'll cry like a baby, and you know it."

"That only shows you care, and that's a good thing."

I hated to think about blubbering in front of an audience of bejeweled and be-jangled donors. My stomach tied itself in a knot. "Alex, you've been amazing. Thank you for collecting the rent from

Gloria. With school and everything else—well, you've really stepped up. But it's time for you to go back to being fifteen-year-old wonderful you. My exit visa should come through any day, and then I'll head home. I can take care of the stuff you've had to shoulder."

"I like going to Gloria's. She plays with my hair. You should have seen the purple extension she gave me. Besides, Mom gives me a ride, and then we go out to dinner."

I had to ask. "How is your mother?"

Her face lit from within. "She's doing good. She's on a new medication."

Nicci had been on and off many medications, swearing the last time she'd stopped taking a drug that she would never do that to herself again. "She is?"

"Yeah, she had a hard time going from her old drug to the new one, but things have gotten better. She hasn't missed one day of work, and they put her on permanent status. She's stoked about that."

"Alex ..."

"I know, Grandma. I know she'll probably get tired of something or another and stop taking the drug, but she's good now. So good that she painted the Lakeview Room this really awful color. It looks like pond scum. You're going to hate it. It's gross."

Alex told me about her first dance, emphasizing she didn't go with a boy but with a group of girlfriends. The whole thing, in her estimation, was lame and awkward until the music started, and then they danced as a group and had a great time.

She pulled another envelope out of her pack.

"What's this?"

"Carolyn wrote you a letter. She's thinking of moving to Colorado Springs to be closer to her daughter and grandkids. At least, that's what she said yesterday. Like, one day she'll be all excited and talk about the fun she'll have being closer to her family, and the next day she looks like her cat died." Alex handed the letter over. "She probably wants some advice. Personally, I think she should go. I mean, you aren't in Grand Lake much anymore, and her husband has these new signs everywhere—they're totally awful. Why shouldn't she give herself a fresh start?"

The idea of Carolyn leaving Grand Lake used to terrorize me. Now, thinking of her taking a chance sparked hope. Carolyn deserved a fresh start and so much more.

My watch sounded a five-minute warning. "We haven't much time." I pulled a greasy paper bag from my tote.

"*Gulab jamun!*" Alex popped one of the deep-fried balls into her mouth. "I don't have to share these with Mom, do I?"

"I got her something, too." I helped Alex pack up her treats and the pair of earrings Ahana had made for Nicci.

"Have you tried traveling yet?" she said.

"No, not yet. Soon. Maybe when I get home."

"You know, don't you, that you'll probably land at home? I mean, the cabin has to be a strong emotional pull for you, right? Then you wouldn't have to wait for a visa or spend the money on a plane ticket."

"I'll think about it."

I held her tight, breathing in the sea that clung to her hair, until she softened and left my arms empty.

THERE WAS NOTHING MAGICAL about flying a commercial airline from Mumbai to Denver. Absolutely nothing.

It took two weeks in Grand Lake before I started feeling human again. Eventually, I woke with the sun as alert as an owl and hungry for curry.

Alex sacrificed her privacy to let me sleep in the Pollywog Room, which she had decorated with—what else?—frogs! I slept under Monet's Water Lilies and Kermit ogled me from Alex's nightstand. She slept on the futon and left the cabin with Nicci before the sun came up for school and work. Most mornings, they moved about the cabin with such precision and stealth that I didn't wake up ... until the door clicked closed behind them.

I sat in the wicker chair by the window, the wood-burning stove freshly stoked, with a cup of Darjeeling tea. The sky above Green Mountain glowed pink and orange as winter's reluctant sun inched skyward. A herd of elk had bedded down on the snowy lake and left only their tracks to mark the spot. Steam from my tea warmed my face as I looked around the cabin. I pulled the afghan to my chin.

The cabin smelled of paint from Nicci's fevered attempts to update the place. The paneling was now white, and she'd covered the futon with a French-blue coverlet. When she'd told me she'd painted, I braced myself for something more dramatic, something closer to black. The lighter walls, however, brightened the place in a convenience-store-at-midnight sort of way.

All woodsy kitsch had been eradicated and replaced with art posters of still lifes and bucolic scenes. Evidently, she'd bought a gallon of red paint. The furniture looked familiar but altered. The affect wasn't quite a French chateau, but it wasn't angry Nicci either. I liked it.

Was this home?

I'd called Mrs. Chawla three times and talked to Pooja. Hearing the girl's voice soothed me. I wanted to call several times a day but knew she needed to attend to her studies and get used to my absence. At night, I dreamed of bahava trees and billowing fabrics and the tinny report of hammers against metal. When a horn honked, I smiled. Ahana danced in my daydreams, and I fretted over Jiya's progress in bookkeeping class without help with her sums. I hummed Jackson Five tunes as I worked around the cabin.

It would be months—possibly a year—before I returned to Restoration House. The prospect deflated my heart. All I needed to do was touch a map for a short visit. I could arrange with Pooja and Mrs. Chawla to meet me at Manori Beach. But oh, the difficulty of explaining to Mrs. Chawla how I traveled.

Difficult, yes, but not impossible. Knowing Mrs. Chawla, she would allow a skeptical smile but bid me to prove myself, which I could do easily enough. But where would I land on my return? *Zella* was nothing but ash washed into a sandy beach. I supposed I could land among the ashes. But perhaps not. I asked myself frequently: What binds me emotionally? What in this old world holds my heart? The cabin with its disquieting white walls and myriad frogs?

I didn't think so. My daughter and granddaughter owned my heart, but they weren't places.

Alex and I sat at the dining table. She chewed her pencil over math problems. I worked at shortening my first fundraising talk by fifteen minutes. Maybe if I talked faster?

She interrupted my thoughts. "Grandma, I'm sorta surprised you haven't tried to travel yet. I can tell you really miss Pooja."

There was a sadness in her eyes.

"You'll return right here, won't you?" she pressed.

"I might not."

Surprise and knowing flashed in her eyes.

"I could get stuck in India again," I said.

"Would that be so terrible?"

No, returning to Restoration House would not be terrible. What I didn't bring up with Alex was the possibility that I could get stuck in the Sea of Cortez on a test flight. And in that eventuality, if I didn't land close enough to the coast, I might find myself in a watery grave.

Right or wrong, that was a risk I was willing to take.

But I had something to do first.

SALLY SAT IN STATUE-LIKE stillness, looking out the window from a chair by the fire. What did she see? After our recent snow, Shadow Mountain Lake was a table of white under a steely sky that robbed the scene of color. Deer tracks in the snow crisscrossed her yard. Perhaps she waited for their return.

Sally wore a hand-knitted sweater of exuberant pink, the one blast of color. I'd seen her wear it in the chill of an alpine morning, but that day the sweater slumped off one shoulder. Her usual sleek bob was now broom blunt and held back from her face with a barrette.

Richard spoke softly as we watched her. "She's taken a turn, I'm afraid. I was warned to expect the anger, but nothing could have prepared me, not for this. She's here but not here."

"I don't want to upset her," I said. "Maybe I should go?"

"It isn't you. And I've been assured it isn't me either, although it sure seems like it is me doing the vast majority of the aggravating around here." He shook his head, sighed. "She's not the person I've known and loved. She seems afraid most of the time. I suppose that would make me angry, too."

Sally turned to us as if she'd just heard us talking, but her eyes didn't focus. I sat with her, holding her hand, and telling her about the girls of Restoration House until the day dimmed and the chill reached us through the window. I could have talked longer but talking about Restoration House only made me homesick. I patted her hand and rose.

Just as I stepped from the living room into the foyer, Sally called out, "Robin!"

She'd never called me by my given name before. "Sally," I said, as I sat knee to knee with her and took her hands again. "How are you?" Her eyes met mine and she smiled.

"You've been away a terribly long time, my dear," she said and squeezed my hands.

"I *have* been gone a long time. I'm sorry."

"Oh, well, I don't see what you have to be sorry about. Those girls are depending on you."

She'd heard?

"Besides, dear, I've been doing quite a lot of traveling, too."

"Is that so? Where are you going?"

She started to speak, stopped, frowned. "I'm not really sure, but I seem to be going farther and farther away each time. Richard isn't very happy when I get back, and I'm sorry for that, but I can't seem to stay put."

"He worries about you, that's all. You know Richard."

She nodded. "Richard takes very good care of me."

"Sally, he's concerned that you're afraid. Are you traveling to scary places?"

"Heaven's no. I only go to familiar places. I can't seem to remember where just now. I would like Richard to go with me, but he always seems too busy. He absolutely must have a project going at all times. He's been that way since the day we married. I can't expect him to change now. No, I'll do my traveling alone and come home to him whenever I can."

Later, on the front porch, Richard ran his hands through his hair. His eyes glistened when he lifted his gaze to mine. "Thanks for letting me know. I hated the idea of her stumbling around in darkness. Sally isn't fond of the dark. She insists on a nightlight."

"You're doing a very good job with her."

"Am I? I've never been so tired. She wakes every couple of hours. She's hungry, wants a sandwich. We're up an hour or more. She asks me to light a fire."

"Are you sleeping at all?"

"That's why I sit her by the window. The doc says the sunlight might reset her clock, so she'll sleep better at night."

"Richard ...?"

"Yes, you're right. It's time to bring in some help. The kids are saying so, too. Just at night, you understand. Just at night. The days aren't so bad. Besides, Sally likes her privacy."

"What would your Sally, the real Sally, say about getting the help you need?"

"She would be appalled that it took me so long to make the call."

"Let her take care of you this way, Richard. Promise you'll call?"

"I have a social worker's business card by the phone."

"First thing in the morning?"

"You sound like one of my kids."

I wrapped my arms around him. His shoulder blades rose hard under my hands. "And eat more donuts, that's an order."

WITH NICCI AND ALEX as my ground crew, I prepared to test my travel skills—if, indeed, I could still travel. Nicci insisted on preparing the enlarged map of the Sea of Cortez, so I wouldn't touch the map and travel off prematurely or land too far from shore.

Since I'd floated there many times on my way to Doug's garage—I groaned at the memory—the waters off Puertecito were familiar. Most importantly, this destination required only a brief stay. After only 5.5476 minutes, I would return ... somewhere. Alex filled a bag with oyster crackers.

I double-checked my skirt's zippered pockets for what I would need for the possibility of landing someplace besides the cabin. I had my passport, Colorado driver's license, a copy of my birth certificate, and a newly minted credit card with a generous limit. I put a comb in my other pocket.

Nicci took a baggie of cash from her pocket. "I've been saving. If you don't return to the cabin, this should get you home."

"I have a credit card."

"Cash is always better, at least that's what you always told me."

Alex expelled one last breath into the inflatable shark. My life vest had been destroyed in *Zella's* fire, and the spare needed to stay with Alex for her travels. The shark was all that would keep me off the bottom of the Sea of Cortez. I prayed it wouldn't prove to be an ironic choice.

Nicci looked me up and down. "I wish you would take some clothes, Ma. No one, but no one, is going to help you dressed like that. You look like a freakin' missionary."

I looked down at my long cotton skirt and sensible sandals. "This is what all the cool missionaries *are* wearing."

Nicci frowned. "Absolutely no one dresses like that, Mom. Saying so is a disservice to missionaries everywhere. I'm sorry I said anything."

I looked at my watch. The girls at Restoration House would be filing into the dining hall for their evening meal. "We have to be quick."

We stood in a tight knot. Nicci put her forehead to mine. "We are good here. You see that, don't you?"

I did. Nicci was still Nicci, brutally honest and transparent— she could not subdue a thought to save her life. But there was an emerging Nicci, a woman who loved her daughter fiercely and valued hard work. Her anger now took a breath before it surfaced and passed more quickly. She'd even apologized for lashing out. She still smoked—outside only—but I'd not seen her drink anything since I'd returned home. Most surprising of all, she turned off the news after the weather and headed to bed, until the alarm went off at 5:30.

"I'm amazed by you, Nicci."

"Then you should go."

I touched the map and doubled over from the force of the pull. My chest muscles cramped at the sudden plunge into cold seawater. The inflatable shark wrenched from my grip. When I surfaced, a clouded sky dulled the sea, but the shark bobbed happily nearby.

I was still a traveler, destination unknown.

I draped an arm over the shark and floated on my back, my face to the hazy orb of light. Instead of reciting "The Midnight Ride of Paul Revere" to pass the time, I prayed for Pooja and Ahana, Mrs. Chawla, and the newest girl, Jiya. *Oh Lord, release her from her captivity to shame.* The gardener's son needed a job. *Father, provide all that is needed for Maahir and his family.* I pleaded for success for the next raid, and, of course, for the safety of the team. I even prayed for Doug and Tiffany, as Mrs. Chawla had strongly encouraged, to establish a household of love. And this time, I didn't choke on my words.

And I prayed with new faith for Nicci and Alex. *Bapa God, continue your very good work in my girls.*

The shark had deflated to a squishy rendition of himself just as my vision got cloudy and an unseen arm pulled me out of the blue waters.

I landed under the bahava tree in Restoration House's courtyard as a butterfly alights on a welcoming blossom, with nary a vibration and certainly no jarring of bones. I sat in the very chair I'd spent so many hours talking with Mrs. Chawla.

The night wrapped around me like an embrace and tendrils of curry curled around me. Yellow light spilled onto the pavement from the dining room. The girls' voices quieted briefly for a prayer and rose again after the amen. Beyond the gates, a symphony of car horns serenaded the night.

I texted Nicci to let her know where I'd arrived.

"No surprise there," she texted back. "I'll let Alex know. Need clothes packed?"

"Yes, please. Let me know when you're done. No hurry."

I rose from the chair to go find Pooja.

www.ingramcontent.com/pod-product-compliance
Lightning Source LLC
Chambersburg PA
CBHW070726280626
47159CB00023B/2799